CHRYSALIS

CHRYSALIS

JEREMY WELCH

Matador
9 Priory Business Park,
Wistow Road, Kibworth Beauchamp,
Leicestershire. LE8 0RX
Tel: (+44) 116 279 2299
Fax: (+44) 116 279 2277
Email: books@troubador.co.uk
Web: www.troubador.co.uk/matador

ISBN 978 1788039 369

British Library Cataloguing in Publication Data.
A catalogue record for this book is available from the British Library.

Printed and bound in Great Britain by 4edge Limited
Typeset in 10.5pt Minion Pro by Troubador Publishing Ltd, Leicester, UK

Matador is an imprint of Troubador Publishing Ltd

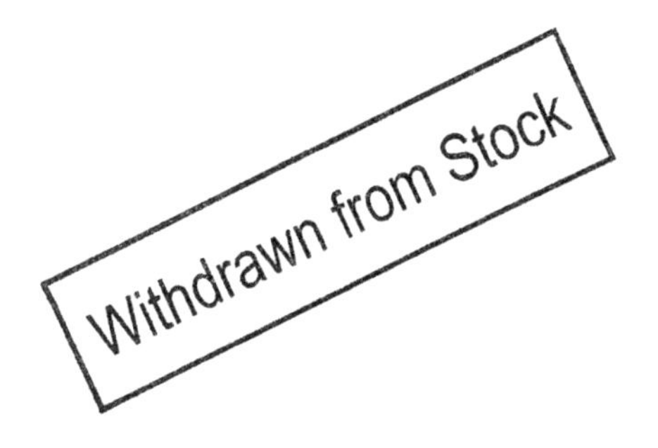

For Poppy, Lara and their beloved mother.

CHAPTER 1

Sebastian reached over to stop the insistent ringing of the phone alarm. The winking red eye in the right hand corner told him his American colleagues had been busy last night passing chores to the London office.

"Oh God!" The first words to pass his lips, same as every working day.

The small bedroom echoed to the slap of forehead into open palms, the floor reverberated with reluctant feet as they hit the floorboards.

"I hate my job, my life's a mess, my boss is an arsehole and my colleagues alien bastards," he wailed into the silence of his bachelor flat.

"A beautiful, compact apartment for a professional man like yourself, sir." That was the pitch of the well-spoken but rather dim estate agent. Looking around he noted the scarcity of space; tea cups in the bathroom, bath towels in the kitchen and dirty dishes resting on the television. Perhaps he was the dimmer of the two having accepted the price and paid for it with another tectonic movement of his finances, pushing the debt mountain up another few thousand feet.

He walked toward the door, the marmalade jar on the table by the entrance that had once held all the flowers of the seasons empty. The label old and sun stained with the words "Made in Edinburgh" just discernible. The jar had last held flowers a long time ago. He shut the door and walked to the underground station.

The journey to work on the underground through the bowels of London was more joyless than usual. The heat unbearable in the carriage as the commuters shoulder to shoulder stood like matchsticks in a box. To his right a man with knitted eyebrows growled quietly at the front page of his newspaper, his nose deeply embedded in the sweat-stained armpit of a pissed Irish bricklayer. The girl to the left applying makeup whilst peering into her compact; with each shudder of the carriage the lipstick scarred her cheek.

"Oh, for fuck's sake!" she exclaimed to no one in particular.

The Boden-dressed mother's lips pursed like a cat's arse as she covered the ears of her 1950s - dressed child to lessen his exposure to the working classes. Their journey to the leafy confines of Wandsworth, the cursing lipstick girl to the hen-cooped factory known as open-plan offices. Most in the compartment tried to avoid any physical or eye contact for fear of engaging a psychopath en route to some collective slaughter.

The other travellers were the typical commuter collection: the bespectacled frotter rubbing himself against the thigh of a businesswoman; the blank straight-ahead stare of those who would defend their seat against an invading army, legs splayed in territorial grab.

Directly in front of the parting doors stood one of his type: a broker or banker looking rather pale faced and sickly. The visage was easily recognisable. It was the look of a man who had entertained a client in various respectable city bars before descending into some strip club on the Tottenham Court Road. He looked most uncomfortable, his Adam's apple rising and falling in quick succession as he tried to swallow the bile escaping from his overworked stomach. As the train glided into Canary Wharf the doors opened onto a solid wall of people. There was a gasping noise, echoed immediately with a cry of disgust and horror as the pale reveller of last night ejected the contents of his excess onto the clean and manicured shirts and blouses of the waiting passengers. With the remarkable recovery of an antelope escaping the jaws of a Nile crocodile he was off at a sprint down the platform to the exit. Passing the silent and incredulous crowd decorated in the multicolours of his presentation there was a faint bouquet of Petrus. Ah, so he was an investment banker.

The notes of 'The Wild Asses' from the *Carnival of the Animals* echoed mostly unheard in the cavernous arrivals hall. Sebastian walked into Caffè Nero as he did every Friday to order two lattes, one with extra sugar. Ascending into the daylight the music switched tempo to 'The Swan' from the same musical suite. Alone amongst the hurrying masses he stood and listened until the final note had played.

"Do you always know when I am arriving?" He said handing over the extra-sugared latte to the busker.

"Yup, every Friday at seven forty-five. It coincides with a caffeine hunger."

He dropped a twenty-pound note into the hat. The busker lifted his bow in thanks. Sebastian didn't turn back but laughed and raised his hand in recognition as he heard the 'Royal March of the Lion', growing fainter as he headed towards his office.

Arriving he joined the controllers of the weapons of financial and social Armageddon converging in a polite line at the lifts of the chrome temple of finance.

The air thick with expensive perfume and aftershave, female necks covered in the blazing colours of Hermes, the male cavalry jangle of Gucci buckles. Amongst this Beauchamp Street finery he looked at his colleagues, recognised some but only to the extent that he could nod acknowledgement of their existence. Did all these people really know what they were doing on the trading floor? He knew bloody well that he didn't!

As the lift glided upwards to the earnest noise of clicking phone keypads Sebastian recalled a conversation with his brother the previous night.

"Do you people really know what you are up to when you chuck all that money around?" he had asked with genuine interest.

"Some, perhaps, but quite frankly I have no idea what's happening. I've managed to wrap myself, cat-like, around the ankles of those snarling their way up the promotional ladder. On some occasions I have felt my feline tail being grasped by the clawing of the aspirant on the rung below only to be saved from a downward fall by the all-consuming ambition of the host body scrambling ever upward."

As the lift door opened he felt the usual rush of fear-induced adrenaline. Today is the day that the Wizard of Oz moment occurs! A question will be asked of which he will have no idea of the answer; questioning heads will turn to him as the Head of Sales and the wind of silence will push the curtain apart and reveal an uninterested and knowledge-free individual.

"Hello boss! Did you get lucky last night?"

The daily salutation from Darren, the head trader. He sat with his enormous pregnant belly between splayed knees. Shirt buttons strained to contain the creature that lived in his midriff, his collar almost invisible as it hid in the overflow of red, sweating neck flesh. The once new shirt had the unusual pattern of cigarette ash mixed with coffee stains.

"Obviously not by the look on your mush! Never mind, tonight's Frantic Friday, never know your luck!"

All days of the week were prefaced to give an indication of Darren's liquid diet: Mojito Monday, Tequila Tuesday, Wet Wednesday, Thirsty Thursday and Frantic Friday.

"Come on you! Into my office, JP is over from New York and wants a meeting at 2pm today, need your help."

The chair sighed in pleasure as Darren swung forward to get some motion going as he wobbled over to Sebastian's glass office. The spare chair squealed in pain as he dropped into it. For the second time that day Sebastian's forehead slapped into open palms.

"What the hell am I going to say?" he pleaded. "I'm not, and neither are any of the salesforce, making any money. I hate these meetings with JP, he's a real sod and I know he hates me since the last call."

Darren burst out laughing.

"That was the best call I have ever been on!"

He mimicked an American accent.

"'So, Seb, tell me what's happening in Europe.' Your reply was fantastic. 'It's very difficult at the moment, quite frankly it's a Sisyphean task.' That's when JP exploded and said, 'Why is it impossible to get a straight answer from you, Eurotrash? And who is this guy with syphilis?'" The midriff creature oscillated wildly in mirth.

"It's not funny. He's here today and I can already feel the displaced air around my neck as the sword drops, another City cadaver to be thrown onto the fire built by politicians to appease the plebeians."

Sebastian searched the computer screen icons to find the spreadsheet containing the dismal proof of his indifference to his career. Just as he found it his PA, Tracy, poked her head round the door. Her face made up like a Geisha and with her dark-rooted blond hair pulled back she looked like an extra in a Japanese porn film.

"Don't forget your BUPA meeting today at 5pm," she whispered conspiratorially whilst glancing sideways to Darren.

"Oh dear, boss!" Darren exclaimed with pleasure. "I know what that's about, you're getting a finger up your arse for prostate, aren't you? Got some advice for you."

"I'll leave you two to discuss Darren's advice," she replied retreating quickly in the full knowledge of where the conversation was about to go.

"When you get there they always ask if you want a man or a woman. Take my advice, go for the woman. The men who work for BUPA are all old GPs with rheumatic fingers and swollen joints. The women are all new graduates with slender fingers."

He smiled. "In fact, now I think about it you may not have got lucky last night but you're going to get fucked twice today – JP and BUPA!" Watching Darren's appendage creature wobbling with mirth Sebastian knew the day wouldn't get any better.

The rest of the morning passed with the typical time filling and useless meetings where things beyond his interest, and too sterile for him to even bother to learn, were discussed with maniacal enthusiasm and with no doubt terrifying consequences for the world. During the meetings Sebastian reviewed the attendees: analysts clothed in numbers, the salesmen already counting and spending their future bonus and the traders irritated with the lack of activity.

"If we trade the gamma against the beta the opportunity cost leaves the window open to make a fortune and the best bit… the client is an arse and will never see we have taken him for a ride," Darren whispered to the smug smile of the traders.

The same mass conspiracy of the City was played out in meetings in the surrounding offices of Canary Wharf, each firm pitched against the other with the knowledge that the winner takes all in a zero sum game. After each meeting Sebastian left the room alone, poured out the cold remains of his coffee before scrunching the plastic in his hand. Disappointed with the industry? Not really as it was beyond his control. Disappointed with himself for being a participant? For sure. The depressing conclusion was the same. How has an industry that came about to benefit the participants and not the actual investors been made legal, respectable and indeed revered? The participants mostly had average IQs and by falling into a City job had joined, like him, the lucky sperm club. The unspoken secret that they all knew, and knew that they all shared, was most didn't enjoy the job, but the pay was wonderful and the posturing associated with that was hard to give up.

Closing the door of his office he Googled, "What to do if you hate your job". He was obviously not the first to try this as there were 4,780,000 suggested answers. The first seemed to offer the answer. "That doesn't mean you have to keep it. There are steps you can, and should, take to move on if you hate your job and you're not happy at work. We spend too much of our time working to stay in a job or work environment we hate, or even dislike. Besides being happier, you'll do a better job if you're working at a job you love, or at least like." Looking out through the glass of his office onto the trading floor, rows of smartly dressed salesmen speaking silkily to clients, traders with multi-coloured eyes reflecting the changes in colour on the screens they stared at for ten hours a day. The advice had to be right.

Dialling his brother's number he waited impatiently for the phone to be picked up.

"Come on, come on."

The receiver picked up and the noise of laughter almost drowned out the speaker.

"David here. Can I help?"

"It's Sebastian, I've got a question for you. Are you happy with your job?"

"Hi Seb, we went through this last night. Sure, I love it but would love it more if I made what you make. Being an art dealer is great fun but as you know it's not the route to Ferraris and the Caribbean!"

"It's not all it's cracked up to be, you know."

"Listen, Seb, we talked until the end of a bottle of whisky last night. If you don't like it don't do it. You know what you want to do, why you want to do it, well just do it. You're beginning to sound like an old man whose life has passed. I mean you're living more in the past than the future." He knew the next statement was unkind but needed saying. "Just make the call, take the decision." He also knew that Sebastian would be playing with his watch. The one with the hands that never moved. It correctly told the time twice a day, seven thirty, unseen beneath the broken glass and held on his wrist by the grubby wristband in his old regimental colours of blue, red and green. He paused for a reply. There was none. "Look, I'm happy to go through it all again as long as you're paying."

"I don't think I can take any more advice from my younger brother. I'll ring you next week."

Placing the receiver back he looked again at the trading floor, and amongst the conversations, visible and invisible, office politics being played, the one emotion totally absent was happiness.

Fingering his credit card he swung his jacket over his shoulder and walked to the exit.

"Don't forget your two o'clock with JP," Tracy reminded him.

"I'll be back by then, just off to buy myself some happiness."

One thirty and fortified with a bottle of Spain's best red it was time to meet the foe; he emptied a carton of mints into his dry mouth and headed back to the office. The Wall Street types take a dim view of the pleasure of wine at lunchtime; for them a rush to the gym to ensure the body was trimmed and fit so able to conquer the world again in the afternoon.

"You drunk? Better not be, JP in room 401 and is in a filthy mood." This after only a brief inspection by Darren. *Why do rooms not have names?* Sebastian hazily wondered. *Numbers make them sound like a prison.* He pulled his tie straight, a needless brush of suede loafers on the rear of his calf muscles. *Looking good*, he thought.

He entered room 401 with the wine-induced feeling of benevolence and generosity. The first look at JP alerted him to the fact that he wasn't here to hand out job title promotions in lieu of a salary increase. JP sat across the table, his small head perched on his overly exercised body. His face impassive as an Easter Island statue. This wasn't going to be fun.

"Hello Seb, you look well," he said rather pointedly.

"Indeed, just been to the gym, that's why I am a little red in the face." He spoke from the side of his mouth to avoid the alcoholic fumes filling the room. With this lie he knew he was in trouble.

"Seb, we have been looking at the European business from a top down and holistic perspective and decided it's not going forward in tune with the overall strategic overlay plan for future expansion. What are your views?"

Whilst trying to digest the corporate speak, Sebastian looked directly into JP's reptilian eyes and spotted his reflection on the meniscus that covered those never blinking eyes. While trying to focus on the reflection, his neck telescoped out of his collar. The sword, it's coming, and soon.

"Well, JP, I have been thinking about that too," he replied with a slight slur as the effect of the wine clouded random and vacuous thoughts. Before he could corral any more he spotted the harbingers: two rather well-dressed Group 4 security guards approaching the office. Dressed in black, they reminded him of SS troopers.

"I think that's enough. You are obviously drunk so let's get this over and done with." Sebastian felt a cold breath of air on his neck. "With effect immediate you are terminated and will be escorted from the trading floor. Speak to no one as you leave." The words sliced through his neck. For the third time that day his head fell into open palms, perhaps never to be lifted again.

"Oh Christ! Who will take my place?"

"Darren will be replacing you as head of sales and head of trading. It has been in discussion for some time now."

"Bastard, hope he never sees another Mojito Monday again."

"These two gentlemen will see you out. Have a great day." JP blinked clearing something from his eyeball.

The escort took up sentry post either side of Sebastian, shoulder to shoulder, squeezing him like a sandwich filling. In step the trio walked towards the exit; no eyes were raised. Everyone concentrating on tasks at their desk, their computers or clutching pieces of paper en route to a fictional meeting. All but one avoiding eye contact, Darren the exception, his feet planted on the desk top and his buttocks flopping over the side of his chair like stabilisers on a child's bike. He smirked; he had known. They had all known, Children of Janus. Bastards.

Stepping into the warm air of summer Sebastian took off his tie, dropped it on the pavement and walked away from the office. Lighting a cigarette he weighed up his options. There were three:

Option 1: tap dance naked through the fountains of Cobalt Square at his new found freedom.

Option 2: burst into tears at his new found unemployment and go to the nearest bar to get sloshed.

Option 3: return to his lair of a flat and caveman-like spend the rest of his days licking the moss that would grow on the walls.

He took none of the three on offer; he did cancel the BUPA appointment. Sebastian needed someone else to unravel the chaotic threads of his thoughts. He dialled the number of the only skilled weaver he knew who could unravel his current mess; she had past history of exactly this task.

"Hello, is Zoe there? It's Sebastian."

"Oh, it's you," was the rather frosty reception. He knew this gatekeeper of a receptionist having accused her of being a lesbian at the last Pinkerton and Smith Auctioneers Christmas party; help was not going to be immediate.

"Oh hi Janet!"

"Jane actually."

"Of course, Jane, how silly of me, found a boyfriend yet?"

There was a pause, a ripping noise, a sniffle and the blowing of a nose.

"Why are you such a shit?" she cried. "You must know he left me last month, Zoe would have told you."

Two things came to mind. He would rather have his brain removed with only a phial of vodka as an anaesthetic by a blind first year medical student than know anything about Jane's love life. The second was he hadn't spoken to Zoe in more than two weeks.

"Of course she did, I'm sorry."

"Hello, Zoe here," was the reply to the simpering apology.

"You are my oldest friend, I am your most useless friend, but I need to see you now, this minute. I've been fired. Please?" he implored.

"What? When? Oh Sebastian, I'm sorry. Come round to the office, South Kensington tube, opposite is a café called Mario's. Give me a call from there, and don't stop anywhere for a drink on the way!"

"Be there in forty-five minutes, and thanks."

It was odd travelling on the tube in the middle of the afternoon. Quieter, more peaceful and populated by less harried individuals than rush hour. As the train pulled away from Canary Wharf Sebastian thought of his first meeting with Zoe.

They had first met at the Theatrical Society at Edinburgh University. Knowing he couldn't act he specialised in makeup and headed that particular department. He had learnt that skill at school and become a master of disguising and changing an actor's physical appearance. He actually met her feet first at the end of a *Romeo and Juliet* production party, as on all fours he introduced himself by vomiting onto her leopard-patterned kitten-heeled shoes. They studied English together and although an inauspicious start, became firstly lovers, then flirts and finally friends. She became confidant, tutor for lectures missed, nurse to stitch the duelling scars of mistaken lust for love, bridging loan broker in times of fiscal depravity and company in times of sloth. Her counsel always sought as he tried to extract himself from the bear pits of life. Post-university, and with the passage of time, her circle of friends increased as did his attempts of drunkard telephone seduction of her. Both of which he resented.

Zoe opened the door; her body blocked the sunlight. The shape of her legs silhouetted against the opacity of her skirt, her silk blouse see-through with the light. She looked pretty standing at the doorway, head turning in search of him. She was dressed with stylish indifference. Her only jewellery was a cheap and slight bracelet he had given her in their twenties on a weekend in Amsterdam.

"What happened? Sorry, I'll start again. Hello Sebastian, what happened?" Zoe was the only person that called him Sebastian. She pushed her hair behind her ears with her middle fingers to ensure no detail of the disaster was missed. With open palm she gently stroked his cheek then gathered his hands tightly into her protective grasp.

"I am now a morsel being digested by the corporate juices of my previous employer. Some odious shit from New York arrived, bit, chewed and digested me in less than five minutes. No doubt to be passed, via his rectum, into the Thames before he flies back. What am I going to do?" It was not the first appeal to Zoe to solve his problems. "No one will give me a job. I know no one left in finance, most have been fired, a few escaped with a premier card and a Swiss bank balance to go skiing for the rest of their lives." His mouth was bitter with stale wine.

"Well you knew it was coming, you hated your job, you hated the people and you hated the industry. Yes it's a shock, but look at the other people you know who have been fired, they're all doing something. You have lots to offer." she said with more confidence than he felt.

"What have I got to offer? I have been a student, then an army officer changing a camouflage uniform for a suit and penny loafers, City battledress."

"Exactly, it's time to do something else, wander more widely. Think of what you wanted to do at uni. You were going to be creative. What happened to your book?"

Sebastian looked at her with exasperation.

"For Christ's sake, I was twenty, I'm now thirty-five, broke, unemployed, unemployable and need a salary! If I thought I could in any way avoid sipping from the trough of corporate slops I would do it. But I can't!"

Her hair had slipped from behind her ears. Her sympathy had ended.

"For someone who was employed in the risk business you sure don't know how to take one! Sebastian, can't you remember what it felt like to be alive? Passion, Sebastian, passion. If you don't have that you have nothing. How do you think you got such a good degree in English? Passion. Why, when we were... well you know... did it seem to go on forever? Passion." She was flushed with anger. "It all died when you went into the City."

"What ended when I went into the City?" he asked with a flicker of hope without looking up from the table.

"When we left Edinburgh you could have done almost anything. You wasted that opportunity by following the soulless crowd into the City, and for what? Money, probably the only thing created by man whose Genesis is passionless! Well it's not worked. Fifteen years later and you're broke."

He opened his mouth to defend himself but with her hand raised it closed.

"I have defended you all these years against friend and foe who have spoken badly of you, and in most cases they were justified. I know it's still there, so do you, all you have to do is find it. That something that you feel passionate about."

"Christ, the crowds are hard to please tonight."

"I know you, you came to me to hear what you most need to learn, it's always been that way since I met you. Do you really want to spend the rest of your life playing paper battleships in some anonymous corporate building? You need to do something spontaneous and more importantly something you want to do. You always wanted to write, be a writer. It's that time, Sebastian, now is the time! For the first time in years it's time for you to make a decision about your future."

He looked angrily at her. She knew she had strayed onto forbidden turf. He had spoken to no one else about it, just her and just once on his return from Iraq. The crack of the sniper's round. The panic of a young officer in command, his panic. The decision made, his decision. He ordered the three eighteen-year-old soldiers to cross the road. The whoof of the IED. The following silence. Then the cries of the three. Screaming for their mothers.

Each fell silent before he made it to them. The last noise he could remember was the zipping of the body bags. The last thing he felt was the pain on his wrist as he looked at the broken watch face. It was all over by seven thirty, but his decision wasn't.

"Thanks. Fucking thanks!"

She knew this was unfair as he had tried and failed after university to write a novel. The unanswered letters to publishers and agents crushing his hope. Her voice softened and she gave him a look of affection.

"God help me, Sebastian, I really do care for you, but you alone can rekindle the fire, find a reason to do it and then do it. In fact you now have that reason." She squeezed his hands with willingness. "Look, I have to go back as I have a meeting. You going to Arabella's tonight?"

"Forgot about that, no I don't think so, not tonight. Christ, what am I going to tell everyone? No I can't bear it."

"Yes you can, pick me up at seven from my flat, I'll pay for the cab. We can talk more on the way." The tone was soft but it was an order.

She kissed him on both cheeks, picked up her bag, placed the two fingers of her right hand to her lips and blew a kiss. All that remained of her admonishment was the perfume of her presence. *Why is she always right?* Since his return from Iraq he had been a piece of flotsam lazily directed by the currents; he had never once made a decision to go against the current. It had been easier to float along and blame circumstances, and others, when he was washed up on some reef waiting for the tide to come back in.

CHAPTER 2

1

Arriving at the door, the noise of smug contentment was too much for Sebastian.

"I really can't face this, let's go out for dinner and phone to say we're ill. Arabella's friends are awful. Bet that prick Joseph is there with his ghastly wife Mary."

Zoe pressed the bell. "Just be nice," she said before brushing down her skirt and running her fingers through her hair. She had a look of anticipation.

The door opened and Sebastian's face cracked into a pantomime smile.

"Come in, you two, how wonderful to see you both. Go through to the drawing room and meet everyone." Arabella guided them through, holding back Zoe by the arm. "He's here!" she said in a hushed excited voice. Zoe flushed.

Before he could take in the congregation a Chernobyl-coloured drink was pushed into his hand.

"You'll like this, it's a cocktail I picked up in Prague at

my last conference." Martin's well-polished and whitened teeth smiled at him. Martin was dressed like an aged modern version of d'Artagnan: skin-tight black polo neck jumper, equally tight black trousers with a small middle-age continental shelf of fat poking out above his Hermes buckled belt. Goatee beard dyed black and crowned with what looked like an undernourished caterpillar masquerading as a moustache. Sebastian looked at the glass and knew Martin had anticipated, wrongly, his taste in cocktails.

"Good to see you, Martin," Sebastian lied. He had never liked Martin. Arabella had met him when they were at university and he was a lecturer in modern women's studies. Sebastian remembered the day he oiled his way across the floor at the English faculty annual dance and performed a poor version of the salsa. For reasons known to no one Arabella had fallen for this oily creature and had been caught in his slick ever since.

"There is someone I want you to meet, her name is Clarissa and she has joined me at London University." His overly warm hand massaged Sebastian's back as if he was a prize-fighter being guided back into the ring by his second. "Clarissa, this is Seb, Seb Clarissa. Seb works in finance." His caterpillar moustache twitched with disapproval. "Clarissa specialises in the exploitation of women by the financial services industry."

Her hair was cut like a Wehrmacht helmet with a sharp branch of black coral hanging from her neck against the angry red of her tight cleavage.

"Indeed," Sebastian muttered through a nervous cough.

Clarissa looked at him the way a gravedigger looks at

a steak after a hard day at the cemetery – the certainty of finishing it with ease, speed and enjoyment.

"It's more about female empowerment than subjugation. I look to reverse the role of the rapacious male that prowls your industry to the detriment of the definitive Eve. Without a doubt the stereotypical female client is seen as a virgin to be deflowered by you." The pronoun accusative made Sebastian uneasy. A swift movement of his forearm saw the radioactive-coloured cocktail drained and the colour transferred to his cheeks. She continued in a closing prosecutor's address. "It is because of people like you that the minority female groups remain hindered in their aspirations and contained in a pen to await your rapacious demand to hand over their money."

He looked desperately around for Zoe. She was exchanging laughter with a blond man in a suit. With no escape he returned to the role as sparring partner receiving a new flurry of verbal punches.

"Some of my best friends are women," he weakly replied, looking over her shoulder for help. Her top lip rose to further the pulverising as Joe and Mary mercifully joined the conversation. Normally Sebastian would have run into the path of fast-moving traffic rather than face these two. Joe was dressed to suit his chosen career, Prince of Wales check suit topped by a tight-knotted blue tie hanging like an icicle down his white shirt. His face gaunt confirming the time spent with his personal trainer. Assured, entitled and rich were the qualities on display. Mary was the clone of the fine ladies of Wandsworth. Her hair highlighted blond, fingers bejewelled with rings of congratulations, appeasement and guilt. Her branded jeans doing their best to contain and mould the expanding flesh of two parturitions. She was looking rather flushed, no doubt after a day spent flirting with her tennis coach whilst Joe fought off an angina attack in the world of advertising.

"Mary, Joe, I cannot tell you how good it is to see you." They both returned his greeting with holy smiles appropriate to their biblical namesakes. "Clarissa and I were discussing the merits of creating tailor-made financial services products to suit specific client groups." He looked at the three with a wide-open smile. There was no reply from any of them. Escape, escape was screaming in his head. "Oh look, everyone's glass is empty, let me find some drink for us all."

He retreated to the kitchen to find a much-needed refill for himself; he had only been at the party for twenty minutes. Whilst alternately swigging from a gin bottle and banging his head against the doorway muttering, "Fuck, Fuck, Fuck", he was interrupted by the blond in the suit.

"You alright? I was looking for the loo."

"I know it doesn't look like it, but I certainly feel as if I'm in the U-bend and about to be flushed to oblivion… sorry, excuse me, feeling a bit, a bit, well… assaulted today. It's under the stairs." He reached out his arm, hand open. "I'm Sebastian, by the way."

"Simon, Simon Smith."

The initials enough to recall the disaster of earlier today. More SS!

"You're an old friend of Zoe's. She has spoken about you, you were at uni together. You work in finance, I gather, perhaps we know some people in common."

How did he know so much about him? More importantly what was the occasion that had allowed the two of them to discuss him?

"Perhaps I do, but actually I am thinking of changing career as I find the world of finance full of arseholes and egotists, especially the rapacious crooked hedge fund managers. Who would trust those thieves with their hard earned cash, eh? What do you do?"

His handshake gripping harder as unnecessary pressure was applied, he looked Sebastian in the eye with a look that would have the Brigade of Guards snap to attention and replied, "I run a hedge fund in the West End."

Sebastian's response was unplanned; a little fart squeaked out.

"Well good Lord, I'm sure you're not all bad, some of you must make money for the widows and needy. Talking of which, do excuse me, must get the drinks to the thirsty masses." as he harvested some glasses.

Depositing the glasses, mostly empty having relieved them of their content, into the waiting hands of Joe, Mary and Clarissa he made his way over to the safety of Zoe.

"I've just met an awful man, some arrogant hedge fund manager. Handshake like a vice, awful-looking creep, one of those marble-carved bodies. Bet he spends most of his time keeping fit and pruning himself at the Harbour Club in Chelsea when not pickpocketing the poor and stealing from church collection boxes."

Her lips bloomed into a smile. A serpent's arm slipped round Zoe's waist pulling the prey closer to its mouth.

"Simon, you've not met Sebastian, have you?"

He felt like a heretic on a medieval bonfire with the peasant torch bearers getting closer. The Papal reprieve came from the unlikely black-clad Martin.

"Come through for dinner, everyone."

In the dining room the table was meticulously laid with a name tag at the head of each place setting. Sebastian scanned the name tags knowing that anyone other than Zoe at his side would leave him with the feeling of slipping quietly into quicksand. Clarissa on the right and Mary on the left. He felt the first tug of the hungry sand.

It didn't take long for the conversation to follow the template of a *Daily Mail* leader column. House prices and personal wealth accumulated thereby reflecting self-admitted canniness rather than luck. The seemingly ever-rising cost of private education, the overpopulation of our green and pleasant land by illegal immigrants and our indigenous benefit baby breeding underclass undermining the foundations of our society. Sebastian was never sure if to agree was part of the protocol at dinner parties and had decided a long time ago to avoid engaging as none of these subjects encroached on his life.

"We are moving to the country next month. You know what boys are like, they need space to grow up in," was Mary's opening salvo as the frantic first table conversation subsided into pockets of talk with those on either side. She said this with the look of shared knowledge as if a single, childless man would have sympathy and understanding of the confines of metropolitan living. Although Sebastian had often heard of this mythical collective noun called the "countryside" he was never too sure where it was or how to get there, as it was always referred to in a vague and non-geographical specific way. By now slightly tight he slurred, "What happens, Mary, the family arrive all packed with their suitcases at Liverpool Street station like refugees in the Second World War, approach the counter and ask for a single to 'The Country'? A knowing wink from the cheery clerk to the escapees and off you go to pastoral pleasure? The other thing I have never understood is that people who move to 'The Country' always move near somewhere, never in somewhere. Near Nyland, near Oxford. Does anyone actually live in the villages and towns or do they settle in anonymous desolate places like Soviet nuclear testing towns during the Cold War?"

"It's for the children," she relied in a syrupy and sanctimonious manner, as if the future foregoing of coffee mornings and organic weekend markets were sacrifices to be made as a good parenting rite of passage. "Joe's commute will only be two hours each way. He will wake to the silent tranquillity of the countryside and return to it in the evening with the birds singing in the trees to relieve the stress of the day."

"Must admit I prefer to wake up, open the windows and hear the birds coughing on the carbon monoxide from the passing buses and cars. All too cheery for me to hear the birds run through the Lauds every morning. The commute will be hell, leaving in the dark and arriving in the dark for at least five months of the year. Does Joe know what he is letting himself in for with this move?"

"Oh Seb, you're always so negative," Martin butted in. "You just don't understand the symbolism of motherhood. The desire for the topographical paradise in which women crave to bring up their children." This was the start of a long psychobabble monologue from Martin to which Sebastian paid little attention as he played with his starter and drained his wine glass. He looked across at Zoe with slightly blurred vision.

Her face was lit by candlelight and the shadows cast gave prominence to her high cheek bones. Her smile fast and wide, even teeth showing as she laughed and with each laugh her Eurasian-shaped eyes seemed to close. Wishing they were alone in a restaurant, he leaned across the table to stroke her cheek with the back of his hand before he kissed her gently on her nervous lips.

"What do you think?" Martin interrupted his dinner for two.

"Bollocks," was the reply in punishment to Martin for ruining his imagined dinner and punishment to Mary for being so content and certain. Without looking at either Martin or Mary, whose glances he knew were telling each other, "ignore him, he's drunk", Sebastian stood up and under the pretext of going to the toilet went for a cigarette in the garden.

Standing outside in the dark looking through the sliding double doors of the kitchen extension he was the sole attendee of the theatre watching a play on social interaction. Clarissa the pugilist, animated in conversation with Simon throwing verbal punches at him; Simon with ease and the skill of a bantamweight avoiding each jab as he drew diagrams on the table top with his index finger pictorially showing her the shortcomings of her thoughts. Arabella and Mary from the opposite ends of the table sipping their wine in unison as their conversation faltered, both more interested in the now escalating discussion between Simon and Clarissa. Joe and Martin talking across Zoe in the middle. Zoe oblivious to the surrounding conversation was looking towards Simon. Her eyebrows knitted with each jab thrown by Clarissa but relaxed as Simon remained untouched. Knowing he was safe she looked towards the window and unknowingly looked straight at Sebastian. She rose, slipped unnoticed from the table and joined him outside.

"What's the matter?"

"Nothing and everything. I can't stand all those smug bastards."

With her bodiless embrace he knew his desire was one-sided.

"Who is Simon?"

"He's nice, isn't he?" She looked for approval. "I met him at a party a couple of months ago and we've been going out ever since."

Spitefully Sebastian threw the end of his lit cigarette into the middle of the well-manicured suburban lawn.

"We had better go back in. I hope he is good to you, you really deserve someone nice."

"I know you'll like him."

He doubted that but kept his counsel.

Reaching for a bottle of wine from the sideboard as they re-entered the room he retook his place at the table. Martin gave a disapproving glance at the theft as he was one of those irritating hosts that fills the wine glasses and, as if rationing for one's health, places the bottle back on the sideboard beyond reach until he himself deems it is time for a refill. Sebastian filled the glass to the rim and looked at Simon who exchanged a glance with Zoe, enquiring if all was alright. Zoe replied with a demure, not-to-worry smile. Sebastian decided to get drunk.

The conversation had deflated after a draw between Simon and Clarissa. It was now being passed around like a soggy leather football: dreary predictable summer holiday plans in villas in Tuscany, neighbour troglodyte basement extensions threatening sink hole devastation of entire streets. Clarissa, now more relaxed after her work out with Simon, turned to Sebastian with her left eyebrow arched and asked, "What are your plans for the summer?"

Emboldened and braver after the excess of Martin's reluctant hospitality he slurred, "I'm off to Amsterdam to sleep with hookers and smoke vast amounts of Moroccan Black. In between I'm going to write a book."

This vision of the future appealed to him in his inebriated state but was obviously less appealing to his fellow diners. The rush to start a conversation, any conversation, saw Sebastian's future blown away and hoovered up with the urgent exhalation and inhalation of words. The only person to show any interest in his new career was Clarissa who whispered in his ear.

"How exciting!" she breathed as she kneaded his testicles unseen under the table.

The excuses for departure started almost immediately with babysitters to be relieved, deserved beds to be got into after a week of repetition. Any excuse to avoid any further views from Sebastian.

"We are off too," Clarissa announced as she poured Sebastian into his jacket.

In the embarrassed silence, his arm around her shoulder for support, Sebastian was guided by Clarissa towards Arabella and Martin where he mumbled his thanks through thick lips. He turned unsteadily to look for Zoe. Her arm linked with Simon's, she had a quizzical look on her face, almost imploring.

"I will write it, you know, I'll write it for you," he slurred into Clarissa's chest, but it was aimed at Zoe.

"I'll ring you tomorrow," Zoe said as he stumbled over the doormat with his other arm wrapped around Clarissa's waist, head firmly in the clasping embrace of her breasts.

2

Wiping the cement from between his eyes, he painfully raised his eyelids. The wallpaper patterned. The bed comfortable and warm. This was not his room and this was not his bed. Peering out of the window he looked directly into the MI6 building. Whatever happened last night MI6 would know. Turning inward he stared at the face of a smiling yellow PAC-MAN printed on a T-shirt.

Tentatively he pulled back the duvet and stood up feeling unsteady and head sore. There was a stirring from the other side of the bed.

"Great sex last night," Clarissa said with a sleepy smile stretching her arms upward and yawning.

"Oh my God… really?"

She laughed lightly as she wafted her arm upward from his feet to his head.

"You were so animal-like, uncontrollable. Are you always like that?"

"Well not always… just sometimes." Sebastian could vaguely remember the departing, the taxi and a lift ride. The rest was a blank.

Clarissa burst out laughing.

Looking down – shoeless, trousers on, one sock off, shirtless but with T-shirt on – he felt rather confused.

"Well it could have been. But Dionysus got the better of Aphrodite. You were very affectionate but sleepy as a newt!"

Sebastian hurriedly gathered up his few unworn possessions and dressed.

"Clarissa, I'm sorry about last night. I hope I didn't make a fool of myself. Perhaps this can be our secret, I mean it's probably best that no one knows."

"Sure." It was said lightly and obviously not the first time this conversation had taken place in her bedroom. "Perhaps you can include it in your book?"

It seemed to Sebastian that this was neither the time nor place to discuss his current employment options and opted for a quick escape.

"Perhaps. I'll see. It was certainly a fun evening. It was great to meet you." Droplets of boozy sweat formed on his forehead and prickled his armpits.

He knew she didn't believe him.

"Do you want a coffee before you go?" It was said in the expectation of a no as she had already turned her back with a view to going back to sleep.

Quickly he walked towards the door to escape from the libidinous humiliation of the night.

"Thanks, no. Perhaps I will see you around," fumbling as he eagerly turned the door handle to escape.

"Perhaps," her back answered.

As he closed the door the last vision of Clarissa was the laughing yellow PAC-MAN.

3

The oncoming summer stretched in front of him like the never-ending school holiday of his youth. Days passed and Sebastian limply looked for a job using the excuse that no one recruited in summer. Each day passing the responsibility of phoning anyone he knew who might have a vacancy for him to the next. Concluding that it was preferable to rise late, languish in cafés drinking coffee and await the end of the working day when, like children rushing out of the school gates at the ring of the bell, there was always someone he knew that wanted to go for drinks.

In between the indolent and soporific days there were moments of reluctant self-inspection. Uncomfortable lunches with his parents. A loveless father dressed in his military blazer with gold buttons gleaming with honour looked at him as if his favourite gun dog had died. A mother demur and acquiescent after a lifetime of self-sacrifice following the beat of the military drum. Her dream of becoming a concert pianist dispatched on the bayonet of her husband's career. Father wanting to know when his son and his investment in his education was going to yield a dividend. Mother privately insistent that now was the time to take charge, change and grab the opportunity of a new life for fear of it being lost forever. Friends, envious of his inactivity, bullying him into re-joining the world of work by trying to frighten him into submission with threats of poverty in old age and mortgage repossession.

The only constant throughout was the draft of his failed novel. It was ever present, a coffee mat at breakfast, moved but unopened throughout the day to eventually reside on his bedside table at night.

Zoe was the catalyst for activity. They had spoken many times since the dinner party but, for the sake of mutual shared avoidance of embarrassment, not talked about that evening or Clarissa. The phone rang mid-afternoon, three hours into watching the cricket test match on TV.

"Hi Sebastian."

"Zoe, how lovely to hear you. What you up to?"

"Packing for my summer holiday. I want to talk to you before I go. You around this afternoon?" He recognised the tone; it foretold of a lecture. He had been in this situation many times with Zoe and knew not to provide her with room to manoeuvre; he built up his defence by tidying the flat.

On entering his flat she looked around at the discipline and neatness, knew it was temporary and knew why it had been done.

"Well this is what you do all day. Have you turned yourself into Mrs Drudge?" Her laugh was easy and happy knowing the future had opportunity. "It's good to see you, Sebastian, I wanted to see you before we go on holiday." With hands gently cradling his face she kissed him on both cheeks.

"We?"

"Yes, we, Simon's taking me to San Francisco and has booked us into the Fairmont Hotel for two weeks. It's so exciting, and we're going first class."

As the kettle boiled and steam snorted upward he felt the green-eyed monster of envy awake in his stomach. Not for want of the Fairmont, San Francisco or first class; he wanted to be with Zoe for two weeks, two weeks anywhere even if they had to get to anywhere by a tuk-tuk.

"That sounds fun. How is the corporate thief?" Handing her a cup of coffee, black and strong as she liked it.

"I know you don't like him, so let's not go there, OK? What are you going to do this summer?"

Sitting opposite her at the kitchen table he looked around the flat, thinking that the next few months confined in the small space would be insufferable.

"I don't know."

"Look, Sebastian, I had a coffee with your mother last week. She came up to town specifically to see me."

"She did what? Why? She didn't come and see me. What did she want?" He tried to look indignant but felt comforted in the knowledge that his mother and Zoe would have spoken about their shared concern of him. He wasn't alone.

"She is worried about you but at the same time excited for you. Excited that you can try something else, something different. Look, she is no fool, I've known her since we were students. She knows you won't get a job over the summer so before the autumn you have a chance to try writing again. I mean, why not? You have the skeleton of the book, rework the text, change it, add more characters. I don't know but I do know you can do it." She was talking quickly and excitedly as if for two.

His lifted the cup off the manuscript. Another ring added to the unplanned Spirograph-patterned cover. The liquid thoughts of the past week slowly turning to crystals. He didn't reply.

"Your father doesn't know she came to see me," she said to confirm the courage of his mother's defiance of his father's authority.

"Oh, I am sure of that!" His hand touched the manuscript. "He thought it a waste of time when I wrote this, almost delighted in its failure."

"Well why not give it a go? For her, her forsaken musical career, for you and... well for me too. I know you can do it, I knew then and I know now."

She was right of course, why not? What else was he going to do over the summer but get fatter with sloth and beer? By mid-summer he would be reduced to bar flying with randoms as everyone he knew would be away for the summer.

"I can't write it here, I'll go mad sitting here all day playing Brick Breaker waiting for opening time." He was looking for inspiration from Zoe.

"Try somewhere different, different smells, architecture and culture. Somewhere you were happy." He felt her hand cover his resting on top of the manuscript; she squeezed it encouragingly.

"Do it, Sebastian, do it for yourself." She was almost pleading.

He looked at her, looked at the manuscript.

"I am going to, as long as you promise to come and see me."

He knew it would please her. But it would be her fault when it went wrong.

CHAPTER 3

1

The air-conditioned train pulled into Amsterdam Centraal, the carriages populated mostly by tourists. The culture seekers clutching their bibles of architectural sites to be visited, the tortoise-back packers with their *Time Out* counter-culture guides to nightclubs and marijuana-selling coffee shops. The few businessmen arriving from the airport connection looked out of place in suits, resignedly clutching their flipchart presentations, looking as if they had arrived somewhere they didn't want to be, to meet someone they didn't want to meet, to sell something they were not interested in. Sebastian recalled that feeling with smugness now it was no longer part of his life.

He had been to Amsterdam many times on business but always seen the city through the windows of taxis, hotel rooms and offices. He pulled out a map of Amsterdam and remembered the fan-like layout of the city. Each leaf of the fan was divided by the ribs of the canals: Singel, Herengracht, Keizersgracht and Prinsengracht.

With only his redundancy money and a small monthly rental income from the flat to survive on he had rented a canal boat in the De Wallen district on the Oudezijds Voorburgwal canal. The internet page had promised a small sitting room with kitchen and bedroom rented from a Ms Anneke Cloos in the centre of the red light district. At 200 euros a month it was just affordable and fitted his idea of a writer's place, being bohemian and somewhat seedy.

There was a pause between the sounding of the doorbell and the opening of the door. Having expected Ms Cloos he was slightly taken aback by the tall, athletic black man who opened the door wide with confidence.

"Hello?" His voice was deep and with an African accent.

"Is Ms Cloos in? I booked the houseboat."

His mouth opened in a welcoming smile, teeth dazzling white against inky black skin, the colour of the chest of a magpie.

"Sebastian, correct? Anneke is doing rehearsals. I'm Umuntu. Come, let me show you where you're going." Picking up Sebastian's bag he swung it over his shoulder as if it contained air. They turned the corner onto Oudezijds Voorburgwal canal. "Here we are, she is called *Tulp*, it's Dutch for tulip." His laugh full and throaty.

The hull of the houseboat was tired black, canoe-shaped and had been a coal-shipping barge. The living quarters of wood painted in green, large windows opened the inside to daylight. The roof crenelated with flowerpots of tulips dancing in the summer breeze.

"It's larger than I thought."

"Your entrance is here, the other three-quarters is rented out to some of Anneke's troupe. That door is locked so you have privacy. They are fun, you'll like them. You've taken the rent for two months, holiday or work?" Umuntu asked.

"Work really. I'm going to write a book, well try to. Perhaps a framework of a book," Sebastian replied without conviction and feeling fraudulent.

"Fact or fiction?"

"Fiction."

"I love fiction, you can be anyone from anywhere. They say you write with your eyes. Is that right?"

There was directness and openness about Umuntu that commanded an honest reply.

"I'll let you know when I start. At this stage I have no idea how to start. Well I have in the past started, it's going to be a rewrite." Sebastian sounded both daunted and excited with the realisation he was here and the task was now at hand.

"There will no doubt be a beginning, middle and end. It's like everything in life, you can be and do whatever you wish." He smiled knowingly. "So you can get your bearings, there is a supermarket in Dam Square, a church over there for the religious and that over there is the best bar in De Wallen, the Vlinder. It's the bar of choice for the troupe at the end of rehearsals. Anything you need just come round and ask." He departed leaving a scent of coconut oil.

Sebastian needed to remind himself of where he was and walked into the honeycomb colour of early evening towards Dam Square. The cobbled streets echoed to the ringing of bicycle bells and the Palace clock announcing it was 6pm, the bars full with after-work drinkers spilling onto the street. The sound of laughter echoed off the canal water. Small pleasure boats full of revellers chugged their way along the canal diluting the sound of a small brass band playing on a pontoon next to the Vlinder. All this was in contrast to the numerous silent windowed cells that lined the street on either side of the canal, curtains drawn awaiting the curtain call at the theatre.

Dam Square was the reservoir for people flowing in from the adjoining streets. The shoppers clutching small logoed bags from the fashion district of de Negen Straatjes, women on their way home clutching armfuls of rainbow-coloured flowers from the floating Bloemenmarkt. The army of Japanese tourists armed with their cameras firing photographic shots at each other against the backdrop of the Royal Palace. At the foot of the National Monument to the war dead teenagers lounged as if war wounded themselves, exchanging texts of momentary thoughts. Weaving through the crowds the cycling commuters, upright and elegant on their 1940s bikes, moved with the authority of the sacred cows of India knowing that their right of way was total. Trams clattered on the tracks announcing the arrival and departure at each stop with a tinkling.

He sipped his beer; the bouquet co-mingled with the early evening smell of freshly seared steaks and a hint of marijuana. From the direction of Rokin an elaborate campanologist's pleasure of bells accompanied by whistles and horns heralding the imminent arrival of a protest. The figurehead of the protest was a naked male cyclist waving a rainbow-coloured flag. Behind him came a melee of men in the uniform of the Gay Pride movement. Well-sculptured men in Bob the Builder outfits, a peacock tail of lady boys and behind them, scantily dressed in crotch - less black leather chaps with their chests crisscrossed with bandoliers and leather peaked hats, came the banner holders. "Gay. It's alright to be Gay." "Gays have a right to be happy." As the festival of rights passed, the final row of three biker protesters had a letter painted on each buttock spelling out "The End". The tourist response was varied depending on nationality: aghast, turning away, smirking, laughing and pointing. The Dutch passed on either side of the cavalcade in an attitude of respectfulness. As the noise of the protest retreated the sun dipped below the housetops to leave a blue dusk in its absence. He was glad to be in Amsterdam.

In search of food he headed off towards Prinsengracht. Each of the houses tall but seemingly undernourished with a slim profile. The golden eye of each room staring into the eye of the opposite house. The canal dividing the houses became a moving serpent striped by the mutual glow of opposing yellow light as the night arrived. Through each window could be seen domestic scenes being played out. The hugging of children returned despite parental thoughts of the perils of the day, arms raised in offer of wine, quiet dinners for two, hair being dried after a shower. Unlike London there was an openness about these houses, no curtains were drawn, nothing was hidden. Life was being lived and observed by all.

As he turned into De Wallen district the schizophrenia of Amsterdam revealed itself. Curtain up had been called. The concealed cells of the afternoon were now revealed and the doorways tempting in the warm red glow of light above the entrance declaring tantalising sin within. The prostitutes fluttering in the compact quarters of their individual butterfly houses. The streets, quiet during the observable light of day, now thronging with the drunk, the mad, the curious and the deviant. Almost exclusively men, some furtive with their collars up and hats pulled down. Bravado groups of young men, emboldened by beer and mutual encouragement stared with hazy lustful eyes at each window. As this throng of neutered masculinity crawled through the narrow streets of sexual availability eye contact between the groups and individuals was avoided in shared shame. The windows of each cell clicking with the sharp rasp of a coin being racked on the window as the girls tried to attract eye contact and business.

From an alleyway adjoining the canal a roar of cheering and derisive laughter accompanied a shoeless man, bare-chested and struggling to button his trousers as he rushed blind-eyed into the crowd. Close behind him a banshee dressed in a skimpy nurse's outfit clattering after him like a giraffe in high heels shrieking between cracks of her bullwhip, "Enema, I will give you a fucking enema, you weirdo!"

"Welcome to Amsterdam," Umuntu said through a smile. "Fancy a drink?"

They knifed their way through the crowd at the entrance to the Vlinder. The initial cluster in the doorway was tourists, drinking and chatting excitedly about the adventures of the day; recommending art galleries, parks and churches to be visited to fellow strangers temporarily united over a drink and the shared pleasure of being explorers. The oratory of the pub altogether more peaceful and thoughtful. Here the drinkers were locals and less excited, more contemplative, discussing the events of the day in a familiar quieter tone. The wooden bar was highly polished with small glasses neatly upturned awaiting orders to be filled. The barmen neat and precise with white shirts, black trousers and starched, bleached white aprons tightly tied round their waists.

Umuntu waved towards an empty table, handing over his shopping bags. Nodding in a familiar way to the inner core of drinkers.

"Beer?"

Sebastian nodded in acknowledgement.

The walls were decorated in a mixture of sepia and modern advertisements for theatre productions and fashion exhibitions dating from the 1930s onwards. The more modern in sharp contrast as they reflected the light off their gloss surface, making it hard to see what they were selling. Behind the bar was a collage of photographs of men and women in various theatrical and creative outfits. The centre and most prominent of these was a picture of an attractive woman with black hair and piercing grey eyes, the pupils wide giving her a look of defiance. Her face was perfectly centred in the velvet high collar, the lapels touching her ear lobes and cut away along her jawline plunging to the bodice revealing a slim neck. The multicoloured embroidered dress flowed to her feet pleated from the waistline. "The new collection from Jurgen," it stated.

"It's one of the oldest bars in Amsterdam. Originally the shop next door was a dining room for the post-theatre crowd. Slightly faded now but still very popular with the thespians and young artists, designers and fashion aficionados."

"Is De Wallen always as animated as it was five minutes ago?"

Umuntu chuckled into his beer.

"It's forever been thus, the red light district served the sailors of bygone years. Now it's the epicentre of men's fantasies. They flock here in their thousands throughout the year, living out their darkest fantasies that they won't share with their wives or girlfriends. The girls may be prostitutes but they are not sluts."

"Well it's certainly not London."

"Amsterdam. What the eye sees is not necessarily what exists. The place is full of escapees from somewhere. It's the city of eternal spring where change is always possible. It's the legacy of a colonial power, I suppose, that and a unique culture of acceptance."

"Are you Dutch?" Sebastian asked unable to place Umuntu's accent.

"I am now. It's been a long road to here. I'm South African by birth, been here for many years now. Odd to think that I am now in the land of the forefathers who subjugated my race to such misery under apartheid. That turn of events would have had the Afrikaners scratching their beards on top of their kopjes."

"But why did you settle in Holland?"

"The route here was via the whole continent of Africa. Life was miserably hard in South Africa. My parents desperate to ensure a better future for my brother and myself worked as gardeners, houseboy, maid, fruit sellers, anything to earn enough to send us to the local church school." The memory of them softened his speech.

"And there he learnt to speak English and Dutch before

becoming the master of the Spiegeltent! Hello darling." The American voice kissed him on the top of his head, her hands covering his eyes. "Is he boring you with his life story?" she enquired smiling.

"Without looking I know it's you, Pepper, I can tell by your endless sympathy for all the downtrodden of the world. That and your perfume. Is Salt with you?"

Pepper was dressed in a large man's jumper covering her knees. Her legs shining in Lycra tights and her ankles wrapped in bright green leg warmers. As she moved a chair to join them, a disembodied arm put a drink in front of her.

"Sebastian, meet Salt and Pepper, the mistresses of sword swallowing."

The disembodied arm refound its body and sat next to Sebastian. Salt, dressed as a facsimile of Pepper, but with red leg warmers, jumper tied around her waist hiding a belly button piercing. Her hands precisely curved around the glass she looked directly at Sebastian.

"And you are?" she enquired with a gentle North American accent.

"Behave, the pair of you, this is Sebastian and he's a writer. He is living on the *Tulp* with you lot until we start touring, so be nice to him."

"I knew a writer once. He drank so much that instead of creating characters he became the subject of a psychiatric study into Delirium Tremens. It's a dangerous profession," Pepper said with an easy laugh.

"Well I'm not really a writer. Well not yet. Perhaps I will be in the next couple of months."

"I hope you do, it would be fun to know a writer," Salt and Pepper replied in unison.

The conjoined reply took him by surprise as if he was the butt of their private joke. The only feature that separated the two was their hair. Pepper, blond with brown highlights held up in a loose bun on top of her head. Salt, surfer blond tied precisely and tight in a French plait.

"You're twins, identical twins!" Sebastian cried as if he had solved a mystery.

"Indeed we are," they replied with mock surprise looking at each other.

"Ignore them, Sebastian. Apart they are a delight, together the creation of Satan with a hangover." He smiled at the pair. "Rehearsals were fine? You didn't antagonise Anneke, I hope."

"Everything is perfect except the usual problems with Dasha, he just can't seem to stay sober. He arrives smelling of last night's bar and only starts to talk to anyone once he has finished his thermos flask, and we all know what that contains!" Pepper replied pertly.

"Forgiveness is a wonderful quality, Pepper, and perhaps you should learn it. Dasha is still the best contortionist in Europe. His desire for perfection tortures him. He knows he needs to reach that point of perfection before his joints and bones refuse to obey him, the life of a contortionist short and the future sore."

"It's the same for all of us, Umuntu. All of us have a limited life at the Spiegeltent," Pepper replied slowly stroking her throat. "He wasn't always like this. When we were all doing our training together at Circus Space in London he didn't drink at all. He started after spending two years in Hong Kong studying Taili Quan. I think all that shadow boxing and being born in the wastes of Kazakhstan makes for much darkness in his head. No wonder he is a contortionist, always trying to escape from his shadow."

"Drink up, you two, Anneke has booked us a table at Envy for dinner. Sebastian, would you like to join us? I'm sure you will want to meet the rest of the houseboat, that's if these two haven't put you off already."

"Thanks, that would be nice, I don't actually know anyone in Amsterdam."

Sebastian let the girls walk ahead before asking, "Umuntu, I am sorry to sound stupid but what is a Spiegeltent? Is it a circus?"

"For heaven's sake, don't say that at dinner or you will be thrown into the canal! A Spiegeltent is a fusion of a cabaret club and an entertainment salon. The audience is part of the acts as they are beside, below and around them. It's intimate, imaginative, flirtatious and personal, so no, not a circus. If you have never been in one it is one of life's must-dos. When we open you must come to the show, only then will you understand what a Spiegeltent is."

"If it's not a circus what happens in the show?"

"There's a troupe and each member of the troupe must have a specialist skill, for example it could be they are an illusionist, contortionist or have aerial skills like the trapeze and so on, but they must be skilled in other disciplines. The troupe is usually about eight performers. Each performer needs to be multi-talented so as to assist and participate in the specialist acts of the others. In addition each one must be able to play a musical instrument to provide the music for each act."

"Oh my God, is there anything they can't do? At the factory line of birth when talent was handed out you lot got a double dose and I was obviously the non-working prototype!" The thought of transforming the failed novel into a success was now even more daunting.

"Sebastian, they are a very unusual group of people. Different as they may be, one thing I know they agree on is that there is no such thing as talent. There is only hard work and the manifestation of that hard work is what people call talent." His sympathetic reply was enough to stop Sebastian's downcast eyes looking amongst the cobblestones in hope of finding some discarded talent. "Listen to me!" he laughed. "I sound like the missionaries back home. No work leads to no achievement resulting in no entry to Heaven!" He put a consoling arm around his shoulder.

"There are drawbacks too. The life of a Spiegeltent performer is an itinerant one and doesn't suit many. The tent is erected, the show plays and we move on to the next location on the tour. The lifestyle lacks privacy as we live and work together. It's transparent with nowhere to hide and can be a fractious existence. You have just heard those two." Pointing at Salt and Pepper. "Multiply that by four and imagine what you get!" He laughed as he pushed open the door of Envy.

The table already animated in conversation and drinking, Umuntu introduced Sebastian to the other members of the troupe by name and skill.

"This is Eva, she works trapeze, Hugo and Ricard perform hand and pole balancing acts." Pointing at an unoccupied chair, "Here is Philippe, our illusionist, who may or may not be here." There was a chuckle around the table. "No one really knows if he is going to be where he says he is going to be as he is very unpredictable. To you all, this is Sebastian. Sebastian is a writer and is staying on the *Tulp*."

Sebastian winced at the mention of being a writer surrounded by those of obvious and proven talent. No doubt when not performing, and idle for an afternoon, all of his fellow diners could produce a manuscript that would have the hardened literary agents fighting on the streets of Bloomsbury for the publishing rights.

He sat down between Eva and Hugo. Hugo: compact and precise, the muscles on his arms defined and constantly rippling and rolling as if trying to burrow an escape route from the confines of the skin. His head bald and the flesh on his face tight, shrunk dry to perfectly fit his bone structure, the jawbone muscles visibly working as he ate some nuts. Eva, by contrast, was broad shouldered with the wasp-like perfectly asymmetrical figure of a swimmer, power and strength obvious with each flowing movement of her arms as she reached for her drink and the table snacks.

"You coming to write about us?" she said.

It must be easier to write than explain himself multiple times a day.

"No," he replied flatly.

Umuntu took charge and ordered a taster menu for all. The first course of sushi arrived. As Sebastian fumbled with chopsticks there was a pause in the conversation.

"Hi everyone, sorry I'm late. Look who I found wandering around. Dasha, why don't you sit over there?" She waved at the illusionist's chair as she sat down at the head of the table.

Dasha made unsteady progress and slumped into a chair. He sat with his body at ninety degrees to the table indicating no intention of eating. Propping his head in his opened hand with his elbow on the table he crossed and intertwined his legs in the way that only adolescent girls can.

"Me too, sorry I'm late." With that his mouth closed and he looked upward to the ceiling. He looked hollowed wearing an ill-fitting collarless shirt, sleeves poking out of the cuffs of his military fatigue jacket. Bags under his troubled and bloodshot eyes.

Taking the initiative and to avoid an explanation Sebastian introduced himself to the newcomers.

"Hello Sebastian, I'm Anneke. How do you find the *Tulp*? Comfortable, I hope. It hasn't taken you long to meet everyone. Welcome." Her voice was a smoker's, deep and welcoming with a hint of the hard vowels of Germany. She evidenced no surprise that he was at dinner. She was dressed plainly in a light blue cashmere roll-top jumper to her chin, her skirt tight around the midriff and drifting to the top of her knee. Her feet, unusual for the summer in full calf-length suede boots. As if to confirm her sex a simple necklace and locket hung imperceptibly between her small breasts. Her black hair parted at the side covering half her face which was covered with a thick skin of foundation, hiding and not highlighting her features, rouged gloss on her lips and a hint of mascara to extend her small eyelashes. Her right eye was visible through her hair like a peeking child. Perhaps it was the wine, perhaps it was being in a different country where the rules don't apply – Anneke made him feel accepted and he instantly, and unusually, trusted her.

The meal clattered on, pleasurable with the arrival of numerous Oriental tapas dishes, clinking of glasses and the rise and fall of amiable conversation. The talk focused on the rehearsals and the forthcoming opening. Throughout, Sebastian had been included as if a member of the troupe but unable to join in the conversation as a non-participant in their recent history.

"Sebastian, you will come on the opening night, won't you? Perhaps you can write a review for us along the lines of before and after. You've met them all," as she waved around the table, "but not the Chrysalis." Anneke spoke as if he already had an audience that would want to read his review. Warming to the theme she continued, "I think it would make a great review."

"As do I!" the wine in him replied.

"I thought you weren't going to write about us." Eva looked at him as if he was a habitual liar.

Before Sebastian could reply Dasha unravelled his legs, turned table ward looking directly at Sebastian. Dasha's mouth opened and his crooked nose, like a pugilist from a 1950s fairground, pointed to tobacco-stained teeth.

"You are not from here either, are you?" he whispered softly with a Russian accent through a drunkard's simian smile. Putting on his jacket he stood up and left without saying goodbye to anyone.

Pepper, flushed with wine, hooked her arm through Sebastian's for stability as they left the restaurant.

"Whatever he said to you, ignore him. I told you there was darkness in his head," she said.

Anneke and Umuntu turned right at De Wallen to head home. The rest walked onwards to the *Tulp*, Pepper drunkenly leaning her head on Sebastian's shoulder. Arriving at the *Tulp* Salt took hold of Pepper's free arm, as if her twin was drunk because of him, and accusingly said, "I will take her from here," as she protectively guided her on-board.

Over the retreating shoulders of the troupe as they boarded Pepper whispered, "He is very sexy, isn't he?" followed loudly by, "Night, Sebastian."

2

It was pre-dawn and Sebastian was woken by a deep groaning as if a hungover man was gutturally regretting the previous evening. Poking his head through the companionway silhouetted against the rising sun sat Dasha in the lotus position.

"You alright?" he asked, to no response.

The groaning continued but with a rhythm.

For fear of interrupting this morning ritual he retreated below and drifted back into sleep to the incessant background sound.

The groaning was gone when he next woke, to be replaced by the weekend morning chorus of infrequent heels on cobbles and birdsong. He looked around the room. Decorated by functional furniture, it felt robust and impersonal. The only personal effect was a photograph of Zoe outside the Rijksmuseum taken fifteen years ago. He turned towards the photo; it had been his amulet from the day it was taken. Usually hidden in his London bedroom wrapped in one of her silk scarves available for viewing in solitude. The picture always available, but she was now physically unavailable. Before thoughts of regret clouded the start of a new day he decided to get up and find a coffee and shop for the week ahead, anything to delay the lonely process of change, from pretending to acting and finally writing.

Wiping the steam from the shower room window the view looked directly onto a street of tall houses; they looked as if they were reflections from a fairground mirror where the shapes were pinched and elongated. Amongst these pillars of domesticity four cells with curtains drawn and dimmed red lights hinted at contemporary sexual attitudes. The door of the house closest to the *Tulp* opened and a mother kissed her Ajax-uniformed son as he departed to a Saturday football fixture. As she closed the door the curtain of one of the cells opened.

A man in jeans and a leather jacket clutching a plastic Albert Heijn shopping bag was laughing as he retreated backwards from the entrance. As he turned to depart the whore passed a hand across his cheek with a stroke of feigned familiarity. Was he her pimp? Perhaps her pusher? The alarm clock buzzed the arrival of 8.00. Sebastian watched the Mediterranean-skinned prostitute leaning out of the doorway dressed in a basque and suspenders wave at the departing man. As she waved Sebastian noticed a tattoo in her armpit, recently done as it was bright with colour – a winged horse's head. The man turned towards her.

"See you tomorrow."

It was only 8.00 in the morning and she was working and already had a client.

A bicycle bell pinged at the punter in anger. As he

turned towards the canal to curse the cyclist, he looked directly onto the window where Sebastian was standing. It was Dasha. He directed a long and hostile look at Sebastian. A warning to silence an accomplice sustained for a full minute before he disappeared round the corner.

The thought-troubled walk to Dam Square took Sebastian past the four prostitutes touting for business in their cells. Another curtain opened with the whore indicating she was ready for business but his eyes concentrated on the Mediterranean girl, which she mistook for interest. Lithe and dark with a pretty, overly made-up face failing to disguise her youth. Her bored face broke into a Lolita-like smile with her finger wagging, enticing him in.

"Suck and fuck for fifty euros," she said in a husky foreign voice. He raised his palms and smiled a watery smile of self-denial.

"Don't be shy, I will suck you dry," she continued to try to tempt.

A rush of irrational fear at being seen looking at the property of Dasha increased his speed. Before turning off to Dam Square he looked over his shoulder to see the curtain being drawn behind the form of a portly man entering the cell. She must belong to Dasha and like a flat she was being rented out for temporary use.

No, it can't be he owned her, he was just a punter perhaps; no one actually owned anyone in Europe, did they? Dasha was a sinister-looking man from a former Soviet state and everyone knew what they were like. Sebastian didn't want to get on the wrong side of him, perhaps he knew some shady people. Pepper said he was dark. Sebastian's mind played with the various options, none with a happy start or ending, certainly not for him.

Distracted, he heard his name being called and ignored it in the knowledge that no one knew him in Amsterdam except Dasha, now. The salutation became more insistent.

"Sebastian! Sebastian!"

Turning towards the voice he looked onto a sunlit terrace of tables fully populated with early morning weekend coffee drinkers. Through a maze of raised newspapers he placed the voice in the half-seen mouth of Anneke.

"Hi Anneke, I didn't see you against the sunlight." She was sitting under a sun umbrella in the gloom of shade.

"Have you time for a coffee?"

She moved sideways tapping the chair seat next to her so they could sit side by side and watch the city wake up.

"How are you settling in?"

"Fine," he replied although still troubled by what he had seen that morning. "I was the first up, I think," he lied.

"It's a wonderful city, Amsterdam. Probably the most peaceful city in Europe to wake up in. The absence of cars, the wakeup alarm of cycle bells and the chime of Westerkerk. It's no wonder the bells comforted Anne Frank during her hiding," she said through a veil of hair.

"Have you always lived in Amsterdam?"

"No, I used to live in Germany, moved here four years ago."

"With the Spiegeltent?"

"No, I did something else before this, something different but still similar," she said vaguely and to avoid any further questions she asked, "You, Sebastian, why

Amsterdam? Why writing? Hope you don't mind me asking."

The coffee arrived giving him some moments to think how to answer the question.

Anneke raised the cup to her mouth, her finger too large to fit into the handle.

As she waited for a reply he saw the movement of her hair as she turned away leaving him looking into a curtain of black with a hint of her mouth and eyes behind.

"It's complicated really," he replied evasively.

"If it's complicated it's probably worth the telling, don't you think? Complicated things are always more interesting."

He felt as if he was in a confessional. Anneke, anonymous and non-judgemental, offering absolution. Like all confessors what he really needed was guidance. There was no contrition, nothing to confess to other than his fickleness of thought (or indeed absence of thought). His penance was a vacuous life of self-imposed reluctance to take a decision, a decision to do something he wanted.

"It's a shit show," is all he said and felt the better for it.

The veil of her hair was flicked back by a red painted nail. Her eyes looked at him.

"I come here every day for coffee in the morning."

After the last word her hair fell forward offering the anonymity of the veil.

CHAPTER 4

As the days passed a routine established itself offering infrastructure, predictability and familiarity of events. Each day started with the pre-dawn head-sore groaning of Dasha which might be some form of foreplay. By 8am his libido was as active as an alcoholic's search for an open pub to assuage his thirst. Dasha's daily pre-coitial routine ended with a KGB-like stare toward Sebastian's shower window, a warning. A post-coitial serene smile was absent as he scowled on departure, always clutching his Albert Heijn bag. From the look of fear the whore gave to his back as he turned the corner it could only contain something that demeaned or frightened her. As well as disliking him Sebastian was now scared of him.

The new addition to the days was Pepper. The first day to apologise for the night of their first meeting and thereafter for company in the late afternoon under the guise of getting an update on the literary progress. The meetings were easy and flirtatious. A welcome distraction from a morning and afternoon spent writing.

"How did it go today?" she asked on entering

without waiting for a reply in the sunny, confident way that Americans, especially West Coast Americans, have. She was met by an echo of Dasha's early morning moan without the anticipated pleasure.

"Well," followed by a pause trying to convey studied thought, "same as every day. It's taken all day to write fifty lines. I won't read them to you but would you like to see?"

He lifted the computer lid and the light of the screen increased as if an heirloom from a long-departed relation was about to be revealed. The screen divided into perfect paragraphs, all ten paragraphs with five uniform lines like a battle formation. Each paragraph starting with a capital letter and finishing with a full stop. The sentences had uniformity of length. The words "Fuck It" covered the entire screen.

The corners of her mouth tried to chew back a forming smile.

"It's progress, I suppose, I mean you could have written nothing! Imagine a whole day without even one word. Perhaps over time your vocabulary will widen." By the end of the critique her smile had broken free. As she laughed the pink of her mouth, enclosing Californian even white teeth, offered the same symmetry of his writing but complete and perfect. Having worked with Americans Sebastian had always admired them for their ability not to see a problem. If too tall, climb over it; if too wide, circumnavigate it; if too thick, push until it falls over. If all else fails blow the problem to smithereens.

"Fancy a glass of wine?" Too early for her perhaps, but in his frustration required by him.

Handing her a glass and to avoid any further discussion

of his work he asked, "How did you get involved in the circus business?"

She sipped from the glass.

"Sebastian, it's not a circus, it's a Spiegeltent. We were looking for adventure, I suppose. In the States we lived the full American dream: nice house, high school, two cars, all the usual. My mother is third generation American but of British stock. Dad was a theatrical agent in San Francisco so it was a sort of natural choice to go to London to study."

Reaching into her pocket she pulled out a reefer, showed it to him to enquire about acceptance. A nervous nod permitted her to fire it up.

"Throughout school we were good gymnasts competing interstate, you know hoops and ribbons stuff."

She offered the lit reefer; he raised the glass to decline.

"Salt broke her leg aged seventeen so that ended our gymnastics career."

"Are you really that close? You never refer to yourself, it's always 'we.'"

She let out a laugh which could be an effect of the dope or acknowledgement of her use of pronouns.

"We are very close. In fact we are as close as you can be as twins. Not born conjoined, but Salt arrived first and I arrived holding her hand seconds later. Doesn't get closer than that, almost one."

She curled her legs under herself making a cushion, lent back and exhaled a blade of smoke towards the ceiling like the extraction of a sword.

"Anyway we decided to enrol in Circus Space in London to see if we could become performers. The location but not the course met with parental approval."

"But sword swallowing? What on earth made you choose that?"

Pepper smiled indicating simplicity. "There were no women doing it so we knew if we could specialise in that we could get work, well at least busk around Europe as a duo. At the last show before graduation Anneke and Umuntu were on a talent-spotting trip and offered us a job at the Chrysalis. We've been with them ever since."

"Dasha was with you at Circus Space too, wasn't he?" Sebastian nervous that Dasha would overhear.

She reached for her glass and downed the full content and tapped the glass for a refill.

"He was a year above us. Sure you don't want some of this?" She offered the lipstick-stained roach. Already half a bottle of wine down and equivalent in resolve he took it, inhaled and held the smoke deep in his lungs and coughed.

"Is it only me or do you hear him early in the morning?"

The effect of the dope now obvious on Pepper as she giggled.

"The soul cleanser! It's something he picked up in Hong Kong when he was studying some meditation and martial arts. It's supposed to make you reflect, isolate yourself from your being and reveal a route to purity of living and light."

Feeling the effect of Morocco's best, fingers tingling and his mind achieving the opposite of Dasha's chanting, Sebastian's brain worked slowly as if watching a film but seeing it in slow motion, frame by frame. Each set of frames divided into vaguely related subjects: father, mother, disappointment; present, past, future; sex, Pepper,

Zoe; blank pages, scrolls of words, success. The triptychs floated hazily by as if being exhibited at a pre-sale show at Christies. Sebastian, whore, Dasha.

She uncoiled herself, came over to the sofa and placed her head in his lap. She reached up and gently took the roach from his mouth.

"I like it here, with you. We are all together so much we are like rats devouring each other."

Confused he replied, "Salt and you?"

"No, of course not, the others." She loosely gazed into the now dilating eyes of Sebastian. He looked back at her and felt himself step into the manhole of her widened pupils careful not to stand on the red cracks forming on the whites of her eyes. She continued dreamily, "Do you think it's what people do that makes their character? Or should it be their character reflects what they do? I mean, Hugo and Ricard are neat and tidy, precise. Is that why they do balancing acts? Eva, lonesome and suspicious, is that why she does solo trapeze? Philippe, evasive with a Jekyll and Hyde character, the ultimate illusionist? Umuntu, the guide and musician, creating the mood of the show? Anneke, shy, reserved and not what she is, the conductor of the whole show?" she asked with a quizzical and slurred voice.

Now high he heard the words but could only concentrate on the last image, the previous replaced by the new arrival. Anneke: who she wasn't or was it who she was? There was someone absent.

"Dasha, explain him if you can," he drawled whilst contemplating kissing Pepper.

She pulled on the roach and blew the smoke into his

nostrils with practised skill. The room now as smoke filled as a 1960s Bob Dylan concert.

"Confused, Asian Kazakh Jew fighting agnosticism, solitary but kind and to cap it all gay, I think. Well I've never seen him with a woman. No wonder he is a contortionist." She giggled sleepily.

Even in the befuddled foggy state of Moroccan Black Sebastian concentrated on the last image. Gay! He knew that to be wrong. How can you work and live closely with someone and not even know their sexuality? Kind? He's a bastard either using or controlling a young woman in sexual bonded slavery and almost in view of Anne Frank's house too. He must be an atheist not an agnostic, at least an agnostic can be proved wrong. The heat of trying to focus was enough to melt the frame of thought to be replaced by an action rather than an unconscious substitute. He leant over and kissed Pepper on the lips. The response was slight but willing. Before he could go any further he felt the wine press on his bladder. Walking unsteadily towards the toilet chuckling as a small, animated film played in his memory: the occasion his mother was introduced to his first adolescent girlfriend. She looked towards her and said, "You look lovely and I know there is no fear of an unwanted pregnancy as Sebastian has an inbuilt contraceptive: a small bladder." A pause. "Would you like some tea?"

Returning to an empty room, feeling confused and light headed he looked around for Pepper. Her only presence was a pair of jeans, a T-shirt, a wine glass and the lipstick-tipped roach. The noise of deep but peaceful breathing came from the bedroom.

"Come in here and cuddle me," she said dreamily. As he slipped into the bed he remembered Clarissa and didn't feel it was the right time to kiss Pepper again. He held her warm body spoon-like with his hand resting open and relaxed on the small curve of her stomach.

Waking slowly it was with the feeling of dislocation, having had a full night's sleep but knowing it was still evening. He was gently being drawn back into consciousness by a slow tickle on his back. Not the maternal stroking of the back with a flat hand to awaken a child for a pre-dawn start to a long journey. This was defined and with the point of a finger, nail slightly pressed against the skin. The motion not random but fluid and seemingly writing. His back muscles awake and alert now trying to decipher the movements.

"Again."

The process restarted with heavier pressure, slow and determined. The letters a collection of perpendiculars and flowing movements. He thought he had it.

"Once more."

In silence a repetition of the exercise with harder pressure and exaggerated movement not with anger but an urgency to be understood. The pointing of the finger after the last letter definitive and not to be repeated. He turned towards her, lifted her head and kissed her gently.

"I do too, I like you," he said, looking into her eyes with pleasure.

As if the spoken word was unrelated to the finger scribing she asked, "Let's go out, how about a pizza? I know a place off Leidsedwarsstraat, we can walk there from here. It's such a lovely evening."

More inhibited by the absence of wine and dope it was awkward for him to get out from under the sheet. There had been the shared intimacy of thought but nothing physical.

"I've got no clothes on so if I shut my eyes you can get yours from next door."

She curled the sheet around her, kissed the top of his head and moved towards the sitting room; at the threshold she dropped the sheet and turned her head towards him with a smile of the future.

Initially the walk towards Leidseplein was awkward. He walked by her side avoiding eye contact. His inward arms occasionally and intentionally bumping into hers. He felt the back of her hand gently stroke his limp and indecisive hand. Opening thumb and forefinger she slipped her hand into his open palm. She squeezed.

A laugh of relief escaped as he squeezed her back.

"That took you long enough!" she laughed.

The walk took them past the Bull Dog Coffee Shop populated by marijuana-smoking tourists liberated by the drugs and legality of street smoking. For a pub the street tables showed scant evidence of alcohol, tables frugally covered with nursed half-drunk beers and their owners looking placid and non-responsive to the techno thump from inside the bar. In a contradiction to their late afternoon dope smoking there was no shared experience, just mutual disappearance into solitary worlds. The unenticing entrance to the Casa Rosso erotic entertainment centre heavily patrolled by uninviting dark-coat-clad musclemen; the photographic display that, rather than entice, looked to be advertising a gynaecological convention. The entrance was full of undecided tourists goading each other to enter.

Sebastian felt protective of Pepper and put his arm around her shoulder. Pepper obviously enjoying the walk looked around her and said,

"I do love this place. It's so liberating, how I imagine San Francisco in the seventies."

Sebastian wasn't too sure of the liberation and felt some relief when they crossed the boundary of the red light district at Damstraat. Over the Singel canal with the lingering scent of the flower market with discarded petals bright against the cobbled street. Passing Keizersgracht and Prinsengracht he felt the air of sedate security that only comes with wealth; a lone middle-aged woman watched her dog crap against a railing-protected tree whilst nodding an evening salutation to her neighbour. Her wrist was heavy with a bracelet of gold.

The sound of laughter and activity increased as they passed the American Hotel approaching Leidseplcin. The square like a chessboard with tables of red and white covers, the noise of the diners' laughter and conversation echoing off the surrounding buildings. Cycles formed a perimeter around the patchwork of tables waiting patiently to be pushed home by languid arm-over-the-shoulder lovers at evening end.

"It's just over there," she said as she guided him through the tables with her hands on his hips.

"Hello Marco, before you ask, I'm Pepper." She smiled at the restaurant owner.

Marco, red faced and content with a film of sweat on his forehead and underarm damp patches.

"You are as beautiful as your sister. So beautiful I cannot tell you apart," he said as he kissed her on both cheeks. "A table for two?" They sat at the only empty table.

The proximity of the tables, so close that conversations were shared with fellow diners and the cacophony of noise one of happiness and contentment. Candlelight reflecting off eyes and teeth, heads pushed back in laughter. Men with jumpers draped over their shoulders at the ready to cover bare shoulders should the evening cool.

"Isn't it great here? I love it, it's always alive and hopeful on a warm evening."

She ordered a large pizza to share and a carafe of house rosé. The carafe sweated in the evening warmth.

"What happens next, Pepper?"

"Let's see," she said with a smile.

Sebastian felt the rush of blood to his face. Embarrassed as the words tripped out.

"Not us, you, I mean. Well not you exactly, I meant what happens with the show?"

"Sorry." She giggled as she placed her hand over his. "We stay here in Amsterdam for the next four weeks. Rehearsals next week, the show for three and then on to Hamburg, Berlin, Prague, Brussels. Nothing in November and then London for Christmas and then Edinburgh for New Year."

Four weeks and she will be gone. She sounded excited and sure. He felt a longing for something that had surety. Who or whatever it was he was missing it already. At the moment there was only the flimsy relationship with Pepper to build a structure around, and that would only be a nomadic home.

"Where do you go in November, before the Christmas season starts again?"

"We go back to the US. It's the best time of the year. We miss Christmas as we are performing, so Thanksgiving is our Christmas. Mom and Dad are always so excited when we arrive they have the whole house decorated for Christmas. Well nearly, they don't have a tree that early. On the morning of Thanksgiving we pretend it's Christmas Day and give each other presents. Going back from Europe in November is always great as the sun shines all day in San Francisco." Her face beamed in anticipated familial pleasure.

This tale of contentment was in stark contrast to Christmases at Sebastian's. A damp mist-covered morning in Hampshire. His father dressed in a Viyella checked shirt, regimental blazer and tie standing in heavyweight orthopaedic brogues with the toecaps shining like two bald heads on the beaches of Spain in summer. Mother dressed in an aged floral dress and perhaps new shoes from Primark. Conversation halting and stuttering around neutral territory. The one present each to avoid excess. Mother bravely trying to inject some levity which fails as soon as the Queen's Speech is watched, a preliminary to an overcooked chicken for the sake of economy. His brother desperate to escape the routine of shared misery by getting drunk on cheap imported Californian red wine, and Sebastian by fingering car keys in his trouser pocket. The only sign of contentment is his grandfather who sighs with each post-Christmas dinner fart as he sleeps off the schooners of pre-lunch sherry.

"What's Christmas like at your house?"

"Oh, similar, great excitement all round," he lied. Thinking of the four weeks until Pepper disappeared perhaps forever. He thought of Zoe. "Do you know the Fairmont Hotel in San Francisco?"

"Sure I do. You going to stay there? You had better get a couple of bestsellers under your belt. It's packed with the oil rich and Wall Street types. Why?"

"No reason really, just that a friend of mine is staying there, or has just stayed there." Sebastian omitted to add, "An old girlfriend actually with a nasty little overly paid and single-minded prick in tow."

"Well tell me about your novel and perhaps when you have a bestseller you can put us up there on your book tour."

"Oh God, do you really want to hear?"He said with feigned indifference, eager to tell her.

A nod of interest as she lifted the empty carafe of wine up to a passing waiter indicating that a period of monologue from him was to be given due consideration in the company of a refill.

"It's very difficult, I see it all in three dimensions and technicolour but when I write it down it's one dimensional and in sepia."

"That doesn't tell me what it's about."

"A man, youngish, who views his life from two events: the setting of the sun and its rising at dawn. He has no ability to live in the present. The future approached with apathetic torpor and the past irrelevant. He has been surrounded by the structure of stability, like a house, but it's bland, painted in magnolia. He knows what he needs. Excitement, love, passion, purpose; but apathy rules as he drifts listlessly from one day to the next without leaving the slightest imprint on the previous day and knowing the next will remain equally unblemished by his presence. Hoping that something will happen to introduce him to a life worth participating in, to being alive to life."

"Oh my God, it sounds so bleak."

He lifted the cold carafe of wine, filled the glass to the brim and swallowed. The cold wine heated his imagination.

"No, no it's not. Something happens that changes him, an event or series of events that lead him to want to leave his mark on each and every second of every minute and every minute of every hour of every day."

"This is getting exciting. What happens, what's the event?" Pepper was now keen to find out more leaning across the table, eyes wide with an impatient smile of anticipation.

Staring at the table top, the coloured squares of the tablecloth blurring into a shade of undefined pink Sebastian looked frustrated.

"I don't know. A car crash, a dying sibling, fuck, I don't know. Perhaps an alligator jumps out of the canal and eats Miss Amsterdam before being hunted by ex-whalers in a long boat. I could call the book "*Captain Ahab's Alligator*.""

Her face was serious for a moment before her lips parted and a small expulsion of air escaped like a bubble deflating on reaching the surface. Her eyes narrowed and her cheek muscles rose supporting her smile, then she laughed.

"I love you Brits, not always sure what you are talking about some of the time, but love you anyway. It's a start for sure. Don't all books have to have a start, middle and end? Well you're a third the way through already!" She believed it too. The American way – the belief, the hope.

"If you are going to be rude I am going to tie you up and feed you to my pet alligator."

He knew he wanted to tell her of the horizon, shapes forming in relief to the previous endless and blank vista, forms as yet undefined but separate and animated as individuals. The colour of the background not monotone grey but shadowed and interspersed with pantones of colour. He knew he wanted to write the book, but what about the middle and end?

He took the usual retreat.

"Let's finish this." Waving the now half-empty carafe. "Then let's get a nightcap on the way home. What do you think?"

"I don't think it's enough to have events make a character. Can't the character make the events rather than be the result of the events?"

"I don't know, the story line is still a little undefined. Do we do what we do as a result of an event or do our actions produce the event? One is responsive and the other conditional. For now I am going for the latter." He leant over the table and kissed her firmly on the lips. Hoping for the result to follow later that night.

The walk back to the boat started slowly but quickened as she pulled Sebastian along. Passing the Vlinder Sebastian looked in and contemplated a last drink to bolster his courage. Sitting at the bar he saw Anneke in the shadow of the corner and Umuntu with his back turned to order drinks. Sebastian felt inexplicably guilty at the thought of being seen with Pepper and decided against the drink. Guilty for what, he couldn't decide. Zoe? Anneke? With himself? As he turned to leave he caught a flash of

Anneke's eyes before they disappeared into the manicured foliage of her hair, a smile on her face as she turned back to face Umuntu.

He laughed at her enthusiasm as they stumbled into the *Tulp*. Sebastian looked around him with urgency. Pepper plugged her iPhone into the docking station and chose 'California Girls'. Sebastian threw his jumper over the photograph of Zoe on the bedside table. Turning towards him she let her unbuttoned shirt fall to the ground as her hips swayed to the music and the unzipping of her jeans.

"Come here," she said with a playful smile on her face.

Their lovemaking a contradiction. His clumsy and intense in the search of shared intimacy, protection and hope. Hers deft, sensual and for playful physical pleasure alone.

CHAPTER 5

It was early with a haze of damp air. The trees stood like sentries evenly paced along the canal, only visible in the fog as far as ten metres away. The leaves were bent and soft with moisture dripping into the canal. Sebastian's hands were thrust in his pockets while his unfocused eyes stared downward at the slimy cobbles. It would clear later as the sun burnt through but now it was cold.

Two hours earlier he had been woken by the urgings of his bladder. Leaving the bed gently so as not to wake Pepper. It was the lonely hour when the lights had been extinguished and the new day hadn't started. The streets belonged to the cats and other nocturnal animals heading home.

Easing himself back into bed he put an arm around the sleeping body of Pepper for comfort and warmth. It was cold but soft. He reached for her head and felt a piece of paper on the pillow.

"It was fun last night. Have to go as Salt doesn't like to be alone at night. C.U. P x"

Sleep evaded him. Frustration dressed him and loneliness made him walk.

"Neither do I," he said to the rear end of a cat as he swung his foot in its direction. It missed. The cat turned around and with eyes unblinking confirmed his status of loser before disappearing through a cat flap.

"Perhaps you're right," he said to the swinging door of the cat flap.

The only light visible on the street guided him. It was the same café where he had met Anneke. Cold and miserable he entered. At this early hour there was only one other person, positioned in the corner, dressed against the cold in a heavy coat, with legs crossed with the ankle of the right foot resting on top of the other knee, feet in black Converse gym shoes. He couldn't see the face as the sports pages of the *Bild* newspaper screamed the success of Bayern Munchen.

Out of the window the gloom was lifting, the fog pierced by the red rear lights of vans delivering supplies to the unopened restaurants and cafés. An occasional flickering of light as a newsagent opened to dispense news and cigarettes.

"Latte please," he said to the newly shaven face of the waiter behind the counter. The newspaper rustled as he dragged his open palm over unshaven cheeks. As his eyes followed a drop of water falling down the window he heard her voice.

"Sebastian, are you alright? You look awful."

It took a moment to realise the voice belonged to Anneke.

"Hello Anneke. I know what I am doing here… well I don't actually. It's so early. What are you doing here?"

"I like it at this hour, it's peaceful and quiet. Makes you

thoughtful. Do you want company or to be left alone?" He felt a sympathetic smile behind the newspaper.

The corner of the café was dim. This was the first time he had seen her face unencumbered by her hair. She lowered the newspaper to the bottom of her nose. A thick layer of skin-coloured foundation covered her face; the tips of her wide cheekbones, highlighted by rouge, poked above the newspaper. Her eyes offset by grey eyeshadow. It was early and this was not the makeup of last night. It was fresh and precisely applied. She must have risen very early to look so manicured. Sebastian found her attractive in her makeup.

"Company would be nice." Out of habit he looked at his watch, it reported 7.30. "It must be about 5am and it's already been a long day!"

He took his coffee over to her table and prepared to sit down opposite her.

"Sit here, Sebastian. We can look out of the window."

She pulled the chair next to her away from the table. As he sat down she lowered the newspaper and let her hair fall. The paper folded on the table with the sports section visible.

"You a football fan?"

"When I was young living in Germany I used to go to some of the matches."

"Really? I just can't imagine you and a group of ladies from Berlin shouting and chanting whilst surrounded by the baying mob."

She let out a laugh that hinted that she probably could have coped with the hoards in the stands.

"Oh, you would be surprised. I was younger, different then."

She cupped her hands around her mug for warmth and raised it to her lips. Her fingers denuded of rings had obviously worked. The nails of her fingers glossy with bright red nail varnish.

"I'm here for the peace and quiet, why are you out and about at this hour?"

He saw his reflection in the window. Raindrops falling down the window gave the impression of tears; his mouth opened and closed as if choosing words was too difficult. Patiently she waited for a reply.

"I saw you with Pepper last night," she said gently as she glanced at him.

"Huh!" was all he could say with a shrug of shoulders.

"Do you want to talk about it?"

"Oh God, it's not about Pepper, it's about me." It was a self-pitying wail. "Anneke, what am I doing? Last time we met I described my life as a shit show. I'm trying to think of a word that can properly describe what it feels like to be rudderless, hopeless, but desperate to take control." He paused and stared into his coffee. "You don't want to hear this, do you? I'm sorry."

"Yes I do." Her voice was smoky but soft. "Why don't you talk, I'll listen and when I can I'll offer up some advice?"

Sebastian looked through the window at a delivery van; the driver opened the door and heaved out a large plastic container of fresh rolls and croissants. He handed it to the café owner who peeled back the plastic cover. He nodded his head and smiled before turning into his unlit café.

Without looking at Anneke, Sebastian started his monologue. He told her of his parents, emotionally crippled by their upbringing, loving for sure but in a detached functional manner. School days idling into success from natural ability. University: first love won, lost and compromised into a friendship. A choice of army career out of deference to his father. A regretted move into finance. The drifting and fear of departed time. Wanting change through self-determination, to be someone different to what he was.

He felt the better for the confession. She said nothing in response, she didn't look at him.

"The full confession, that's it. This is when I jump off the bridge, isn't it?"

"Before you do, let's have another coffee." She raised her hand to the waiter indicating a refill.

The two coffees arrived to silence. She sipped hers and passed the sugar bowl towards him.

"Can I tell you a story, well a homily really?"

"As long as it's not as bleak as mine and has a happy ending, sure," he said as he stirred the sugar into the steam.

"I work with a man whose life has been tempestuous. He came from a loving family, both parents hoping his life would be more fulfilling than theirs which had been a grind of subsistence living. Both died leaving a young man in search of fulfilment for them. He started a job of grinding manual labour. The only outlet was a religious sect that initially offered pastoral care. Like so many sects before it turned out very nasty. He saw things and did things that few others can imagine."

He interrupted. "Is this leading to some biblical moral?"

She ignored him. It was she that now looked through the window into the middle distance and the past.

"He escaped the sect and after a terrifying journey

arrived here in Holland. I met him when he was a street performer in Dam Square, a broken, frightened man. Our meeting coincided with a very painful and unhappy change in my life. Bearing in mind what he had seen and been through, his distrust and fear of others, he helped me through a great unhappiness. He is happy now."

"And you, are you happy now?" he asked confused by the story.

"Sebastian, you're missing the point. All change is possible, all things available for change but that desire can only come from within. You can do and be whomever you want, irrelevant of the past and circumstances. You just need the passion to change."

This was like listening to Zoe, but kinder.

"Yes, I get that bit, but the story doesn't mean anything if I don't know the person."

"You do, vaguely," she replied.

Her hands pressed palm down on the table as she lifted herself up.

"I'll be back in a second," she said as she climbed the narrow spiral staircase to the bathroom.

The café had filled slightly with suited men reading the financial pages of *Het Financieele Dagblad*, others browsing the sports section whilst waiting for takeaway coffee and breakfast. It was still too early for the recreational coffee meetings. He didn't know any of these people. He only knew the troupe, Salt and Pepper; it couldn't be either of them as Anneke had recruited them from London. Eva, Hugo and Ricard all seemed perfectly normal without visible marks of a troubled journey. He couldn't rule out Philippe, the illusionist, as he had never met him.

The scent of newly applied perfume told of Anneke's return.

"Perhaps you need some help in this transformation. Perhaps writing it down will help. You do want to be a writer, don't you? Well this is a start. I know little about writing but I have always worked in the creative world, the Chrysalis and before that fashion, so perhaps I can help. Why don't I give you a subject to write about? If you want to you can show me what you've written."

Without looking at her he picked up the mug, held it to his lips and put it down undrunk. Slowly he put another teaspoon of sugar into the mug, stirred it, lifted it and took a long draught. He held the hot liquid in his mouth until it cooled enough to swallow.

"OK."

She wrapped her scarf around her neck and mouth. Her hand slipped into her coat pocket as she stood up.

"Here."

A folded piece of paper was placed in front of him.

She put her hand on his shoulder, squeezed hard before walking towards the entrance.

"As you know I'm usually here in the mornings."

As her hand touched the handle he wanted to know.

"The story, it's Dasha. It's about Dasha, isn't it?"

She flicked her hair back, lifted her coat collar, smiled and left.

Opening the folded piece of paper he read:

It was a long journey

The Country – Africa

The Job – Blood diamond mining in the Congo

The Sect – Lord's Resistance Army
The Sect Leader – Joseph Kony
The Route to Amsterdam – via Africa and Europe
The Name – Umuntu, the compère of the Chrysalis
Your Title – "The Transformation".

He recalled his first meeting with Umuntu – open, affable and welcoming. An exiled shadow from Africa with a new Dutch identity. His skeletal past of thirty-eight words in front of him, those thirty-eight words unimaginable except for the host of the Chrysalis.

Sebastian had heard of the Lord's Resistance Army. It had started with a self-proclaimed messiah called Alice Lakwena who combined Old Testament fundamentalism with politics to overthrow the Ugandan government. After a defeat at the hands of the government she retreated into exile to be replaced by Joseph Kony. The combination of dwindling support and a zealous desire to rule started him on a campaign to build his army through raiding villages and abducting thousands of children to build the ranks. To keep the children obedient and compliant a combination of drugs and Messianic teachings taught them to kill. Each raid for new recruits involved kidnapping, rape and mutilation of the old and those that offered any resistance. Drugs, slavery and retribution created a force of killer children that roamed the Congo and Central African Republic.

He took a sip of coffee; it was cold.

Walking back to the *Tulp* the words of Zoe, the homily of Anneke and the life of Umuntu left him feeling humble and angry with himself. Retracing the route to the café he passed the house with the cat flap; in the downstairs window with its left paw raised cleaning its face the cat looked like a *maneki-neko* outside a Chinese takeaway. The tabby colour in the morning light offering up patches of gold, white and yellow with a red collar sporting a gold bell. Sebastian looked directly into its green eyes.

"I'm not, you know. No I'm not!"

The paw dropped to the floor. The cat looked at him and blinked.

2

Turning into De Wallen district a new day had started. The prostitute cells were almost all covered with sun-worn closed curtains. Cleaners with a bucket and mop were washing out each cell like the slop-out of prisons, the physical guilt of the previous night washed into the canals across the ever forgetting cobbles. Thoughts of error and guilt plagued the minds of men in hotel rooms with hesitant arms wrapped around wives and girlfriends. Almost all of the cleaners were foreign. Had Umuntu been one of them on his arrival? Was this the reward for a journey perilously undertaken? Was the journey worth the prize?

Fifty metres short of the boat there was an argument between three men. Two large in leather coats, the third dressed in a T-shirt and jeans. The two leather-clad men shouting in Russian, jabbing fingers into the chest of the third man.

"Fuck you! I know nothing of what you are talking about," he replied in English with heavy Slavic vowels.

Sebastian retreated and crossed one of the numerous little bridges to the other side of the canal.

As he looked back from the safety of the opposite bank he saw a fist hit the lightly dressed man, head forced upward. Blood covered his mouth and the swelling of his eye gave proof to the fact that this was not the first blow. The wail of a police siren echoed off the buildings. One of the leather jackets pointed at his eyes with two fingers then pointed at the victim, turned and walked away. The noise of the siren increased as the wounded man looked around him and ran in the opposite direction of the oncoming noise towards Chinatown. He looked over his shoulder to make sure he wasn't being followed. It was Dasha.

Recrossing the canal Sebastian quickened his pace back to the *Tulp* and the anonymous safety it provided. Looking through the window of the bathroom he saw two uniformed men get out of the car. Around them the near vicinity of the incident looked deserted. Most of the cleaners had disappeared into the cells and shut the door. Those that remained were questioned by the police and replied with upheld arms and open palms. They knew to admit to seeing or hearing anything would result in awkward questions of domicile.

Faced with a wall of silence and unopened cell doors, the police left the red light district to its cleansing and preparation for pre-lunch business.

Sebastian turned the shower on and went to the bedroom to undress. The bed, left in a state suggesting sleepless turmoil, had been immaculately made. A note under the now revealed photograph of Zoe read,

"Popped in to see you on my way to rehearsal. It was early, where were you? Px"

He removed the photograph, wrapped it in its scarf and placed it underneath his jumpers in the drawer. Feeling guilty about Zoe or Pepper – he couldn't decide which – he shut the door of the shower cubicle.

CHAPTER 6

Sebastian dealt with the voicemails from his mother, in an impersonal and non-confrontational way by email rather than by returning the calls. In recent weeks the tone had become increasingly pleading.

"Your father is very worried about you, Sebastian. He says it will be autumn soon and it's time to look for a job. He wants to know when you are going to look for a job." Her voice dropped to a whisper. "How's the writing going? Do let me know. Don't tell your father I asked." The volume increased. "Do call us soon, darling." He knew his father had just walked back into the room.

The email reply held a promise of an unspecified time period for a return, but he was specific that he wanted to write and would not be returning to his previous life. There would be two replies: one strident, the other supportive.

A week had passed since his meeting with Anneke and there had been some progress. The quantity of writing had increased, the story had been started and some of the characters had breathed; others were awaiting the kiss of life. His original story, breath by breath, was becoming a novel.

Having received a few unreturned text messages from Zoe while she was in San Francisco he decided to contact her. Firstly to tell her of his writing and secondly because he wanted to know how the trip had been and thirdly in the hope of hearing that Simon had turned out as he wanted: a shit.

His *laissez faire* love affair with Pepper continued and he accepted that it was temporary; both gained something from it. For her, physical pleasure, and for him confirmation of being wanted albeit on her terms.

In the mornings Sebastian spent the time touring Amsterdam visiting the Van Gogh Museum, the Rijksmuseum, Anne Frank's House and the bizarre Museum of Bags and Purses. In the afternoon he wrote, when not in bed with Pepper. On a non-physically active late afternoon there was a knock on his door. It was welcome as the past three hours had been spent staring at the computer screen editing the previous day's text.

"Hello. Sebastian?"

"Come in."

The door opened wide and Umuntu came down the steps into the sitting room. He loomed large in the confined space of the *Tulp*.

"Hi, you got a moment? I've come to talk about the show."

The perfect opportunity to get away from work.

"It's hot in here, shall we go across the road? My shout this time."

The afternoon warm and sunny. He had become

mostly acclimatised to living in the red light district but the sight of two children, with their legs dangling over the canal wall throwing stones at a plastic bottle whilst prostitutes touted for trade, was incongruous.

As they passed the closest four cells, Dasha's early morning venue was now occupied by an aged brunette, pale and obviously high, soliciting business from the shadows. The cell next to her was populated by a pretty young athletic women with blond hair. The music blared out from her place of business; she reached her arms into the air touching the lintel of the door, hips gyrating to the music. He noticed on her perfectly shaved armpit a tattoo of a horse's head with wings at the bottom of the neck.

"Why do they do that to themselves? It must really hurt."

Umuntu looked at Sebastian, looked at the prostitute.

"Not all the customers are sadists, some visit them for lack of love, some in search of some illusionary temporary love but most just for sex they don't get elsewhere."

"No, not that, the tattoo I mean. In your armpit, that must hurt, you have to want that a lot to go through that pain."

"Sebastian, you've been living here too long if that's all the pain you think they are going through!"

Feeling foolish he opened the door to the Vlinder as Umuntu found them a table outside in the sunlight.

"The show, it's opening soon. Hope you're not going to ask me to put on a performance. I can't even do star jumps, let alone fire eating," he said putting the two beers on the table.

"No, we don't need a new act," he chuckled. "I know

you and Anneke have been talking about your writing. Well she suggested that you might like to write a small piece on the show for *I Amsterdam*. It's a monthly English publication for tourists. I know the editor and he'll be fine with it."

"My God. My first commission, yes I would love to, how many words? When does it go to print? Who reads it? This is so exciting."

He smiled then laughed.

"Don't get too excited, it's a publication given away for free in hotels and the tourist office."

"Who cares, my first commission. Here, let me get you another one." Sebastian picked up the glasses and entered the bar. As he waited for service he beamed back at Umuntu who was pulling off his jumper in the warmth. As he did so, his shirt rose out of his trouser top, and across his lower back were lines. More than lines. His defined shoulder muscles collected at his coccyx. The lines were weal marks, raised, healed and purple against his black skin almost like surgical scars running perpendicular to his muscles. He turned, saw Sebastian looking and slowly tucked his shirt into his trousers.

Placing the glasses on the table, Umuntu looked at Sebastian as if weighing up his potential to understand something. Thought he probably couldn't. He raised the glass.

"To the writer!"

"Thanks." Sebastian smiled.

"Welcome to the creative world where impoverishment is guaranteed. Recognition is as elusive as a straight answer from a politician."

2

Delighted with his first commission Sebastian was in the mood to celebrate. He knew The Wine Cellar based in the catacombs of the New Church in Dam Square offered a good selection of wines. The whole idea appealed to him: a new career celebrated by buying New World wine from the catacombs; it was apposite, a new start. Cutting through the walkway at the Krasnapolsky Hotel he walked through the foyer, dim after the bright early evening light. The chairs arranged in small groups for businessmen to talk about deals to be done. The Americans obvious in their chinos and tasseled loafers, the South Europeans dressed in bright coloured jumpers ready for an evening out and the Japanese in "Amsterdam" logoed windcheaters clutching guide maps. The suited businessmen wandered with the air of business trip loneliness. Business done for the day, the luxury surroundings of their bedroom not tempting on a long solitary night, they mingled with their fellow residents in the hope of belonging. Their mobile phones attached to ears hoping to engage with colleagues in a familiar language whilst surrounded by the Babylonian noise of temporarily stateless tourists.

He was not one of them, he was in Amsterdam, knew where he was going, had his first commission and was about to celebrate with his girlfriend, well sexual PE teacher. Turning right outside the hotel he joined a large buttock wobble of Americans from the Mid-West. Their waists supported by inverted triangular legs resting on small sneaker-clad feet, thighs crisscrossed each other as they, penguin-gaited, followed the upheld umbrella of the guide leader, the umbrella in pastel blue with "Baptist Churches of Mid-West America – Amsterdam Convention".

"The economy must be bad here, everyone is so skinny and they can't afford cars either, look at all the cycles. I mean look at that scrawny girl over there next to the lamp post."

His eyes wandered in the direction of the pointing sausage. Talking on her mobile as she leant against the lamp post was Dasha's property, the Mediterranean girl. Dressed in blue jeans, a white sleeveless T-shirt and a purple jumper wrapped around her neck. She could be one of a thousand girls waiting for her boyfriend. Without her work makeup she looked young and fresh but frightened. She was talking rapidly into the phone, her eyes darting around her as if she thought she was being watched. The only time her eyes stayed still was when her gaze fell onto the police station opposite the old Amsterdam Stock Exchange. Her eyes focusing on the main doorway of the police station, with each swing of the doors her face reflected disappointment and her nervous scanning continued.

Arriving at the concourse in front of the stock exchange building the Americans formed a Dunkin' Donut circle, the middle of which was occupied by a spherical women in matching lilac trousers and jacket. Sebastian hid amongst the flesh watching the police station.

"The Amsterdam Stock Exchange is probably the oldest in the world. It was established in 1602 by the Dutch East India Company for dealings in its printed stocks and bonds," the lilac lady robotically started.

His view of the girl was interrupted as the Americans swayed from one foot to the other alleviating the pressure on their feet.

"Oh dear Lord, how long does this go on for? It's not God's work all this money making. I'm starving too."

The police door swung open. Three men appeared. One with an unnecessary raincoat folded over his arm. The second an elderly tall thin man in black trousers, white open-necked shirt and a black coat falling to his feet. His black ringleted hair capped by a white skullcap and a collection of white string threads which fell from each belt loop of his trousers. The third was Dasha, lip swollen and a black eye. His hand clutched what looked like a photograph album.

The conversation between the three was animated. Dasha brandishing the album at the raincoat man as if preaching against sin from the pulpit, lips moving quickly without a pause. The raincoat man listened impassively; he had obviously heard it before. With each wave of the album the skullcap nodded vigorously. The raincoat rose and fell with each shrug of the shoulders. Sebastian turned to look for the girl but a mound of purple-rinsed hair blocked his view. Looking back at the trio he saw the raincoat man walking away. Dasha holding the album in both hands smashing it on the top of an imagined table to try to attract the attention of the retreating raincoat. The elderly man put his arms around Dasha and led him away in the opposite direction. The doughnut broke up into bite sizes to re-form into a line of weebles. As they departed Sebastian looked again at the lamp post. She had gone.

CHAPTER 7

He had decided after a few days' writing that it was time to ask Anneke to review what he had done in the hope that her input would deflect from his frustration with the output. The peace of the early morning would be best, there being no witnesses to the potential humiliation. This decision had met with some unplanned events that week that had already sapped his strength.

The celebration of his commission for the magazine *I Amsterdam* with Pepper had been a success with the inevitable tumbling into bed, followed by the late night departure. She had looked different that night as her hair had been dyed red.

"Not sure I have ever slept with a redhead before," had been his only comment before she laughed then made love to him.

The thirst of desire slaked, the post-lovemaking followed the familiar routine. She rested her head on his chest. The chemical smell of the newly dyed hair mingled with her perfume and his effort. Stroking her hair the shards of moonlight shone through.

"Not sure that red suits you," he said after consideration.

"It's for the show, we are fire eaters after all. It's part of the act. Salt is the same," she replied as she pulled back the sheet to get dressed.

The disappearance of Pepper to the company of her sister was something Sebastian had concluded was the price to be paid for sleeping with an identical twin. Her departure always left him with a feeling of second best, being used. It was always a disappointment to wake up alone and discarded.

The first of the unplanned events was the arrival of Pepper earlier than usual, at lunchtime. Her face had the muscular tightness of a decision made, a confirmation of a pre-determined plan of action. Perhaps it was the red hair that gave her the look of control. Sebastian was pulling the cork from a bottle of wine. Without a word spoken she walked in and drew the curtains. The only light in the room was the pale blue background of the computer screen. He turned to observe the activity, opened his mouth for a greeting.

"Ummmgh," was the only noise to come out as Pepper's tongue shot into his mouth even before she had kissed him.

Her hands frantic, almost aggressive. She pulled him bedward tearing his shirt and trousers off. Her hair aflame against the background light of the computer screen. Sebastian felt exhilarated and a little startled.

Her hands grabbed his and raised them above his head, her knees pinning his shoulders against the mattress. He was trapped. Her eyes stared at him, wide with the pupils almost pushing the iris of her eyes into the white surroundings. Hitching up her skirt it was now a solo performance. Sebastian's role passive, the provider of the stump.

"Christ, what's got into you?" he gasped with excitement and dangerous pleasure.

She collapsed on the bed beside him breathing heavily. He turned to look at her. Her shirt had ridden up and her belly button twinkled with a diamond piercing as it rose and fell with her recaptured breath.

"Oh my God!" Sebastian pulled the sheet to cover himself. He wanted to get out of bed and run but felt vulnerable, naked in front of his… his what? New lover? Assailant? His co-conspirator with Pepper?

"For fuck's sake, Salt. What have you done? Christ, what am I going to say to your sister?"

She smiled conspiratorially – with him or with the absent Pepper he couldn't work out.

"Indeed, Sebastian, for fuck's sake. Oh, for heaven's sake lighten up, you Brits are such prudes."

"A prude, a fucking prude! Are you mad! You have walked in here pretending to be Pepper and well… and well you know what you've done." His risen pride subsided with confusion.

She giggled lightly as she tucked her shirt into her skirt. "I think you mean what we have done. We had fun, Sebastian, that's all. You, us and fun, it's a good combination. We should do it again."

"Again? Us, what do you mean us?!" His voice raised in disbelief. "And what do you think I should tell your sister?" he simpered.

"Oh Sebastian, you keep asking that, stop being so

contrite. We have done nothing wrong. Here have this." She passed over a glass of wine as if a prescription. He needed it but found drinking hard with the sheet tucked under his chin like a child poking its head from the bedclothes to see if the creature of his nightmare had departed. But it hadn't.

Salt sat next to him on the bed. Ruffled his hair and smiled.

"I see what she sees in you. When you are as close as we are we share everything. Believe me, she won't be upset, she knew it was going to happen, it always does. I think you should take it as a compliment. We don't do this to everyone, just the ones we like." It was said softly as if comforting a child.

"What, share everything, like a party dress?"

She laughed.

"No, Sebastian, not a dress, important things. Everything is better shared, isn't it? I mean if you watch a beautiful sunrise it is always the more beautiful for being shared."

"It's not the same though, is it?" He knew there was truth in what she had said but couldn't reconcile that with his wounded pride. He had been seduced; it was unfair, wrong and not the natural order of things. Well not the natural order of things in Hampshire anyway. Perhaps it was different on the West Coast.

The feeling of indignation rose as his mobile rang flashing the name of Zoe as the caller.

"Do you want to take that?" she said, looking at the phone as she sipped her wine.

He looked at her incredulously, the thought that a

phone conversation with a normal human being could take place in the circumstances.

"No, not at the moment, I will ring her back. I mean I will ring them back later."

2

The walk to meet Anneke was troubled. He couldn't reconcile the event, as he decided to call it, with Salt and his wanting for love and shared mutual affection. Prude, was he? The juxtaposition of her desire for sex and his desire for love now contradictory. He always knew that his affair with Pepper was temporary, hers for pleasure and his the search for something shared. Could it be nationality as Salt has suggested, or was it upbringing? His certainly very British whereas theirs New World and liberated. Even worse was he now thought of them as a single unit, Salt Pepper; perhaps they were one.

"Oh God!" he groaned to the early morning dawn. No one need know what happened, well no one but Salt and Pepper. As he passed the house with the cat he looked into the downstairs window. There it was, open green eyes, knowing and judgemental. He lifted his arms in the air and lurched towards the window to scare it away, making a noise like a ghoul on a ghost train ride. Impassively the cat remained.

Pulling out his phone he tapped in a message to Zoe.

"I miss you," was all it said. As if anticipated the reply came with the speed of a solar ping.

"Me too, when can I come to see you?"

Arriving at the café he didn't need to look for her. In the shadowy corner she sipped her coffee; her hands thoughtfully tapped a remembered tune on her packet of Marlboro Reds. Eyes like a metronome scanning the passing commuters searching for someone. Occasionally holding the vision of a passing woman before dismissing her as unknown, the wrong one.

"Sebastian, here again for your tutorial?" She gave up her search and looked at him with a welcoming smile.

The welcome enough for him to know it was the right thing to do, to talk to her. The meetings always the same format. He the student and Anneke the tutor. Her role to start the session and his to slowly, nervously reveal his thoughts. After the many previous meetings to discuss his writing he had left less disconsolate and the future seemed almost tameable.

Sebastian took his seat by her side, in the now familiar position of both looking out towards the street; it was as she insisted.

"You happy?" she asked as the lead question.

"Yes and no actually."

"How is it going with Pepper?"

He didn't want to look at her so he stared out of the window. The streets busier now with the hurried energy of early commuters.

"That's the no bit, well not all no, I suppose it's mainly the no bit but within that there is a yes and no." He looked at her reflection in the window to see if she understood. It was difficult to gauge as the yellow streetlight fought for dominance with the light of early morning. He felt her smile.

"I thought this would happen. You know they are identical twins, more than identical twins. They are two parts that make one. They were born holding hands. It's as if Salt was afraid to arrive alone." She knew what had happened.

"Yes, I know all of that but it's not normal to do what they did."

"Sebastian, try to understand. Your relationship with Pepper was always going to carry the seeds of a potential separation. Salt would never have allowed it to continue."

"Great, just bloody great. So what do I get out of this other than being a performing stud?"

She laughed softly.

"Sebastian, is that what you see yourself as, a stud for the procreation of a superbreed?"

Petulantly he replied, "No but certainly more than just a shag for the pair of them!"

"You are wrong, Sebastian. It's not like that at all. The two of them have a unique approach to life. Everything they do is for each other, they must share every experience, it's what keeps them together. To turn the question round, what did you want out of Pepper?"

The tutor probing and the student ponderous. A pause, a false start and then Sebastian spoke hurriedly as if the thoughts spoken would then be forgotten.

"More, Anneke, more. I wanted more, something I had once. It's as if there is a noise from under the floorboards. The sound moves from under the floorboards to behind the walls. The noise persistent, almost thumping to escape the darkness but I can't find the exit for the noise. I can't release the noise."

She waited to see if he would continue. Sebastian interlocked his hands and twisted them hard making the knuckles white.

Softly, she asked, "What happened?"

Still twisting his hands but harder, his fingers now completely white from lack of blood.

"Nothing and everything."

His hands parted. His index fingers drew small circles round each other.

"Our orbit was small, just the two of us. Over time the orbit got larger and larger. Well mine did and over time we were in different orbits." He closed his eyes in the childlike belief that when he opened them it would all be different, as it was previously.

She said nothing, but looked at him.

"Open your eyes, Sebastian. Look at me."

He turned towards her. As tears formed in his eyes he couldn't quite see her.

"If only I had finished the book, it would have been different. It would be different now. We would be as happy as we were then," he mumbled into the scented handkerchief offered by Anneke.

Her hand touched his cheek. Her palm firm and her fingers not quite covering his face.

"You still can be. You now know who you are writing the book for, don't you? Treat the writing as a talisman."

CHAPTER 8

The sound of tinkling wine glasses woke him. Opening his eyes he was blinded by a concentrated beam of early morning sunlight channelled through the glasses. He moved to avoid the blinding light but it followed him making his eyelids warm. Covering his eyes with his hand he looked toward the companionway. There were now two lights dancing around the room, hopping from one surface to the other.

"Do you believe in fairies?" she said. "Tinkerbell and her friend have come to see you." With unencumbered sunlight pouring into his room he could see the two silhouetted faces of Salt and Pepper.

"Do you know the story of Tinkerbelle, Sebastian?"

Pulling the sheet cover over his head.

"Of course, everyone knows *Peter Pan*."

Sebastian remembered his mother reading *Peter Pan* to him in the twilight of summer evenings in the hope of getting him to sleep. It never worked as once the story had been finished he had waited those seemingly endless twilight hours 'til darkness in the hope of seeing Tinkerbelle; she never appeared except in his dreams.

"You're right, they do, but few know about Tinkerbelle. Do you know why she is sometimes spoiled and jealous?" Salt asked.

"No I don't."

"The reason is because fairies are so small they can only have one feeling at a time, so there are no counter-balancing emotions."

As they came into his room both dressed in denim shorts and T-shirts, painted glittering nails glistened in flip flops.

"And today she is here to ask your forgiveness. Do you? Do you forgive us?"

"Yes, yes I do," he said, grateful for the cover of the sheet.

"Well not one of the three of us must ever leave Neverland as you know what happened to Tinkerbelle after Wendy left?"

Sebastian laughed poking his head out from under the sheet.

"I do. I wouldn't want that to happen to any of us." Sebastian was struck by how collegiate they had become. When he first met them they were "we" and now the three of them were "us". The thought gave him a sense of belonging.

"Get dressed, Sebastian, we are off for a picnic." Pepper spoke over her shoulder as she looked for the photograph of Zoe.

As the two of them made no concession to removing themselves from his room Sebastian took his clothes into the bathroom. He couldn't quite decide why, as there was nothing they had not seen before. Whilst dressing he was relieved that they had taken the initiative to bring "the event" to a conclusion. He had been puzzling how to extract himself from the situation. The thought of delivering any of the standard relationship-ending lines too embarrassing to contemplate.

"I'm setting you free." No, that would not have worked. "It's not you, it's me." That contained all of the truth but little panache. Also who would he have said it to? Salt? Pepper? Both? He pulled his jeans belt tight as he imagined the embarrassment of the scene. Salt and Pepper both on the sofa, side by side, as he delivered the line to accompanying mumbling and ceiling staring.

"I can't tell you how nice it is to see you both, I really can't." They knew he meant it too. "So how do we get to Neverland?"

"We fly there by tourist rickshaw from Dam Square. The location is a secret for now but we know you will love it. Food and wine is prepared, and so are you at last. So let's go." Pepper now full of enthusiasm pulling at his arm.

The day was heating up as they walked towards Dam Square. Sebastian felt elated at the resolution of the "event" and with Salt and Pepper on each arm he knew what it was like to walk the red carpet. Even the bouncers outside the Casa Rossa looked benevolent as they cast envious eyes at Sebastian. Walking towards the rickshaw stand at the corner of the square Sebastian was conscious of the passing looks of women. Firstly they scanned the two redheads taking in their slim bodies, matching denim shorts and T-shirts, a glide down to the glistening toes. Completed in seconds and met with approval. Their eyes then focused on Sebastian. A more ponderous quizzical glance. What did he have? The glances asked. Was he famous? Rich? Had they missed something in his physique, was he handsome? He must have something to be with these two. Perhaps he had an insatiable talent for pleasing women sexually. As they looked at their male partners it was obvious that was the real reason for his company. A wry and flirtatious smile crossed their mouths as the trio walked past. The eyes of the male partners betrayed their thoughts: lucky bastard.

The three of them squeezed onto the sofa-style seat of the rickshaw as the cyclist driver raised his head from the cross bar. His face expressed relief at the size of his new passengers – not the usual overfed tourists.

"Take us to the Vondel Park," Salt instructed with a flourish of her arm.

"You'll love it, Sebastian. It's the biggest open air park in Amsterdam. Busy at the weekend so that's why we are going today. We'll find a nice spot near the water for lunch. You been before?"

As the rickshaw set off Sebastian looked around him at the confusion of traffic flow. Although a passenger he was conscious of a comment of Zoe's before he left London. "What's the last noise you hear before you get killed on a Dutch road? A bicycle bell." Looking around him he absently replied, "No."

The journey took them past the flower market and Leidesplein. Sitting in the middle he held onto Salt and Pepper's arms as he tried to work out how he would survive the traffic chaos. Cars driving with logic and discipline until a cyclist appeared. The cars then retreated behind the cyclist as if feeling guilty for being on the road. The sides of the road had a cycle path where the cycles went in both directions. A confusion of traffic lights started trams tinkling and clattering crossing roads and cycle paths, sometimes both at the same time. The python of cyclists seemed oblivious to any light instruction and slithered between cars and trams. The rickshaw cyclist thought at various stages that he was a tram, car and cyclist as the mood suited him. Salt and Pepper laughed as his grip tightened and relaxed with each perceived danger.

"No wonder they built this park in the centre of Amsterdam, you need somewhere peaceful to relax having risked life and limb getting here!" said Sebastian recovering from the journey.

The park was peaceful, the pre-work runners had left and the one o'clock lunchers were hours away. The park was kidney shaped, with a cycle path at the circumference. Within this, lakes bordered by pods of land for different use. The sun glowed off the clay tennis courts as if a flattened Kalahari Desert. The noise of tennis balls being hit from baseline to baseline as predictable as the noise of crickets at night and just as mysteriously the noise stopped with a missed stroke. There were areas for children, play parks with swings and nodding horses on springs. Following the footpath they lazily looked for a shaded spot under a tree.

"How long are you going to stay in Amsterdam, Sebastian?" Pepper asked as they settled below a willow tree next to one of the lakes.

"I don't really know. It all depends on how the book goes. I can't stay here forever as I don't have much money left. And once you have started your tour I won't know anyone in Amsterdam."

"That doesn't give you that long really as we'll be off after the show closes. How is the book coming along?"

For the first time since his arrival in Amsterdam he felt comfortable about the progress of the book. With guidance from Anneke, the shape of the characters had changed from his post-university draft; the journey to completion had started, no more inactivity.

As he lowered his head towards the ground to lie down Salt took his head in her hands and rested it in her crossed legs. He closed his eyes and the multi-coloured light danced inside his closed eyelids as he thought of the progress.

"All the ingredients are there and the texture of the book is more malleable than it's ever been. I now know I can and will finish it."

Salt stoked his hair with her fingers as she rested her head against the tree trunk.

"Who will you dedicate it to, will it be us?"

Pepper lay down on the grass with her head on his stomach looking upwards to the leafy canopy. Her head bounced gently on his stomach as he laughed quietly.

"No, not this one, perhaps the next one." He surprised himself with the belief that there would be another and then possibly another. He was clearer now than at any other time in his life that he wanted to write and nothing else. "I have someone in mind for this one."

"It's the girl in the photograph, isn't it?" Pepper asked still gazing upward. "Who is the girl in the photograph?"

Before he could reply a coloured ball rolled into the three of them. Following the ball was a little girl dressed in a blue skirt and a top too small for her, her belly poking out from the waistband of the skirt. She stopped short of the ball and held her arms out. Pepper rose up handing the ball to her with a smile.

"Is this yours? Here have it back," she said.

"Danique! Danique!" cried the woman running over to the child. As Pepper held out the ball the little girl hesitated before she reached for it. Her eyes darting between Salt and Pepper trying to work out how a mirror image of one woman was possible.

"Sorry," said the woman in English. "Come, Danique. Thank you," she said as she led the child by the hand back to the circle of young women with their children.

The women sat on a mosaic of rugs with toys scattered around them. There were more women on the rugs than there were children. The children ran after each other laughing and screaming, always under the watchful maternal eye. When distance between the children and mothers got too far a cry of a name or chorus of names went up to hail them back to the perimeter of safety.

Most of the women were young, in their late teens or early twenties, slim and hopeful with youth. Sitting on a bench not far from the group sat a-lone blonde woman. Her knees close together and her hands placed between them. Sebastian thought he recognised her. She stood out from the others; although as young as them, she looked tired and gaunt with bruising under her eyes from lack of sleep. Every time she smiled at her thoughts it was with resignation, as if just tolerating life. The mothers engaged and catered for the incessant demands of the children; a small boy ran into his mother's open arms and as her arms enwrapped him Sebastian heard her say, "Darling, I love you", as she squeezed him tight to her chest. The lone woman on the bench looked on with a smile of something missed, unobtainable.

Sebastian lowered his head back into the crossed knees of Salt, the sun draining his energy.

"Everyone needs someone, don't they?" Salt said it as a fact not a question.

"Yes they do," Pepper replied. "Who have you got, Sebastian?"

He delayed answering as he thought of his family – brother, father and mother. They were not needed were they? They were there anyway. His friends, well they were there too. Who did he need, for he knew he needed someone? He knew he needed her, now possibly more than ever.

The sun disappeared along with its heat as a shadow fell over his eyes. It had been a cloudless sky so he couldn't quite work out why. Opening his eyes he saw the silhouette of a man dressed in running shorts with his sweatshirt stuck into the waistband. Behind him came another one with a sports holdall, the zip open and juggling sticks poking out of the top. They gave off the aroma of health after a workout, fit and glowing.

"Hello there. You look like a version of Manet's '*Le Déjeuner sur l'herbe*' except there are two women and one man," said Hugo laughing as his bald head went from gloss to matt as he wiped the sweat away.

"And they are dressed too," replied Ricard.

Both had stomach muscles like the ribs of sand on a beach as the tide retreats. Sebastian felt his stomach muscles contract to hide his mildly inflated tummy into his rib cage. It didn't work for long. Like the water in a balloon it collapsed to its natural comfortable position around his trouser top.

"Hello boys," Salt and Pepper replied in unison. Sebastian nodded to the two in recognition and a readiness to know them better, but not today and definitely not now.

"Looks like you have had a more energetic morning than we have," he said as he reluctantly moved to make room for the two.

Sebastian had met them before and seen them often around the *Tulp* but had never engaged in conversation other than salutations and platitudes as their paths crossed. They were almost always together. He felt a little threatened by them, their presence more pronounced than his. They reminded him of his first girlfriend when he was seven. He had been sitting with her on the green of a park when she had been distracted by the class toughies who had come over and performed handstands and bent-over crab walks. These feats were enough for his fledgling love to be attracted away and for him to hear the over-the-shoulder comment of "What are you doing with that drip? Come and have some fun on the swings with us." Sebastian felt proprietorial as this was their picnic and these two were interlopers. Salt opened the wine and poured three glasses. Sebastian lifted his glass up to catch the sunlight through the white wine; it gave off a yellow glow lighting his face.

"I know it's early for this, but it's good to break the rules," giggled Pepper. Sebastian noticed Ricard and Hugo look at each other and nibble water from their sports bottles.

"Let's play Donkey with the juggling sticks," Salt suggested as she deftly drank from one hand and juggled two sticks with the other.

His participation short lived – it lasted exactly six throws – Sebastian retired as the donkey. He felt another *déjà vu* from his seventh year. The others continued, with laughter and squeals of horror and delight from Salt and Pepper. The sticks being balanced on noses before being propelled to the catcher. Bluff and counter bluff throws from behind their backs to disguise the direction of travel. With each drop of the sticks Salt and Pepper became a "donk" and a "donke". Ricard and Hugo never got close to being a beast of burden. A long arching throw from Ricard sent one of the red and white sticks into the sky. It fell like a stuka bomb, flipping over and over with such speed that it became a pink blur as it fell downward. Salt, glass still in hand, shuffled like a drunk on the spot positioning herself for the catch. Catching it with her free hand and using the downward momentum she whisked it through her lifted knee back towards a laughing Ricard.

Sebastian sulkily looked around him. The children now tired by the heat played quietly on the rugs. The girls playing tea parties with their dolls and the boys pushing tractors and cars through imagined traffic jams to a slow narration.

It must have been about 12.00 as Sebastian noticed a few early lunchers. Men with their tie off, jacket over their shoulder held by one finger, the other hand holding sandwiches and a drink. A couple walking arm in arm, her eyes closed and face upward to catch the sun, him guiding her to some shade nearby. The pace slow and soporific, the conversation gentle and quiet as if to speak too loud would frighten the sun back into the clouds.

"You two go on, let's see who the donkey is!" Salt laughed as she collapsed to her knees in excited exhaustion. As he reached for the bottle she kissed him on the cheek. "I love the summer so much, warm and sunny and everyone so happy."

As Sebastian raised the glass his eyes looked over the lip to take in the happiness of summer. From the perimeter cycle route he noticed two men walking quickly towards them. Unusually for the heat of the day both wore black leather jackets. They weaved between the cyclists with deft determined footwork avoiding any collisions – skilful, quick and determined.

The single girl on the bench was looking agitated as she spoke frantically into her mobile, her hands running through her blond hair.

"Run, Irena, run!" A voice pierced the slumbered torpor of late morning. He looked around him to find the source of the voice.

The children, as if injected with sugared energy, responded to the word run as if it had been the crack of a starting gun to a new game. The tea party ended and the traffic jams were left to self-correct as they ran off like escapees from a prison camp.

"Run, let's run," the children shouted in unison pushing each other aside, yelling with delight at the new game. Their legs pumping and arms wind milling as they formed groups to then splinter like shrapnel from a grenade, reforming and splintering again. The mothers indulgently played the game chasing the children with arms wide open, making monster noises, threatening to eat them if caught.

"Donk," cried Pepper as Hugo dropped the throw from Ricard. "You're a donk! Donk!" she chanted.

The blonde on the bench stood up quickly with her mobile held limply in her hand. She looked at her white plastic high-heeled shoes as if seeking advice. Her head moved to trace the source of the voice advising her to run. Her eyes wide and fearful, frantic.

The two leather jackets quickened their pace through the melee of children.

"Irena, run, please. Run. Christ's sake, run." The voice was hoarse, exhausted and pleading reflecting no hope of response.

Sebastian still couldn't find the source of the voice through the darting of children and the game of Donkey. He was now caught up in the unravelling separate and seemingly unnoticed event between the blonde woman called Irena, the disembodied pleading voice and the leather jackets.

As the two jackets reached Irena they grabbed her arms. The taller of the two had a scalpel-cut mouth sneering at her. The squatter one, the muscle, arced his hand through the air and struck her on the cheek with the back of his hand. Her head snapped back and the mobile phone dropped from her hand. She didn't lift her hand to wipe the blood from the corner of her mouth. She didn't even try to run, she stood quivering. Another slap to her face ensured complete subjugated compliance. The two men grabbed both her arms and lifted her off her feet. Irena struggled and raised her freed arm, reaching out towards the direction of the warning voice, her arm straight with hand outstretched as if the last act of a drowning woman and in her armpit Sebastian saw a tattoo of a winged horse's head. He knew he recognised her.

"Sacha!" Irena pleaded like a child separated from her mother watching hopelessly as she disappeared in the crowd. "Sacha!"

Sebastian stood up and shouted.

"Hey, you bastards, leave her alone." He echoed the voice, "Run, Irena."

As he started to run towards Irena he felt his legs collapse under him and his body pinned to the ground. The weight immovable as he struggled.

"Don't do it, Sebastian, just don't get involved," the voice of Ricard, even and controlled.

Sebastian struggled under the weight of Ricard and was within inches of freedom when he felt the knees of Hugo press on his shoulders pushing his face into the dry hot earth. With his chin on the ground propping up his face he looked towards Irena. He could just see her through the wall of two leather jackets. Just before they disappeared behind the hedge the scalpel-scarred man turned around, raised a corner of his mouth in a half-smile of victory and with his closed hand to his mouth flicked his thumbnail off his front teeth as if sending a morsel of food towards Sebastian.

Writhing to remove the weight from his back he felt powerless and hoarsely pleaded for release, his mouth full of dust. The weight remained, keeping him pinned to the ground. It had happened so quickly with such precision and minimal resistance that the children were oblivious to what had happened and were still running from their motherly monster captors.

"If we let you go you stay on the ground until we say so, OK?"

"Fuck you, Hugo." Sebastian spat out the dust from his mouth.

"Do it, Sebastian, just do it," pleaded Salt. "Do as they say."

He sat up looking towards the hedge. Hugo and Ricard had retreated beyond striking distance. Salt and Pepper's eyes told of their sympathy but also that what had happened to him was for the best. His eyes scanned the park for any sign of Irena; there was none. He looked towards the path that had been the source of the voice advising her to run. Slumped against a tree, her head bowed, legs buckled underneath her like the victim of a motorbike accident, one arm holding her phone to her ear.

"Irena, Irena," Sacha gasped between sobs.

He recognised her; Sacha was the Mediterranean prostitute that Dasha visited daily. The young woman outside the police station. Irena was another prostitute that worked in the same row of cells as Sacha.

Sebastian ran towards the bench where Irena had been sitting in the hope of catching a glimpse of her. She and the muscled leather jackets had gone. He lent down and picked up Irena's discarded phone. Put it to his ear and listened.

"Irena…" The voice was weak with exhaustion. He looked toward the collapsed Sacha muttering into the mouthpiece, her mouth pathetically mumbling, "Irena… Irena…". She was being pulled roughly by a man in black jeans and a T-shirt.

Sebastian still held the phone to his ear and heard an East European voice snarl in the background.

"Get in the car Sacha." He thought he recognised the voice. "You stupid bitch." The phone went silent. The voice was Dasha's.

He started to move toward them. Too late, she had been bundled into a car; the rear door slammed and the car screeched away from the park.

He slipped the phone into his pocket and walked back through the children. The same little girl who retrieved the ball grabbed him by the trouser leg saying something in Dutch.

"No, darling, he's not the monster, he won't eat you," her mother said with a reassuring smile.

CHAPTER 9

He sat alone at a table and for the first time in many days willed the phone to show signs of life. For reasons he couldn't justify he had hoped by some subliminal messaging that Zoe would know what had happened in the park and would contact him. The beer was now flat and warm having been cradled in his hands for the past half hour. The Vlinder mid-week quiet, with evenly spaced solitary drinkers looking for answers or just company in their drinks. Sebastian along with them but also in hope of bumping into Salt and Pepper. He turned to look at the pressure on his shoulder; it had been a gentle squeeze of a black hand, the cuticles purple.

"We heard it was a rough day," Umuntu said through a sympathetic smile.

"Can we join you?" Anneke placed three beers on the table without waiting for a reply. "Want to talk about it?"

He shrugged his shoulders, took a long draught of the replenished beer and regaled them with the events in the park. The hardest part to explain was the anger he felt towards Salt, Pepper, Hugo and Ricard. The anger was due to their lack of engagement in the assault of Irena and avoidance of intervention with Sacha's manhandling. Christ, he was angry with them. There were only two in the Irena assault, no more than twenty metres away. There were five of them, all young, four certainly fit, one perhaps less so. The least equipped making all the running, the other four all offering resistance to any relief. This anger was swirling with the potential loss of friendship with Salt and Pepper. He had screamed at them after Sacha disappeared, screamed at all four of them but really talking only to Salt and Pepper.

"What if it had been you two?! Huh? What if it had been you two and everyone sat on their arse whilst you were being assaulted?!"

Turning to Hugo and Ricard, "Look at you two, built up like alabaster statues and just as fucking useless. God, you make me sick, the pair of you."

He turned and walked away from them.

"You don't understand," was the flat reply from Hugo to his back as he walked away.

He needed a cigarette after off-loading the recent history. Standing outside he drew aggressively on the butt, his hands shaking, his mouth pursed as he tried to extract as much nicotine as possible. Anneke joined him; cigarette at the ready, she struck a match within her clasped hand like a workman to protect the flame from the wind and lit one of her Marlboro Reds. The tip of the cigarette burned brighter in the dusk than the darkness of night time.

"They did have a reason, Sebastian."

"Well if they did I don't get it. It was an act of shameless cowardliness as far as I can see."

"Sebastian, look about you. People coming and going with freedom, homeward bound, meeting friends for a drink. Doing what they want to do when they want to do it. But things are never as simple. Everyone's tied to something: circumstances, events, people. It's never quite as it seems. Everyone is living in a… what do you call it? A shit show. Trying to make sense of events beyond their control." She dropped her cigarette and crushed it under her foot with a twist of her sole and kicked the butt into the drain. He looked down at flower-patterned Doc Marten boots with red laces and noted how aggressively the act had been executed.

"Look, I have to go, stay with Umuntu for a while. It's never good to be alone for too long."

She leant over to him and in the pool of orange streetlight she looked older. She kissed him on both cheeks; she smelt of foundation. He watched her walk away; she walked with confidence and a big stride.

"Come, Sebastian, let's go for a walk. It's a wonderful evening, it will take your mind off things." Umuntu took his arm and lead him towards Oude Kerk. Turning left into Oudekerjsplein they walked along the cobbled street. The church on one side and on the other side, no more than the five metres from the fortified sacred walls, the windowed cells of prostitutes. The prostitutes around Oude Kerk, most black or coloured, older than in the other areas of De Wallen. There was a less frenetic atmosphere, calmer perhaps because of the presence of the church and a subliminal message.

"The whole world is here, Sebastian. Blacks, coloureds, whites, Asians and all ages too. Some from the old colonies like Suriname, the Caribbean and the Malaccas. The newly arrived migrants from Central and Eastern Europe. They are all here."

The cell doors opened slightly as they walked by with invitations and promises of carnal pleasure. One door opened a little wider than the others and a large-breasted middle-aged black woman in white shorts and an ill-fitting bra screeched with delight, her ample flesh struggling to be contained.

"Umuntu, you got a new job? You a pimp now? Man, things can go wrong in life if this is what you're doing! Your friend want some fun?" She waved her arm to entice them in as she opened the door wide.

"Hello Rosie." Umuntu hugged her warmly. "How's business?"

"Man, it's awful. It's hard when you get to my age." She ran her fingers down her sides and over her plump thighs. "Competition is tough with all the younger girls, the new ones from Eastern Europe. They are younger, too young and too pretty too. They gotta work harder, you know, some have just gotta work harder, you know that, Umuntu. Still the best clients know experience is what you're paying for, right, Umuntu?" She licked her lips and winked at Sebastian knowing that Umuntu was never going to be a client. "But you know, kids at university, I've got to pay for that. Then what? When they finish, no jobs. Don't want them doing this." She waved her arms around the warm red womb-like cell. "Hell man, times have changed. They gotta do something else."

"Keep well, Rosie, keep well." He smiled and squeezed her upper arm.

"I will man, I got De Rode Draad to keep me occupied too." She looked at Sebastian. "Come see me sometime, anyone who is a friend of Umuntu is a friend of mine." She laughed as she took up her perch on the high bar stool at the entrance to her cell.

Arriving at the junction of Oudekerksplein and Sint Annendwarsstraat Sebastian suggested a beer at The Old Church Coffee and Juice Bar. The night had arrived and the warm air seemed to be pushed around the narrow street by a slow-moving broom, each sweep warmer than the previous one making shirts stick to backs. The air heavy with the smell of marijuana being smoked at the nearby tables. The neon lights of the bar reflected pagan lights against the stained glass windows of the church.

"She is quite a lady Rosie, how do you know her?" Sebastian spoke through eager sips of his cold beer.

"She used to work in a soup kitchen for the homeless in Chinatown. I used to go there when I first arrived in Amsterdam. She is a wonderful woman with boundless energy, a life being lived. Her husband long since deserted her so she has had to bring up her two children by herself. Quite an achievement really." Umuntu tilted his beer in salute.

"Do they know she's a prostitute?"

"No, she always told them she worked for a homeless charity and for De Rode Draad. Actually she does both but neither pay, but she didn't tell them that bit! She is now a prominent member of De Rode Draad, the prostitute union."

"There is a union for prostitutes?!"

"Indeed, Amsterdam is an extraordinary place. If you

look over there you can see the outline of a statue, like a primitive Degas sculpture."

Sebastian looked through the crisscrossing of people and saw a stationary large-breasted woman in heels. The figure set in bronze leaning against the frame of a doorway exactly as Rosie had been in her doorway.

Waving his arm around the circumference of the church Umuntu continued his history lesson. "Within the thousands of cobbles in the plaza around Oude Kerk there is one cobble set in bronze, missed by most as they walk over it unseen, of a hand caressing a woman's breast. Both these statues are dedicated to all those in the world that make their living by prostitution."

"The union of prostitutes, how does that work?"

"It's there to provide support for the working girls – health checks and advice. For those first entering the business it offers advice on safety and paying their tax."

Sebastian raised his drink and eyebrows. "Tax? They pay taxes?"

"Yup, and VAT! Rosie tells me the charity tries to encourage all the working girls to attend, as they are self-employed. Most of the local Dutch girls do but she has problems with the East European girls attending. Most are illegally here and don't want the scrutiny of the authorities. Their life is a lot harder with no protection or mutual support."

Dropping some euros onto the table Umuntu stood up.

"Come, I want to show you something."

As they walked into Sint Annendwarsstraat they passed the window of Anna restaurant. Inside Sebastian saw the well-heeled Amsterdam crowd along with foreign business people, groomed and sophisticated, at tables with small, beautifully presented dishes. The waiters, clean and sharply servile, glided by with one hand behind their backs as they poured wine into half-filled glasses. The faces of the diners were happy and laughing. Familiarity being built before business discussed. The residents of Prinsengracht and Keizersgracht dressed with success and wealth sparkled with light reflecting off Rolexes and rings.

The atmosphere in Sint Annendwarsstraat was different. The ground floor of the buildings like the filling of a child's birthday cake. A layer of neon reddish pink ran the length of the entire street, the lights on ready for business. The wind of the evening had not dissipated the smell of stale beer and marijuana that hung heavy. Cigarette butts carpeted the doorways of the working girls, a sign of indecision. One of the windows, curtain closed, still had a lit cigarette recently discarded.

"If you look to your right, carefully, there are two men in bomber jackets. Pimps." Umuntu spoke as they walked.

The men were in their early twenties leaning against the wall like flamingos propped up on one leg. The other leg cocked and the sole of the foot flush against the wall. They were not moving, they were not buyers. Eyes glided across the first six cells, some with curtains drawn. The open cells had scantily dressed girls in pants and bras prancing like horses before the start of a race. They looked continually in the mirror, adjusting their hair or makeup, moving to the window to entice.

"They are pimps for some of the girls here. They spend most of the day and certainly all of the evening here counting the number of visitors to each girl. That way they know how much the girls have earned and more importantly how much they have earned."

Sebastian lowered his eyes after being caught in the radar look of the two men. He looked to find Umuntu among the flow of men. Some stopping to stare at the girls the way one would look through a window at a coveted sports car. Others retracing their steps trying to pluck up the courage to enter. He felt a tug on his arm and found himself pulled towards the entrance of a narrow alley. So narrow there was no room to walk normally. To pass through the alleyway was only possible in crab-like fashion. On either side of this suffocating alley no further apart than a one-arm stretch was a twenty-metre row of cells with doors ajar. The air didn't move here but hung like a heavy coat made of fear, lust, desire and regrets suffused with cheap perfume and sweat. The girls scantily dressed for all sexual persuasions. Little notices similar to the postings on a church noticeboard in neat and precise writing detailed all the services that were available. With no daylight the girls shone, their underwear glowed under the ultra-violet light, their eyes white with dilated pupils and soulless. The men passed each other back to back with downcast eyes of guilt.

It was with relief Sebastian came onto the open street of Oudezijds Voorburgwal; here the air was moving at least.

"Sorry about pulling you through the alleyway. I thought it necessary as the two pimps seemed to have clocked you. That's something you really don't want. They don't like to be noticed and an unwelcome stare can be met by an equally unwelcome attack."

Sebastian tried to wipe away the experience of the alleyway from his moist brow.

"I thought you said they were all self-employed."

"No, not all. Some of the East Europeans are trafficked and pimped out by their owners. That's why Rosie said they had to work harder, much harder. To the traffickers and their pimps they are just machines to produce money, when the machine is worn out with over use they are discarded and all too readily replaced. They are ruthless in a way you cannot imagine in the darkest hours of your worst nightmares."

Sebastian thought of the alleyway with no daylight. The small cells, the smell, the lustful stares, the loveless sex, the hell of being owned, all repeated on a daily basis until worn out. He felt sick and breathed the night air, lighter and moving as they walked along the canal edge.

The contrast to the alleyway could not have been more different. The canal dividing the street into two, it was open and the air cooler as it passed over the water. The bars with lights on were noisy and busy with laughter and chatter competing with music. Swimming along the canal a phantom whiteness of swans dipping for food. They seemed oblivious to the streetlife.

"Over there by the sex shop you can see another pimp." Umuntu pointed to a combed-back greasy-haired youth talking into his phone. His face purple from the neon glow of the advertising hoarding shouting, "Sex Videos. Private Cabines".

"There too, over by the bridge."

The bikes cycled across the small cobbled bridge over the canal navigating through the crowds of tourists and night prowlers. The pimp the only person stationary, observing his property to ensure no theft of what was rightly his.

As they walked towards the bridge they were approached by a long-haired lank figure with jeans hanging below his waistline and grey boxer short tops showing. He was skinny and sallow with the eyes of the hunted.

"Want some coke?" He spoke from the corner of his mouth, stopping briefly to await a reply.

Umuntu dismissively waved him away. He didn't linger and walked on slowly repeating the request in search of a buyer.

"I'm not sure I am enjoying this guided tour of yours, Umuntu. I've never noticed the underworld before. Now you are pointing it out I see pimps everywhere, pushers and other lowlife. God, I must have had my eyes shut since I got here."

"The pimps aren't everywhere but they are here for sure. I just want to show you one other thing."

They left the noise of the canal and took a quiet side street which offered Thai massages from genuine Thai ladies. The street was quieter and the absence of red lights and throngs of people gave it an air of prohibition. The few people they passed looked lost, a bit confused and almost disappointed. Turning a corner the familiar structure of working spaces but lit up in blue against a darkened background noticeable by the lack of commercial lighting of bars and coffee shops. The atmosphere of a closely guarded secret, somewhere only those that know go to. The girls touting for business looked taller and physically bigger, filling the window with their presence, their bodies silhouetted against the blue lighting, faces hidden in the shadows. Their enticement routines were more animated; no tapping at the window with coins but wide swung door open gestures of temptation. The blue light gave the working girls a ghostly appearance making it hard to define their features. There were no loitering pimps or pushers.

"I walk past the entrance to this street most days and have never been down here before. There is no one here, yet twenty metres away it's heaving with party animals. Why the blue lights?"

Umuntu led him closer to the windows.

"Look closely as we walk by." His voice was flat and even.

Sebastian, now wholly accustomed to what usually took place, let out a stifled cry. The cavorting and seductive twisting of the girls' bodies took place but something else happened.

"Christ, that woman has just flashed her penis at me!" He looked at Umuntu as if this was an unfair joke played on him. The return look was placid and reflected no surprise at his response.

"Now come, let's go back to the Vlinder." His arm guiding Sebastian to the red light of night to stop him looking over his shoulder.

Sebastian had opted for a whisky which didn't last long. Umuntu recharged the glass and settled down with a beer.

"This has been an enlightening couple of days for me. I've witnessed two assaults and have now passed through the underbelly of Amsterdam. I can't believe I didn't notice the pimps and pushers before. I have confused the red light district as some sort of well-organised bohemian playground. An adult sexual Disney."

"With more expensive rides," chuckled Umuntu.

"No, I mean I thought it was safe. I've had no trouble since I have been here."

Umuntu sipped his beer, sat back in his seat and looked at him.

"It is, Sebastian, it is safe for you, for us. For the visitors and tourists and most of the girls it's safe and well regulated. But there are always those that slip through the net. Those girls that don't have the protection of De Rode Draad, for them it's not safe. It's cruel, hopeless and desolate. They are chattels of the traffickers. Sold onto syndicates and then pimped out by the gangs. For them it's living hell."

"They should leave, make a run for it and go to the police."

Leaning forward Umuntu looked directly at Sebastian, holding his eyes.

"Sebastian, it's impossible. Once they are owned they are owned. There is no escape. I know what that feels like. Do you imagine that they like what they do? Everyday someone tells them what to do, how many customers they must screw. They have to lie there with total strangers. Imagine it. A fat drunk sweating man stabbing you with his prick over and over again. If they don't reach the set number of customers there are repercussions. Serious repercussions."

Sebastian felt a vibration in his jacket pocket. Pulling out Irena's phone he looked at the screen. The photograph on the cover was of Irena holding the hand of what looked like her mother and father in the countryside, all laughing, possible a post-Sunday lunch walk. The name Sacha glowed green next to an envelope. He held it up to show Umuntu.

"It's Irena, the girl assaulted in the park. Should I open it?"

A nod from Umuntu.

The envelope opened and the text came through. "Are you OK? Where are you Irena? S x"

"I kept it to give back to her, she dropped it after being attacked. I know she works near the *Tulp* but she wasn't there today. Should I keep it or hand it to the police?"

Umuntu considered the question.

"Keep it, there is no point giving it to the police. It will just remain in lost property. Wait till she gets back to work, she will need it. Mind, that may be a couple of days."

"What makes you think that?"

"As I said, for the pimped girls there are repercussions. She must have tried to make a run for it because the last resort for a pimp is to hand out a beating. The pimps never deface their property, unless it's to teach a lesson. The girls can't earn with a swollen face."

"Oh my God. Now I know why they didn't get involved in the assault."

"Sebastian, these people are not to be taken lightly. They are evil. A well-organised cross country of criminals. I know what it's like to be owned by such people." His face took on the sad features of a previous misery that had gone on for too long. "They were wise not to get involved in the assault, and lucky for you that they stopped you or who knows what state you would be in now."

Sebastian looked around the bar half-expecting the two leather jackets to walk over to the table and remove him to the back of a waiting car.

"I am going to hand the phone in to the police then."

As if this act would expunge the incident from his memory and any future entanglement.

"No, don't do that. If she's not back at work in the next few days I'll ask Rosie to track her down. She knows everyone here. Irena will need it."

Sebastian looked uncertain, afraid.

"OK?" Umuntu questioned.

"OK."

As they walked back to the *Tulp* Umuntu put his arm around Sebastian's shoulder, pulled him closer and gave him a reassuring hug.

"You know, Sebastian, what those four did in the park was right. Right for them and right for you. You may not realise it now but you will. Don't jeopardise your friendship with Salt and Pepper."

Sebastian nodded in acknowledgement.

Arriving at the gangplank to the *Tulp* Sebastian turned to face Umuntu.

"Why the tour this evening?"

Umuntu paused, turned to face him and smiled.

"Things are never quite as they seem. Are they?" he answered before walking away.

Before he could reply his phone announced a new message. It was from Zoe.

CHAPTER 10

The night was still but Sebastian woke with a start. His clock glowed three. As soon as he saw the time he knew he had to get back to sleep otherwise he would miss the alarm call in four more hours. He checked his phone, the light red. Opening the message again he re-read it, it made him happy.

"Can't wait to see you tomorrow. Z x"

Turning on his side he plumped up the pillow to try to regain his oblivion. He shut his eyes and a smile played on his lips. He would find sleep again but first he wanted to bathe in contentment.

Even as a child he had trouble sleeping when he thought that there were unclosed issues in his life. Things not resolved, no matter how slight, required closure or the sandman would miss him on his nightly visit leaving him tossing and turning, praying for the new day to arrive to close the outstanding issues. Making the ledger balance.

After the night with Umuntu there was the issue of Salt, Pepper, Ricard and Hugo, the need for closure. Umuntu had been right and the next day he had sought them out individually to apologise for his outburst in the park. Easy with Ricard and Hugo but more difficult with Salt and Pepper as they were always together. He hadn't explained his understanding, just that he was sorry. Hugo and Ricard accepted with formality, seriousness and a firm handshake. Salt and Pepper threatened him with untold consequences should it happen again. Before hugging him.

The text that same night from Zoe had said she was free for a few days and wanted to come and stay. The following calls had been effusive from Sebastian, guarded and evasive from Zoe. The result for him the same: she was coming over and arriving at ten. The ledger balanced. Sleep arrived.

He stumbled out of the shower, looked at his reflection, then at the bed. The jeans she liked him to wear laid out, blue and white shirt ironed waiting a choice and a back to hang off. Aftershave or not?

"Not too much, no none," he said to the bottle placing it back on the bathroom shelf. Coffee first then clean his teeth so he didn't have stale breath when he kissed her hello. How was that kiss to be? On each cheek, hand on shoulder? On each cheek with hand behind her neck? A hug and one kiss? Leave it to the occasion. That never worked, he knew; there would be a fumble and he would end up missing her cheek and kissing her lips. Too early for that, or perhaps it was not to happen at all this trip. *Don't put the shirt on until you have your coffee, nothing worse than a coffee stain. Shut up, Dasha, take your groaning elsewhere.* He clenched his fist and looked ceiling ward with his eyes shut, and like the atheist he was he appealed for guidance and success from the heavens.

"God, please, please make it happen." The phrase reminded him of his childhood birthdays before entering the kitchen. "God, please, please don't make it a rugby ball/tennis racket/football." It always was. The smile contrived as his father leant over him holding the racket and showing him how Jimmy Connors used to hit the ball. His mother awaiting the paternal absence before handing over just what he wanted.

"Calm down, just calm down. Stop thinking." His reflection spoke off the boiling kettle. "Please God, it's the last request ever, promise. Tell me she has broken up with Simon."

He waited until Dasha had cleansed his soul. Locked the companionway door; reopened it, rushed down the stairs into the bathroom and sprinkled some aftershave on his cheeks, not too much. Looked at his watch, time enough. Ten minutes to the station and seventeen minutes by train to the airport. Then a wait, a pleasurable anticipatory wait. He couldn't wait.

The doors of the train bleeped and glided open. He stood next to the door to avoid any delay from fellow travellers as they disembarked fiddling with the handles of their wheeled turtle bags before moving off. He followed the signs to arrivals. Took up position behind the welcoming barrier. Looked at the airport clock – thirty minutes to go – he waited.

The opaque doors of customs opened intermittently revealing the new arrivals. He knew a London flight had arrived as a hen party of flat Estuary vowel voices screamed.

"Let's get pissed. Girl Power," they said as the coven of

women dressed in black T-shirts and leggings topped with pink tutus spewed out onto the concourse protecting an overly made-up woman with a "L" sticker on her chest and "Learner Bride" badge on her back.

He bobbed on the soles of his feet to see behind the heads of the arriving passengers. The door closed as he got a glimpse of her. She was dressed in white jeans, a blue shirt tucked into her waistline, her body divided by a brown belt. On her head was a velvet hat of purple and black. She was bending to pick up her bag. His heart raced in anticipation, his palms damp.

The door opened and closed again with momentary glimpses of her. After what seemed an unfair time delay the door opened and she walked towards the entrance. Sebastian started to lift his hand to wave; it fell back to his side. He just wanted to look at her and lock the image away for recall on cold October days.

Her eyes scanned the crowd and fell on Sebastian. Walking towards him with her eyes meeting his and then falling, she smiled. The smile that said, "I knew you would be here."

"Hello Sebastian." She shyly kissed him on both cheeks. "Jo Malone Lime, Basil and Mandarin." She laughed softly into his ear.

"It's a new me." Picking up her bag he noticed it was small. Too small to pack the men's pyjamas she always wore, he hoped. "Come on, we've only got two and a half days to live forever. God, it's wonderful to see you." He hugged her and laughed.

Walking across Dam Square Zoe pointed towards Rokin.

"Do you remember we stayed over there in a small apartment? The walls were thin and the guests next door constantly shouted at their children. We had to spend the entire weekend away from the place." She turned around and pointed across the cobbled square towards the palace where the sentries might have been. Now guarded by various mime artists – Charlie Chaplin, the Statue of Liberty and Jack Sparrow were on duty. "In the corner, next to that pub that's where we went shopping, the shops are gone now. It was a fun weekend, wasn't it?"

He looked at her right wrist; it was still there slipping up and down her arm as she waved her arms about in recollection.

"Come on, I want to show you my new home." He laughed as he grabbed her arm and pulled her onward.

Walking through the red light district, still now and scantily populated by both punters and prostitutes, they were the only ones laughing.

"Sebastian, you really have drifted into the decadent life. I bet you spend your evenings with a glass of absinthe and a notebook. Just you and the green fairy dreaming and writing."

"Not quite. What I do know now is why writers either blow their heads off or drink themselves to a welcome early death. Right, stop here, close your eyes and hold my hand. Watch your step and I'll guide you."

Zoe grasped his hand tightly and walked unsteadily as Sebastian guided her toward the *Tulp*.

"You can open them now." With his hands outstretched like a conductor bringing the orchestra into full note he presented the two yellow bicycles. The bikes old and designed for elegant mount with no cross bar, Amsterdam Cycle Hire on a board behind the seat. On top of the handle bars a bouquet of tulips held in place by yellow ribbon.

"Your steed awaits you. Come on, we have no time to lose." He took her bag and boarded. Unsure what to do with the bag he placed it on the sofa; he looked towards the bedroom and decided to deal with the sleeping arrangements later.

"Oh Sebastian, it's wonderful. Look at all the flowers." Every glass, mug and pitcher was full of flowers. The light of a summer's day giving the room a rainbow glow as it reflected off the petals. She hugged him with a hard squeeze. "I'm so glad I came," she laughed.

With the enthusiasm of a recent immigrant to a new city, Sebastian was desperate to show off his new home.

"Let's go for a cycle ride so I can introduce you to Rembrandt."

The start was shaky as they wobbled south along the cobblestone streets; with each junction crossed and the observation and replication of their fellow cyclists their courage grew. By the time they reached the Heineken Experience on the outskirts of town their confidence was further bolstered by the smell of beer. Cycling side by side along the Amstel canal they looked like any other young Dutch couple on a sunny cycle ride.

"I haven't done anything like this since I was child. I have forgotten how blissful it is to have the wind go through you hair and the feeling of freedom a cycle can give." Zoe was smiling as they passed under the motorway.

Sebastian drew away from her and shouted over his shoulder.

"Race you! The finish line is a café on the right."

"Right, you're on." Zoe rose off her seat and leant forward on her bike. "I'm catching you," she laughed.

He let her draw parallel, stared at her with the eyes of a Tour de France winner and sped away. With the café in sight he knew he was going to win. Fifty metres before the finish line he heard a cycle bell trilling and a deep female voice shout, "*Wegwezen de manier waarop je voor de gek!*"

He knew what the words meant and with the accompanying anger of the bell he pulled on his brakes and slowed, stopping at the side of the cycle path to let the irate cyclist past.

"Loser," she laughed as she cycled past him with her head now over the cycle bars. "Catch me if you can."

He knew he had been defeated. With a slow, sedate and dignified cycle he arrived at the café to find Zoe sitting at a zinc-top table. She smiled the smile of the victor.

"Where did you learn to speak Dutch?"

"If you remember, Sebastian, those were the most repeated comments on our last trip here fifteen years ago. Every time you tried to cross the road you were met by that cry. It's the only Dutch I know: "*Wegwezen de manier waarop je voor de gek*", Get out of the way, you fool."

"And the last noise you hear before…"

"… you die is the tinkle of a cycle bell," she finished for him.

He turned to go into the café with a smile on his face; she had remembered. He knew she would have a double espresso too. He also knew he wanted to ask about Simon, but now was not the time.

"I don't see Rembrandt here, all I see is a café and a park."

They had left the city behind and Amstel Park bordered them on one side; on the other side of the canal a fan of small fields divided an islet into strips of discipline.

Sebastian picked up his bike and pushed it back along the Amstel canal, retracing their route.

"If you look over there you will see a windmill, on the left is the statue of Rembrandt looking into the distance. He came here often to ponder the various events of his life."

They sat down beside the statue and finished their coffees surrounded by the coming and going of tourists noisily embarking and disembarking from buses, dedicating just enough time for a camera snap to prove they had been there before disappearing to hunt further tourist treasure.

"'Try to put well in practice what you already know; and in so doing, you will in good time discover the hidden things which you now inquire about. Practise what you know, and it will help to make clear what now you do not know.' It's a famous quote from Rembrandt," she said as she studied the statue.

"Sorry, Zoe, this must be like a busman's holiday to you. I was going to take you to the Rijksmuseum next, an afternoon of going blind trying to find the characters in the Dutch Master paintings. I think we've done enough culture for today, you decide what to do next." His plans now derailed.

"No, I didn't mean that, it's beautiful here. I'll tell you what, why don't we cycle back into town and do what everyone else does on a sunny day in Amsterdam?"

"They lunch, smoke dope, shop and lounge as far as I can work out. Which one do you want to do?"

To his surprise she looked at him with wide enthusiastic eyes, smiled, laughed and said, "All of them and in that order too."

There was something of a curfew when they arrived back in the centre of town. The post-lunch hour where the offices were full and the streets empty.

The first two were easily fulfilled. They entered the aptly named Rasta Babylon Coffee shop. The lighting dim, the walls covered with flags of red, yellow and green with a portrait of Haile Selassie placed with museum precision. There they were met by a kindly faced ancient Rastafarian with a sphinx smile and bleary eyes.

"Welcome, man, to your subconscious, peace be upon you," he said showing them to a small table with legs no longer than two feet and cushions from Morocco spread on the floor. He placed a well-worn menu in front of them.

The menu was laid out like a New World wine list offering names of the vintages: Super Silver Haze, Lemon Larry, Best Vintage. The marijuana headings divided into traits: smell, taste and effect concluding with the flowering time. If marijuana was not to the patron's taste hashish was offered in various guises, prices and aromas.

Sebastian held the menu in the proprietorial way of a male on a first date, perusing and selecting with knowledge.

"Well I'm not sure I will go for the Nepalese Pollen, I find the effect of fastened seat belts doesn't suit my palate."

Zoe looked at him to enquire if he knew what she was talking about.

"No idea," was the reply.

The Rastafarian returned to the table and hovered like a sommelier offering help if required.

"We really want something light and something to eat as well," he confidently stated to the Rasta.

"Well, my friend, we make very good cakes and muffins, I can bring you a small selection."

"Perfect, let's have the house selection," concluded Sebastian as he handed the menu back.

The hash cakes arrived neatly arranged like a dish of dim sum. Sebastian pushed one towards Zoe, who pushed it back to him.

"It's the etiquette that men always go first in these places."

"I didn't know you were the Debrett's of hashish eating." Sebastian spoke through the crumbling of the dumpling in his mouth.

"What's it taste like? I've never done this before." She inspected one with the suspicious look of a first-time diner at a Seoul restaurant.

"Like soft shoe leather with an aftertaste of moss," was the contemplated reply as he studiously chewed.

The initial effect was a disappointment after they had tentatively then enthusiastically finished the hors d'oeuvres plate. Within ten minutes all that had changed.

The conversation took an unusual turn. Both started talking; neither was listening to the other but throughout their respective narratives they nodded approval or disapproval to their own dialogue.

"The flight was like being a pampered pet. In first class they obviously think you're rather thick as they give you an escort and dedicated check-in counters with fewer people. They even hold your ticket for you in case you lose it. Ask questions as if you are too stupid to know where you are going. They look at your ticket and then say, 'Are you going to San Francisco?' Well where the hell else would we be going if the ticket already said San Francisco?" She showed her disbelief by moving her head from side to side.

Sebastian continued his monologue beaming with delight.

"The book's coming along word by word, page by page. I really want you to meet someone. You'll really like her, well I do, so I know you will."

"I knew there was something wrong when we got there. The suite at the Fairmont had two bedrooms, one each. The sitting room had been set up with computer dealing screens and various alarm clocks showing different times of the day. But that's not all. He made me unpack his suitcase as he fiddled with the screens. He had twenty exactly matching white shirts and ten matching pairs of black trousers, all the same. He threw them out after each day." Her eyes widened at the memory.

"She has helped me start writing again, I mean she is not a character in the book, more of a guide. Not of the writing but as a guide to what I already know, I mean why I am writing."

"All day, I mean all day, he stared at the machines. Well not all day, as he got up very early to go to the gym every day, about 5am. If I ever have to look at multi-coloured bouncing pixels again I promise you I will jump out of the window. He spoke endlessly about risk return ratios and whole conversations took place in letters – EPS, EBIDA,

PE – and other impenetrable language." She shook her head in disbelief.

"On a sunny day like today I went to the park, the Vondel. Anyway in the park there were these two prostitutes. Then a gang of thugs hit the first one and then another guy who I know, well I think it was him, took the other one away in a car. I don't know but I think the car was driven by a rabbi. Do rabbis drive cars or is it against their religion?" He looked thoughtful as he spoke.

"Before he went to the gym in the morning he insisted that my room was tidied, the bed made before the chambermaid came in in the morning, even made me wash and clean the shower after I had used it. You know wipe the walls down with one of those windscreen wipers. The magazines all had to lie in a line, edge to edge. Towels hung like soldiers to attention. He even took his own cutlery to dinner as he said all the other people were probably poor and had nasty diseases." She looked down at the plate with the marijuana motif in the centre, relieved to see the chipped ceramic pattern.

Sebastian searched unsuccessfully in his pocket; he came up empty handed, looked with confusion at his hand and explained.

"Well I have to give it back, I mean it's not mine and she needs it, the phone I mean."

"I had never slept with him before we went to America. He always took me home in a taxi in London pleading an early start. I did after a dinner in San Francisco, twice in fact, well twice but not on the same night." She shuddered as if a cold blast of air had swept across her.

Looking around him for fear of being overheard

Sebastian whispered, "You don't want to get involved with them, the pimps. These guys are brutal, they would kill you just as easily as say hello. Dangerous, very dangerous, that's what Umuntu says."

"Dinner was sometimes in a private dining room. He didn't like the other people at the hotel. He always ordered for me, I don't even like fish. You know I don't."

Sebastian fixed his eyes on hers.

"There should be an organisation, a global one that stops these girls from being trafficked. It can't be that hard, can it?"

She stared back at him, without focus but thoughtful.

"He always wanted to do it doggy style, well the two times we did it he did. I don't like it like that, head banging against the headboard, not being able to see him. It hurts too as there was never any foreplay, just straight in." She moved on the cushions as if uncomfortable.

"The prostitutes around the *Tulp* all seem to have a tattoo of a horse's head with wings, always in their armpit. Is that a new fashion? Like the one where girls get wings tattooed on their lower back? But they're always on the lower back, these aren't, they are in the armpit."

"The worst thing was as soon as he had finished he would stand up and go back to his room, leaving me alone in mine. But I knew he was a bastard. You know why? He had all his pubic hair shaved off and a tattoo saying Master above his cock!"

She burst into hysterical, uncontrollable laughter wiping tears from her eyes.

"The final straw was as he left, his shoes remained. You won't believe this but they had a wedge insert at the heel to give him some extra height. He was really just a short-arse."

He joined her in laughter but unsure what he was laughing at as the effect of the hashish reached its zenith. Through stifled laughter he asked, "How was San Francisco? I hope you've got rid of that shit Simon."

"Have you finished the book yet?" she replied with her hand hiding her mouth and stifling her giggles.

Leaving a tip, they mounted their bikes with a view to fulfilling the next thing on the agenda: shopping. The trip to the eclectic fashionable district of Jordaan was one of increasing hazards as the effect of the late lunch dominated. Balance unsure, reactions slow, Zoe had twice cycled to the very edge of a canal and been saved only by the protective metal barrier from a mid-afternoon swim. Sebastian offering little help as he collapsed into fits of giggles. Each T-junction en route echoed to the cry of "*Wegwezen de manier waarop je voor de gek!*" and the urgent ring of cycle bells forewarning of imminent crashes.

The shops, small and compact, offered designer clothes, not of international brands but of the owners' creations, eclectic in colour, cut and design. Zoe tried on shirts, dresses and skirts and with each transformation pulled back the curtain of the changing room to show Sebastian. He nodded approval or disapproval with the addition of a smile or grimace. The shop owners indulgently watched this display in the hope of a sale. But with each sad nod from Zoe she handed back the clothes; the owners acknowledged that a sale was more likely from someone in a more sober state.

Having exhausted the designer shops, their only

purchase was two pairs of fake Ray-Ban aviator sunglasses with white frames from a street hawker. They walked like stable lads in the show ring next to their bikes, holding them tight to their thighs for fear of the bikes being startled and rearing up in fright from the passing pedestrians. The streets now busy with end-of-day activity. Babboe City cargo bikes with a wooden trough at the front occupied by school children sucking on lollipops whilst the mothers exchanged lunch dates. Family tandem bikes with a child at the rear holding a multicoloured windmill humming quietly, the cross of the handle bars populated with the voice of instructions from the youngest child.

"Let's go back," Zoe suggested with an air of contentment as the hashish wore off to be replaced by a calming tiredness.

Approaching the *Tulp* Sebastian scanned the windows looking for Irena. She wasn't there but the room was occupied by a brunette and scanned by the two pimps from the park. Zoe watched him, followed his eyes.

"Ever been tempted? Bet you have. Come on, you can tell me, I've told you about San Francisco."

Before he could answer Salt and Pepper hopped off the *Tulp*.

"Hi Sebastian." Their eyes ignored him as they studied Zoe. They turned to Sebastian, smiled an approving smile.

"See you two tomorrow at the opening," Salt airily said as they passed them.

Zoe looked at Sebastian. Sebastian looked back with a face that told of a question.

"You've been more than tempted, I think," she said as her eyes followed the departing redheads.

CHAPTER 11

1

He sipped his coffee and looked at the bed. He had been right, the suitcase had been too small. The sun had warmed the room and the sheet had slipped from covering her. She lay curled up with his spare spotted pyjama bottoms and a crop top. Her stomach revealed, even and smooth, moving imperceptibly as she slept. He smiled at the thought of the previous night. They had spent the evening on the bed and then in it, Sebastian reading his book to her from the computer screen. She had listened carefully and not without comment. Each of the points was noted on the screen with a dotted red line finishing in a bubble of red at the margin of the text. Her comments as if spoken in a child's comic. He had agreed with most, but not all. Contesting those he disagreed with had led to a lively debate, which he invariably lost.

"How can he be so decisive at the same time as being so useless in all aspects of his life?" she had asked of the protagonist.

"Well there are layers to his character that overlap, some where he is in control and others where he is not."

The reply was a note in the margins. "Based on who?" it questioned.

As the evening had turned to night she had become sleepy. She had asked for some bedclothes and if it had been a hint at an invitation Sebastian had declined. He was content just to have her in Amsterdam, in his houseboat and in his bed. He needed nothing else although a slight desire to want more lay beneath.

"Second drawer down," he had shouted from the bathroom through a mouthful of toothpaste. As he heard the drawer open he coughed and the toothpaste splattered from his mouth over the mirror like a rabid dog in attack mode. It was the drawer with her photograph wrapped in her scarf. He waited for a comment. Hearing the unzipping of her trousers and the swoosh as the pyjama bottoms were pulled on, he felt safe enough to re-enter the bedroom.

"Come to bed," she said in an invitation to shared contentment. He pulled back the sheet and climbed in. She laid her head in the crook of his neck. Her hand searched and held his.

"Talking of inconsistency, thanks for keeping my scarf, it always was a favourite of mine," she murmured before slipping into sleep.

He watched her as she stirred into consciousness and wondered what it would be like to see this every day, each morning. The thought made him feel peaceful and content the way a constant source of pleasure never diminishes its delight no matter how often seen. The sight of her passport and airline ticket on his bedside brought the thought to an end; she would be leaving tomorrow. They only had today.

"Morning," he said to the vole-like opening of her eyes.

She smiled. "What have you planned today? No more cycling and a different lunch please."

"Whatever you want to do during the day. Tonight we are going to a show at a Spiegeltent."

"Oh, I'm not sure I like circuses." She sounded disappointed.

Sebastian found himself echoing Umuntu.

"It's not a circus. It's like being at an intimate party. The acts are performed as if you are actually part of them. Afterwards there is a post-show party that we should go to. I want you to meet some of the troupe, I know you'll like them."

She looked at him.

"I already have and I'm not so sure," she said, not accusatory but looking for a confirmation or denial.

The day was summer hot and still. They wandered the streets with no destination. Coffee and lunch were spent in comfortable silence interspersed with languid commentary watching the passing of the people. It was peaceful, calm and the soporific atmosphere created a closeness as they, themselves inactive, watched those who were active. Both knew the time for departure was close and each in their thoughts wanted to ask questions and receive direct answers but feared the ruining of what time remained together, not enough to resolve the unspoken issues.

"You know, Sebastian, sometimes I didn't think you would do it. I thought you would come here, get pissed and come simpering back to London after a week. Perhaps you have managed to rekindle the fire. Certainly I loved what you read to me last night."

He looked at her and remembered Anneke's comments: "You now know who you are writing the book for." In gratitude to both he replied with a smile.

"I knew you always knew I could do it. I just didn't. Thank you both."

She looked at him quizzically; time was too short for them both, she didn't want to risk a question.

The tempo of the day changed as night arrived. From peaceful and intimate to busy and public as they arrived at the Chrysalis. The long queue sticking out like an arm from the entrance. The Spiegeltent looking nondescript, a large yurt constructed of wood and canvass with a circus pinnacle top. The crowd of all ages, parents trying to calm the chattering of their children as the excitement mounted the closer they got to the entrance. The entrance like the fairground fortune-telling machine. Hands passed into the curved cut glass opening to exchange money for entrance tickets foretelling of excitement within. Sebastian peered over shoulders in front of him, impatient to get inside the tent. Zoe excited because Sebastian's enthusiasm was contagious. Once inside it was just as Sebastian had imagined.

"It's a Dutch word, Spiegeltent, meaning Mirror Tent. All of them have a history and a name and this one is called the Chrysalis."

He spoke over his shoulder to Zoe as he pushed past the dithering crowd who studied their tickets to find their seats. Sitting in their seats he looked around him. It was exactly as Umuntu had explained it to him. A fusion of a cabaret club and an entertainment salon. The circular pavilion interior made of wood and assembled like an IKEA flat pack but without the assembly problems. The magic inside in contrast to the bland exterior. Inside the tent a small circular stage took pride of place in the middle lit by a solar system of lights. Surrounding the stage the circular seating in terraces and behind the seating, at the widest circumference, velvet-covered booths with banquette seating. The walls inside covered in brocade and broken up with mirrors and multi-coloured leaden glass panels. The tented roof supported throughout by barber shop poles.

"Easily confused with the interior of a Victorian brothel," Zoe commented as she gazed around the now full space.

Their seats were part of the velvet-covered booths, for the privileged elite. Their table circular with two bottles of wine, one red and one white; place settings suggested food to come. A small card on the table read, "Review with kindness, Anneke."

The small circular stage in the centre of the tent was bathed in a pool of blue light. The audience red, yellow and green-faced as the lighting moved amongst them. Leading to the stage a small walkway and behind the walkway, almost invisible but for the light sparkling off their instruments, was a brass band, silent and waiting. Sebastian recognised the half-shadowed faces of the musicians; they played at the Vlinder on the wooden decking. The crowd chatted and looked around at their fellow attendees, eyes not yet focused on the stage. The sound of so many voices was loud and the words undefined but fast and anticipatory, an air of excitement about the unknown.

The brass band broke into the confusion of voices with precision and abating the smouldering excitement. The coloured lights dimmed to darkness, the pool of blue on the stage cut out. The crowd fell silent, a spotlight shone on the stage.

"Ladies and gentlemen, welcome." The resonant voice of Umuntu filled the tent. "Tonight you will see some of the greatest performances from some of the most skilled performers of the world. Dispel the unbelieving and marvel at what you see."

The light went out. The time in darkness was enough to provoke the shuffling of feet and murmur of voices. The beat of a double bass accompanied the rasp of a trumpet as the stage exploded into flames from the centre. As the flames died the blue lights bathed the stage as Salt and Pepper arrived dressed in sequinned bodices blowing fire into the canopy. As the tempo of the music increased Hugo and Ricard joined them on stage dressed only in pinstripe trousers with braces, their bodies muscular and seemingly carved from stone as the shadows exaggerated each movement of their naked torsos. Salt and Pepper sprayed jets of flame at Ricard and Hugo who turned somersaults. The music slowed to a drumbeat of the double bass strings. Ricard and Hugo formed a gothic archway by performing handstands with their feet together at the apex of the doorway. The lights dimmed and a silhouette appeared in the doorway standing erect and straight in a black suit, white shirt and black tie. Dasha lowered himself with his chest flush with the stage floor and his head staring directly in front. The strings increased their pace; he raised his legs from behind catching them at his shoulder, and seemingly folded himself into two separate but conjoined body shapes like a sheet being ironed, his face impassive as each of his cheeks was bordered by his feet. The music stopped and as if charged with electric voltage his face and body disappeared behind his folded legs to arrange himself back into the straight erect figure of his entrance.

"My back's sore just watching this!" Zoe said massaging herself.

Sebastian looked at the audience; Dasha's act of body reconfiguration had been met with open mouths by some; others had their hands covering their eyes as if they didn't want to see his body snapped in half and guts splattered across their faces. Dasha repeated the movement across the stage resembling a human Slinky toy.

Eyes moved canopy ward as Eva dropped from the darkness holding herself upside down with her ankles wrapped around a suspended hoop. Around her naked shoulders was a red velvet cape flowing towards the stage. As she lowered to the floor the cape spread evenly across the stage. The lights turned off, the whole tent aflame with jets of fire from Salt and Pepper. The illuminated darkness lasted for five seconds. The band reached fever pitch as the lights came back on and standing middle stage with the cape around his neck held by a golden clasp stood Philippe the illusionist.

The applause burst from the audience interspersed with couples whispering into each other's ears.

"I know how he did that, there's a trap door below the stage." And, "He was under the cape when she came down."

All improbable and impossible. Again the voice of Umuntu spoke in Sebastian's head.

"Not all is as it appears."

The stage lit up as a piano was wheeled to centre stage; there was no trap door.

Umuntu tap danced towards the piano, tight black trousers giving emphasis to his strong thighs. His back and shoulders fighting against the confines of a tight white shirt. On his head sat a small black trilby set at forty-five degrees. He sat down and started to play a rag-time melody, pausing intermittently to let the brass band play alone.

Sebastian nudged Zoe.

"I didn't know he could play the piano."

"You seem to know everyone performing. Not just those two," she said with a hint of relief as if she had miscalculated when they had bumped into Salt and Pepper.

The stage now had the whole cast dressed in colourful striped blazers, each carrying a bottle of champagne. Umuntu paused his piano to wipe the top of the upright piano with a duster, the spotlight bouncing off the perfectly smooth surface. As the cast tap danced around Umuntu they placed each bottle of champagne on the piano top. Umuntu continued his rag-time as Ricard and Philippe mounted the ends of the piano balancing on their toes. The tempo of the piano increased; in unison and from different ends Ricard and Philippe placed their hands palm down on the top of the champagne bottle necks. As if in slow motion they raised themselves into a handstand using one hand on the bottle top, the other held parallel to their bodies. They looked like two gannets the second before breaking the surface of the water. The crowd fell silent, then clapped as if this was the end of the act. Umuntu crashed a chord; Philippe and Ricard with military precision placed their spare hand onto the next bottle simultaneously releasing the other, repeating the movement before dismounting from the piano gymnastic style with a backward somersault. Throughout Zoe had been holding Sebastian's hand and with each movement of the two on the bottle tops she squeezed as if from her via his hand the next bottle would be safely reached. Her relief after the somersaults was wild clapping and smiles of happiness for their safety.

"Something not to try at home," she shouted into the deafening applause.

The brass band played a melody as the stage was cleared for the next act. The coloured lights swirled around the audience, talk impossible with the volume of the music.

Sebastian watched as ice creams were licked, melted droplets dabbed from the chins of children. Excited exchanges of looks of wonderment between couples and nods of respect from others.

"It's him. There, over there. The one I told you about at lunch." He pointed at the empty stage, struggling to be heard above the music. Sebastian had spotted the rabbi. He was dressed exactly as he had last seen him at the police station: long black coat, white tieless shirt. He was alone in not clapping. His ringlets now more disciplined as they poked from under the rim of his black Fedora. From behind his Fedora were two small child's faces bobbing in and out of view as they tried to see the stage through the rim. As the lights moved across the audience his face was spot lit or in darkness. When in the light he had the look of a man who was rarely questioned, a hard definitive look that ordered authority from his fellow man. Not the look associated with his calling. His wife sat one seat away demurely dressed with a headscarf of modesty covering her hair. A child, their daughter, aged about six, sat between them obviously bored. To occupy her time she bit her nails; with each approach of hand to mouth he slapped her hand, hard with discipline. Sebastian imagined hearing the slap. The child's mother waited until after the slap to offer a momentary furtive look of sympathy. The child looked down at her shoes, sullen and sore.

Zoe looked in the direction of Sebastian's stare but not knowing who she was looking for shrugged her shoulders as the lights dimmed. The next act was missed by Sebastian as he couldn't take his eyes off the rabbi; for some reason the sight of his face, the resolute configuration of his features made him think of Dasha, Irena and Sacha and what role he played in their lives. No matter how minor or major that role it was executed without question from him or questions from them. He wanted to know how involved that role was; he also wanted to have that resolute belief so apparent in the features of the rabbi. The look on the rabbi's face only confirmed to Sebastian that it was his duty to get the phone back to Irena. Although he hadn't seen her since the attack, he had been indecisive, but not now. Now he knew he would return it to her.

His moment of introspective thoughts was brought to a conclusion by Zoe squeezing his hand.

"That must be included in your review." She spoke over the applause.

"Yes, it's the best so far," he replied aware that he had missed it and was there for a purpose as important as his newly made decision. Reaching for his pad he started to write some notes and concentrated on the stage.

The centre of the stage was occupied by a small table and on top of the small table was a square-shaped object covered by a cloth that trailed to the floor. The stage was lit in a haunting green, the air thickening with dry ice falling off the stage and covering the feet of the audience. The band started a thoughtful tune as the cloth rose into the roof. The square-shaped object was a clear glass box no more than two foot wide and high. Lowered from the ceiling in a tight pair of trousers was Dasha. His body was so lean he looked like a single tendon taken from an anatomical drawing.

"This is impossible surely," Sebastian spoke into the darkness.

Dasha opened one side of the glass box, threw his arms out to the audience and then to the opening of the box. The audience responded with murmurs and looks of disbelief. The music stopped, to be replaced by a slow drumbeat and a noise like a marble swirling in a glass bowl. The music increased its speed to the clapping of the audience. Dasha first placed one of his feet into the impossibly small glass box. As if his body was boneless and fluid flesh he flowed his torso backwards into the box, his arms retracted like the fleeing of a squid after his torso, and with his thumb and index finger he pulled the glass door shut. His eyes, Sebastian noticed, fixed on the rabbi. Those that didn't clap held their hands up to cover their eyes and peek through their fingers as the condensation from his breath misted the glass. The foetal-positioned Dasha was now invisible through the frosted glass. The music stopped. The marble noise in the glass slowed to almost a lament. The clapping abated. The audience looked at each other, some questioning whilst others looked worried, as if something had gone wrong with the act. For the first time that night the Spiegeltent was silent. A crash of concert cymbals broke the silence. The door opened slowly, Dasha flowed onto the stage, stood up and with an exaggerated suave movement of his hand rearranged his hair, fell into the gymnastic position of a crab and scuttled off stage.

Sebastian spent the rest of the evening performances making notes and trying to decide how he could distil ten pages of notes to the prescribed hundred words of his review. He knew he was biased and wanted to make a special mention of Salt and Pepper. Their solo act was a seemingly suicidal ballet dance. They both arrived on stage to the snorting of fire from their mouths, firstly at each other, then above the heads of the audience. Even in the banquettes at the back the heat could be felt on his cheeks. Standing shoulder to shoulder facing opposite sides of the audience with swords in each hand they waited as Umuntu set the swords aflame and retreated. Salt and Pepper juggled the lit swords above their heads creating an arch of fire. Catching the falling swords they stood still, paused and tilted their heads back. Tapping the still burning swords together to confirm they were made of metal they held them above their heads. The swords and flames disappeared into the slender slits of their mouths. During the act Sebastian had glanced at the rabbi, his face impassive, his wife's curled in imagined pain and his daughter surreptitiously nibbling her nails. The finale of their act was to place two neon strip lights down their throats; their gullets glowed like a radioactive drain. It was the first time that the child had shown any interest at all; she looked at her nails, looked at Salt and Pepper, ran her tongue around her teeth and smiled.

When the show ended the audience was reluctant to leave. They sat in their chairs under bright white light but collectively thought if they stayed in their seats the lights would dim and the show recommence. The silence from the band confirmed that it was the end.

Walking out Zoe linked her arm through Sebastian's. They walked slowly at first.

"I thought that was a great show. It's impossible to believe that the body can do those things, mine certainly can't." Her voice was reverent in respect of what she had seen.

Sebastian was distracted and his eyes followed the Fedora. He wanted to know where it was going. He pulled Zoe along with him as he hurried through the crowd. The rabbi walked towards a group of three policemen; his wife and daughter followed behind. Sebastian arrived as the group of laughing policemen broke up and started to move off.

"Have a good evening, Inspector Bloogard!" one said to a man in his early fifties not in uniform. The inspector was standing next to a pretty girl of twenty, her arm loosely held in the crook of his arm. The rabbi stopped without warning, alarming his entourage who bumped into each other but avoided bumping into him. It was the raincoat man from outside the police station near Dam Square; he didn't have his coat with him on the balmy summer evening.

"Rabbi." Inspector Bloogard nodded his head in acknowledgement.

The rabbi looked at him, then at the young woman.

"This is my daughter." The inspector looked at her with paternal pride.

The rabbi nodded curtly to the daughter, gave a fleeting look of disdain to Inspector Bloogard and walked past without a word exchanged; his family with heads down followed in the wake of his black coat.

The crowd swallowed the rabbi and his family. Sebastian looked at Inspector Bloogard. He looked like a man that would welcome imminent retirement. The face was etched with lines of questions unanswered, a face that spoke of an inability to understand what he had seen. When he spoke to his daughter these lines disappeared and his face shone with happiness, the lines replaced by an almost youthful smoothness, a face of hope for another.

"Sebastian, do you know them?" Zoe studied the daughter, youthful with alert and innocent but curious eyes. She remembered her late teens. She looked just like that when she had met Sebastian.

"No but I have seen him before. It doesn't matter. Let's get to the Vlinder for the after-show party." He smiled at her; he wanted to tell her of his suspicions: the rabbi, the inspector, Irena, Sacha and Dasha. But unable to understand his thoughts himself he dismissed them and focused on the remainder of the evening. The last few hours before Zoe went home, leaving him alone to finish the book. The thought filled him with urgency to enjoy the remaining time together tinged with an impending loss. He pulled her towards him, kissed her forehead.

"God, I'll miss you," he whispered into her ear as he squeezed her close. She placed her hands on his hips and pulled him closer pushing her pelvis towards him. He felt a rush of blood to his groin. She laughed.

"We don't have to stay too long at the party, do we?"

"No," his voice replied through a contracted throat.

2

Sebastian had suggested they walk. He didn't want the evening to end and by walking he hoped to slow the movements of the clock but knew from maternal homilies that procrastination was the thief of time.

Arriving at the Vlinder he could hear the voices from outside; it was busy and excited.

"Do we have to go, can't we just go out for dinner?" Zoe sounded nervous.

Sebastian remembered the last time he had said that to Zoe; he thought of Clarissa and with shame remembered the evening's end.

"We don't have to stay for long, promise." Sebastian knew this evening would not end the same way as it did in London. This evening had a meaning, a start or perhaps a restart. He squeezed her hand to give her courage as he pushed the door open.

The troupe looked happy and excited as they mingled with the guests. Hugo and Ricard stood talking to Dasha; all three still had stage makeup on and their eyes were made larger by mascara. They looked like backing singers for the Velvet Underground meeting on a night out. Umuntu walked over to them with a wide smile.

"All hail the man whose words will make or break the show." His arms wrapped round Sebastian and Zoe. "Come, let me get you a drink."

They made their way to the bar where Salt and Pepper were standing flirting with a journalist. The size and direction of travel of Umuntu was enough to open a gap in the crowd.

"Sebastian, meet Jan, he writes for the arts magazine *Blend Bureaux*. You can compare notes, but make sure the reviews are glowing." Umuntu turned to order drinks, cutting the invisible cord between Sebastian and Zoe. She looked nervous being left alone with Umuntu. Sebastian turned to look for her but Jan pulled at his arm to draw him into conversation.

Umuntu noticed her discomfort.

"Here, let me introduce you to Salt and Pepper whilst I order some drinks."

Zoe held out her hand unsure which one to shake first.

"Hi, I'm Salt."

"Hi, I'm Pepper."

They replied in unison covering her hand with theirs.

"I'm Zoe, a friend of Sebastian's," Zoe said feeling at ease with the touch of their hands.

"We know who you are, you're the one in the photograph." Salt smiled at her welcomingly.

Zoe felt less assured and wanted to know how they had seen the photograph. She knew it was stored in Sebastian's drawer. Before she could ask they were interrupted by Anneke who took the twins by the elbow.

"Come on, you two, the show doesn't end when the audience leaves. Go and talk to the journalists, they're the ones that keep us in a living."

She turned to Zoe.

"Hello, I'm a friend of Sebastian's too. We don't know each other, well you don't know me but I know you." Her smile offered some shared knowledge, a shared pleasure.

Zoe looked over her shoulder for Sebastian; he was unwillingly engaged in conversation with a group.

"Everyone seems to know who I am but I don't know anyone here apart from Sebastian," Zoe said nervously.

Umuntu placed a glass of white wine by her side.

"You've met Anneke, she has been helping Sebastian with his book."

Anneke flicked her hair in acknowledgement of the compliment. Zoe recognised the name and studied her face. She saw a broad face, almost square, not pretty but attractive. Far too much makeup, she thought. Anneke's eyes defiant and willing to defend a secret if challenged.

"He read it to me last night. I really enjoyed it, I always knew he could do it. What do you think of it?" Zoe sipped her wine waiting for the answer from Anneke.

"I've never read it. I know it will be good." Anneke spoke through her veil of hair, a hint of a shared knowledge established between them. "I think he will finish it quite soon." She reached out and touched Zoe's elbow, squeezed gently. Her eyes fixed on Zoe. "Excuse me but I have to talk to one of our sponsors. I'm glad it's you. I hope we'll meet again."

She was gone before Zoe could think of a reply. She stood alone in the noise of laughter and movement of people. Zoe didn't like Anneke; she was somehow involved with Sebastian in a way that she was not. She wanted to leave. She looked towards Sebastian and caught his eye; he lifted his arm up holding up two fingers. Two minutes in a room full of strangers was a long time, thought Zoe.

To avoid the embarrassment of being a lone woman in a bar she turned towards the counter. Her eyes scanned the mirror behind the bar. It was dark outside and the lights of the bar reflected off the mirror intermittently as the reflection was disturbed by the photographs posted. She moved her gaze from one happy photograph to another, each showing groups of people laughing around tables with glasses. The sepia photographs were of diners in black tie telling of the former glory of the Vlinder as an eatery of the theatre crowd. The barman lifted a bottle of gin and one of vermouth off the shelf to make a martini. Hidden behind the bottle was a poster of a woman in a high-collar multi-coloured embroidered dress walking along a catwalk advertising the new collection from Jurgen. She studied the face of the woman; recognising her but not knowing any models she was unable to place her. Her eyes moved to look for Sebastian hoping he was extricating himself from the group; as she did her eyes met Anneke's in the mirror. She was smiling, a smile of further shared knowledge, a secret shared. Zoe looked again at the poster. The girl in the poster looked like Anneke, well perhaps a few years ago. Not exactly the same; Anneke's face was broader, much bigger features, almost a parody, and she was not as attractive as she was in the photograph.

She felt the familiar hands of Sebastian on her waist.

"Let's go before I have to admit to anyone that I'm not a journalist."

She was glad of his arrival and protective arms. Zoe had felt uncomfortable as soon as she had arrived at the Vlinder. The troupe still covered in makeup looked sinister to her. She had been further disconcerted by the way she was known to many without any reciprocity of knowing them. She hadn't wanted to go in the first place; she wanted to be alone with Sebastian; she needed to be with him, to regrow what they had had many years ago. His passion had returned, she could see that now; she wanted to be part of that passion.

Zoe wanted one more look at Anneke before they left; she scanned the room for her unsuccessfully. At the door she had a last look for her; she was standing next to Umuntu engaged in conversation with others but looking at Zoe. Whether it was in response to a question or addressed to her she didn't know but Anneke raised her finger to her lip. "Don't tell, it's our secret," it seemed to say. Her eyes slowly slipped from contact with Zoe and returned to the speaker next to her.

3

It had started slowly and with tentative movements. Their lovemaking was gentle and delicate, the act itself almost a rite of passage to the desired shared intimacy of lying in each other's arms. Sebastian knew that it was for the future. Zoe thought it was a restart, a beginning of something constant. Since Sebastian Zoe had had four or five lovers, all of them based on a weak relationship hidden in a desire for sex. None of these ever replicated the post-sex intimacy of her relationship with Sebastian. With him there was always a mutual vulnerability resulting in a total trust of each other, an opportunity to say things that would otherwise have been unsaid.

"It's back, your passion, it's back," Zoe whispered almost to herself.

"Yes, it is for the two things I want. Both of them in his room." His eyes moved from her to the stain-covered book on his bedside. "Not quite complete though, is it?"

She held her breath, was now the time? Was she too early? Would he say no? She wanted the answer only if it was a yes. She tried to let her breath out slowly as if everything was normal. But it wasn't. She needed to know. It came out with the rush of her exhaled breath.

"Why don't you come back with me?"

There was no response from Sebastian, no muscles contracted. He stroked her hair. She spoke quickly in the belief that the more she spoke the more likely the answer would be as she desired.

"You could come and live with me in London, finish your book there." She tried to paint the picture. "There is a spare bedroom, you could work in there. I would be out all day at work and in the evening we could cook and discuss what you had written. I have money to keep us going and with your rented flat we would be fine."

She raised her head from his chest and looked at his

face. He was looking at the ceiling. He didn't answer. It hurt waiting for the answer. She gently dug her nails into his chest.

"Well say something, Sebastian."

She shut her eyes and waited, wishing the past two minutes had not taken place, prayed that she had only thought and not delivered the question. By the silence she already knew the answer but not the reason. She needed him, wanted him, wanted it to be like before; she knew that he would make her happy. She knew what she had been missing and that her lingering love for him had been just that.

"Please, Sebastian." Tears welled up in her eyes. "Please."

"I can't, not yet." He spoke softly hugging her gently. He felt her tense up, her muscles taut to repel his touch. She rolled away, pulled on his dressing gown, went to the bathroom and shut the door. He heard the stifling of crying, the flush of the toilet to destroy the evidence.

The door swung open, her face blotchy with eyes red rimmed.

"Why, Sebastian? Just tell me why."

He knew she had exposed herself, revealed not just her new found love for him but had shown her continued love for him. He wanted to go back with her but not yet, not until the book had been finished.

"I'm not ready yet. I haven't finished it. I haven't finished it for you. When I have I will, I promise I will." He tried to sound soothing. He knew if he went now he would have failed, failed himself and would be a failure to her. As her cheeks flushed red he knew it hadn't worked. She was angry – blindly angry with him or herself, he couldn't work out.

"Alright then stay here, stay with all those weirdos at the circus, yes the circus. As for that thing helping you, helping you! Christ, some butch lesbian helping you. You know she's not even read it. How's that any help?"

He knew not to reply. He could see the rage within her, not rage at him but more within her. She had revealed something dormant, something she had harboured.

"What, nothing to say? Want to stay here and fuck those twins, that what you want, is it?" She collected her bag and started stuffing it with clothes.

He knew he could easily make peace and just as easily leave now, like all the other times take the easy way out. Blame fate, circumstance and look back blameless. If he took that route he would be the same, the same for her, the same for himself. He knew that the finishing of the book was important to him and for them; without that he would never be complete; it was a risk he needed to take. If he didn't he would have failed, again, both for himself and her. She was too important to him to fail; not this time he promised himself. Not this time.

"Look, where are you going? It's 5 am."

She continued to stuff her clothes in the bag; perhaps without thinking or consciously she pushed in the pyjama bottoms he had lent her.

"I want to go to the airport, the flight's at 11.00 and I don't want to miss it." Even as she said it she knew it sounded absurd but she needed to go. She felt alone and wanted to be alone.

He approached her.

"No, Sebastian, don't, just don't."

By the time he had put on his clothes she was standing at the companionway ready to leave.

In silence they walked towards the station. It was quiet. The streets empty and the only activity was the flashing of neon advertising lights. The occasional snoring at doorways as the forgotten slept in sleeping bags or cardboard boxes.

He tried to think of something to say, something that would make her understand that he was doing this for them. He didn't know what to say and remained silent.

The concourse of the station cold, grey and the concrete with a film of moisture from the floor-cleaning machine operated by a man in blue overalls. The ticket offices closed and only the automated ticket machines available to dispense tickets.

Sebastian followed the instructions to buy tickets to the airport. His finger pressed two for the number of tickets.

"No," she said without taking her eyes off the neon instructions. Her finger pressed the back button and she pressed one.

He walked her to Platform 1 and handed her the bag. She looked at him.

"Perhaps I shouldn't have asked, perhaps it was too early. Maybe I now know the answer."

Sebastian felt a wave of panic for something not yet lost; a small reach and he could grab it, take it back. But it would come at a cost too high, he knew.

"Finish the book then talk to me. Promise until you do you won't contact me. Promise?"

He could still smell the sleep on her from his bed. He could take her back, say yes, pack and be in London in her flat within ten hours.

"I promise," he said leaning over to kiss her on each cheek.

She turned and walked down the platform, pushed a button, waited for the hiss of the opening door. It closed silently behind her. She hadn't looked back. She had missed Sebastian silently mouthing, "I love you".

The lights changed from amber to green; slowly the train built up speed and the red tail lights disappeared into the darkness of the tunnel.

She was gone.

CHAPTER 12

Sitting in a pew in Oude Kerk he felt at ease waiting for a prostitute. The service was not due for another two hours. The church was sparsely populated, mostly elderly bending slowly and painfully, the air sterile and cold. Were they forgetting the years past in the hope of everlasting youth when they died or were they praying for those departed who were forever young to them? Sebastian often wondered why people prayed to an unseen better being that never seemed to answer the collective prayers of the faithful as war, famine and misery continued to rise. Even on an individual basis He always seemed just too busy with someone else to provide succour to the pleas and promises of those requesting help. *What a waste of time*, he thought.

He stared at the sunlight coming through the stained glass windows. The different-coloured lights reflected off the uneven wall surfaces like a kaleidoscope. Sebastian thought if at one stage during the day all the colours met at a single moment to create a white light shining on the crucifix it would be perfect, everything balanced. He would wager it never happened. The priest glided past him in the aisle and smiled at him to see if he could offer pastoral care.

"No thanks, Father, I'm fine," Sebastian said pointing to a middle-aged woman dressed in black rocking on her knees in front of an arc of candles.

In the peace of the church Sebastian hoped the quiet might slow his thoughts. Had he blown it with Zoe? Their departure had not been quite as he had imagined. "Don't contact me until the book is finished," she had said. Had she said it because in the past he hadn't and she thought he couldn't? He was disconcerted and felt unbalanced. Too many things happening that he couldn't control. The troupe would leave soon, leaving him alone in Amsterdam unless he could finish the book before they left. The book was nearly finished. Well not quite, mostly. Zoe had left him with the hope of a reunion, or was it in the knowledge there might never be one? He hated the responsibility of being in charge and the temptation to drift was strong, the current hard to resist. Let it all be someone else's fault. He let his breath out in a resigned sigh.

"Fuck it," he muttered to the nave.

He stood up to leave and walked towards the rear door. He turned with a cynical look at the crucifix. Below it was a woman walking towards him. She was pulling at the strings of a stained white apron revealing the uniform of all charity workers: practical loose-fitting trousers, soft nurses' shoes and a patterned jumper. He waited for her at the door.

"Sorry I'm late," she said wiping her hands on the apron. "They're hungry that lot."

"Hello Rosie," Sebastian guiltily replied as he had been caught in the act of leaving.

"I'll just get my coat." She wandered off into the shadows, her presence now the smell of school cooking, cabbage mostly.

Sebastian cast a last look around the church; the colours of the sunlight had moved and hadn't become a white light, the crucifix still in the gloom. The black-clad widow calm now that the priest had his arm around her, still and peaceful.

"Come on, let's go, nothing happens here unless you make it happen, that I can tell you," Rosie said as she slipped her arm through Sebastian's. "You were about to leave, weren't you?"

Sebastian thought about lying but knew Rosie knew more about men, and everything about men's lies, than men themselves. He nodded guiltily.

"Well it's my fault, well it's the number of hungry folks' fault. There are more arriving every day. Black, white, yellow and all shades in between. Who knows where they come from or how they get here but they do. Someone's gotta feed them. You know there's never enough money to feed them, always enough for political conferences to discuss the crisis, but never enough to feed them."

Sebastian shivered as he hit the sunlight, shaking away the cold air of the church. They were an unlikely departing couple from the church: the prostitute and the procrastinator.

She cut through the perimeter side streets of the red light district to Dam Square with the ease of knowledge and the purpose of avoidance.

"You can buy me a mint tea. Don't want to have one back there as I never mix work with pleasure," she laughed but it was a tired laugh.

The square was bustling with summer traffic, tourists aimlessly wandering, the locals moving purposely.

Unsure of how to start the conversation he looked at Rosie as she sipped her tea. Her hands plump and more suited to rolling pastry than flesh. She looked different in daylight: slightly puffed and with the air of a favourite aunt. A welcoming ready smile for the waiter, a soft confiding presence. She drank her tea from a spoon.

"It's so fresh the smell of mint, cleansing, don't you think?"

Sebastian sipped his bitter espresso and smiled, still unsure how to start the conversation.

"Umuntu says you have something that belongs to one of the girls." She would always make it easy for people, never leave them ill at ease; she had a rare inherent and noticeable kindness.

"It's a phone, it belongs to someone called Irena. She works in the red light district. I want to give it back to her, well actually can I give it to you to give back to her?" He put the phone on the table; he had even charged it up so that it could be used as soon as returned to Irena.

She looked at it, picked it up and turned it on. The screen shone with the photo of Irena and her parents.

"Tell me how you got it?" There was no suspicion in her voice; his friendship with Umuntu had endorsed Sebastian's qualifications as trustworthy.

He told her of the assault in the park, his fruitless intervention; he left out the argument with the others.

Throughout the retelling she remained silent. Once he had finished she reached for his forearm and squeezed it gently.

"I wish I had met someone like you when I was a younger. What you did took a heap of courage. Umuntu tells me he took you on a tour of my workplace. I think you know what I mean by courage now. I admire you." She meant it too.

He blushed at the praise.

"If I give the phone to you can you get it back to Irena?" Sebastian knew only too well that his act of intervention was foolishness; he wanted nothing further to do with the traffickers, prostitutes or the red light district. He was scared. He wanted abdication. He had lost the rabbi-induced resolution.

She didn't reply, she just looked at him, studying his face and reading his thoughts. Her eyes gentle and moist like a calf.

"Well I'll have to find her first. I know most but not all of the girls. She's not one from De Rode Draad, I would know that. You'll have to give me something to go on, what she looks like now, age and all that then I'll ask around. She will look different from this now." She looked at the image on the phone. "They always do. But I will find her, then you can give it to her. These phones are important to the girls, it's what keeps them safe and in touch."

"No, no, Rosie, if I give it to you, you can give it to her." He said it quickly to get out of the whole episode before the door shut with him still inside. *I've done my bit, I have enough of my own problems, too many in fact*, he thought.

"Sebastian."

She paused, looked at him, assessing. She wanted him to know the answer to a problem, not just know the answer but comprehend the route to the answer.

"You must try to understand the women that work in my business have a mixed relationship with men. For those that choose to do it, it is always due to circumstances. Mine, well I needed the money for my family. For some it's to feed a drug addiction, others because they like what money can buy but that always comes at a price. Some to get out of debt. Many were abused as children. There are a thousand reasons why the girls work. None do it as a career choice, but they do it in response to their circumstances and hope it will be temporary. They have the ability to put what they do in a sealed compartment separate from the rest of their lives. They work for themselves and hope to decouple from the compartment one day. Some succeed, those that don't? Well time, wear and tear exclude them from the business. You following me?"

Sebastian felt the warmth of the sun on his face but the words made him shiver. He nodded; she took that as acknowledgement but he didn't understand, not really.

"For some, quite a lot in fact, it's everything and nothing to do with circumstances. They have found themselves in a situation where there is no option, none. They are known as the 'forgotten ones'. These girls are owned. That is their life, there is no separate compartment. They are owned by someone else and have to do it. They do not work for themselves and they are in the compartment, they cannot ever get out of the compartment. There is a difference, you understand that, don't you?"

"Yes, yes I do."

And he did, he had brushed up against the owners and he knew what they were capable of. *Christ, how do they get into this situation?* he thought. How had it come to pass that he was sitting with a matronly prostitute on a sunny afternoon discussing the personal and professional circumstances of working girls. He needed to get away, to go back.

"The forgotten ones are usually from small towns and cities in the East. They are easy targets for the boyfriend trap, the start of the journey to captivity."

"Rosie, I'm struggling with this, I mean 'captivity'? We aren't talking about a performing circus animal here, these are humans, they can walk away." He paused, looked at her nodding his head in the hope of her mutual agreement. It was not forthcoming.

"They can, right?"

She looked at him kindly as if trying to explain a difficult maths homework problem to a child. The child would get there in the end, would understand but needed it explained. Explained simply and in detail so a full comprehension achieved. She needed him to understand.

"They can't and yes they are just like performing circus animals. The red light district for the forgotten ones, well that's their big-top tent, the circus. The clients, the participating audience."

He interrupted; he didn't want to understand, he didn't want to comprehend.

"But they can walk away anytime they like. They can go to the police, catch a plane, a train, a bus, they can get away." He was speaking too fast trying to counter his thoughts that were conjuring images of darkness, misery and hopelessness. He knew they couldn't walk away, not the forgotten ones. He didn't know why and didn't want to know why but he knew they couldn't, not ever.

Patiently and kindly she started to explain. She wanted him to understand, not for chastisement of men but for him to comprehend.

"They can't, Sebastian. For many reasons. It usually starts with a love affair. The girls live in some rural town out east. There is no work, the system has collapsed. The parents exhausted by subsistence living but in the evening on the TV they see a life beyond the decaying, given-up-on town. They are old and tired, it's too late for them. America, Paris, Amsterdam, London… names that offer work, money, freedom and a better life. The colour of the clothes, the success so young. Why you can even be President even if you are like me, black. Everything is possible. The TV screen shows laughter, happiness, perfect family life, there is no wanting, no back-breaking labour. They want it for their children, they love them so much. Oh, the love of a parent for a child knows no bounds."

Sebastian thought of his parents, what had they wanted for him? Was their love boundless? As boundless as Rosie's? Would his mother work as a prostitute to provide if his father had left? Yes, he thought she would.

"The love affair starts. Quietly at first. These towns, they're conservative places, love affairs between teenagers and older men are frowned upon. But he has a car, not a tractor or a Trabant, he has money, lots of it. No one knows how but he does. He speaks of an uncle who started a business importing and exporting to the West, it's vague but wealth is easily believed. He cares for her, she's young, and this is her first love. He gives her presents – makeup, coloured jumpers – and buys her expensive drinks in the cafés. She feels great, she is getting on, not to the factories like her friends. She has a rich man that loves her. He may be older but he loves her or he wouldn't give her all the presents, right?"

Sebastian thinks he knows where the story is going and in silence he listens, fearful for the young girl; he knows how she ends up. He is peering into a world he knows nothing about and wants even less to find out the details. But he needs to know, know how this young girl becomes a prostitute. He sees Irena, young, very young, pretty but frightened and broken. It's made more personal, he's involved in the story now.

"Word gets to the parents. They want to meet the lover, unsure of the suitability of an older lover for their teenage daughter. They know of him, everyone does, he's the successful one in town, the rich one who goes on business to the cities on the TV and he has a penthouse apartment. The father thinks he might be the right sort. If he is he can get that for his daughter. They want it so much for her. They meet him. He is a good one, calls them Mr and Mrs, not their Christian names, drinks their tea and compliments the mother on her cake. He looks nervous meeting the parents but smiles at their daughter. He talks of the hard work involved in running his uncle's business, but the rewards are there for those that work hard. The father nods, he knows hard work pays off in the end. He knows if he doesn't work the family starve. He likes him, the new lover. Yes, he's older but with age comes wisdom."

In his head Sebastian can hear a voice screaming, "Beware, beware this man."

"He helps chop the wood, not as well as the father. Well he couldn't, could he? He works in business, his hands are soft, but he is willing. During the wood chopping he tells the father the business is expanding and his uncle needs a personal assistant. The PA will sort out the administration of the business. The daughter is perfectly suited as she speaks the local language and English too. You are a clever and loving father to have forced her to learn English at school, it shows parental love and wisdom. The father slaps him on the back and thanks him for his comments. The boyfriend is in, he's now part of the family. Now his real work starts."

Sebastian is now angry with everyone – the father, the mother, the daughter – and their stupidity. This cannot happen. He places a cigarette between his lips; they are trembling. He wants to shout, to warn them. The match flame gets blown out by the wind. In frustration he strikes four matches together to guarantee they don't go out. He draws hard on the cigarette.

"I don't want to hear anymore. I know what happens. Look, just take the phone and give it back to her."

Rosie looks at him; she knows he has found the answer but she wants him to comprehend.

"Let me finish. You will let me finish, won't you?"

Sebastian doesn't move. He drags on the cigarette.

"The parents take the hardest decision of their lives. They push their daughter gently, push her towards the future they want so badly for her. The daughter is nervous but excited. Nervous at leaving her parents, she is only seventeen. She has never been abroad before but with their blessing it's the right thing to do. She will send them money, come home often. Well it's not far away, is it? It's only two hours on a plane, that's only 120 minutes. Her lover helps her apply for a passport, he is so very good to her. The visa is fixed. The day of departure is fixed but the lover can't travel that day as he has business in another town close by. His uncle will meet her. It's OK, she will really like the uncle and his wife, they are in their late fifties with no children. They will look after her as if she is the daughter they never had, he reassures the parents. The parents weep as the car draws away. The lover raises his hand out of the expensive car window. The daughter, excited, smiles at her parents. 'I'll call when I get there,' she shouts. The crucifix necklace that her mother gave her before she got in the car glistens in the sun."

"OK, Rosie. I've got it. I can't see how this is helping to get the phone back to her." Sebastian was now angry with Rosie who has taken him into the darkness.

She ignores him and continues her narrative as if he is not there, looking blankly to the distance. Sebastian wants to leave but can't; his legs won't move and he hasn't told Rosie what Irena looks like. He wants Irena to get the phone; he really wants her to be reunited with the phone with the picture of her parents, the green hills and the blue sky.

"That's not the end, Sebastian, that's only the beginning of her journey. There is a change of plan at the airport, the uncle is on business in Tunis. She will be met by him there. The lover, he will follow in two days, just needs to tie up some business. But they will be together in two days, he promises. She trusts him, why not? He has organised the passport, the visa, bought her presents, her parents like him. He has never lied to her before, he has been nothing but kindness and he had taken her virginity. That means something between two people, something meaningful. The sign of ultimate seventeen-year-old trust of another."

Rosie sips her tea, it's cold now, she gently spits the liquid back into the cup.

"Of course the uncle's not there but a cousin is. He drives her to an open-cast mining site. It's in the middle of nowhere. It's hot. He roughly conveys her to a Portakabin where men are playing cards. She fights the advances of the men, but each rape her in turn. It hurts. With each thrust she feels the crucifix bounce on her Adam's apple. She wakes in a bed of soiled sheets. There are men heavy with the scent of perspiration, they are having sex with her. There are multiple languages, but all kindness absent. She wakes and just makes out a syringe with a bead of liquid from the needlepoint waiting to drop. Her feet are held down and the needle plunges into the flesh between her toes. She relaxes. 'Don't damage the goods', she hears someone say. 'She is moving on tonight.'

Sebastian's toes contract in his shoes. He feels a pain between his big and second toe.

"What are they doing to her?"

"This is how they break them, Sebastian, this is how they break them. It's a slow process but always achieves the aim. The rapes, then being prostituted out to the migrant workers in isolated, unpoliced places. To ensure the least resistance heroin is used. Always injected in an area that doesn't damage the investment. Between the toes is best.

No tramlines, no swollen veins. Think about it, when did you last look between your toes?"

He felt sick. His stomach contracting with the acid flowing into it. The acid of anger.

"Is this what happened to Irena?" he asked with concern.

"I don't know, Sebastian. It's a familiar enough story. The details are always different, the breaking of the human being the same, the conclusion the same." It was obviously not the first time she had told this or a similar story; she sounded depressed at the telling, the familiarity of it all. "Now you see why they don't have a separate compartment. They are in the compartment and it's locked and it always will be. The forgotten ones can never get out, never."

"Well surely the ones here, here in Amsterdam, can. I mean this is Europe not North Africa." He knew it to be untrue.

"They are the same girls, Sebastian. Tunis, Amsterdam, Prague, the geography is irrelevant. Once broken they are sold to a new owner. The routes might be different, the final destination different. But the ones trafficked via North Africa are easy to get into Europe. The girls are now stateless, their passports destroyed, lives destroyed. They are shipped across the Mediterranean by speedboat. The traffickers wait for the boatloads of economic migrants to leave the shores of North Africa. They know the patrol boats are too occupied with the overloaded boats to chase a high performance speedboat. Once in Europe they are delivered to the new owners across Europe and of course that includes Amsterdam."

He knew it was futile but said it again.

"But once here they can still walk away. Go to the police."

"Sebastian, they are owned. They are in debt, deeply in debt. The owners have spent a lot of money to buy them from the traffickers, depending on age and looks up to 100,000 euros. Work it out at fifty euros a client, that's 2000, then they have to pay for the rent of the room, that's another fifty euros a day. There is interest to be paid on top too. They all come with a known history, almost like a DHL parcel. The new owner will know where they come from, their family history. They threaten to tell their parents knowing that would destroy the family. In many cases the girls will never be welcomed back if the family find out what they were doing. That's why they are known as the forgotten ones."

"Oh God, I feel sick. It's happening less than half a mile away from here."

Rosie shrugged her shoulders. Yes it is, the shrug said, right here and right now.

"She is blond-haired, about five foot nine inches, slight build, about nineteen, pretty with blue eyes." Sebastian blurted it out without thinking. "You must find her, Rosie, she needs the phone," he pleaded.

For the first time since they had met she smiled gently and directly at him. He was so close to comprehending, so very close.

"I need more than that, Sebastian. There are many pretty blondes working in the red light district that age. Think, anything unusual about her?"

He shut his eyes and rocked trying to dislodge something from his memory that would help Rosie. His eyes opened wide. Excitedly he said, “A tattoo, a tattoo! It’s of a horse’s head and at the base of the neck it has wings.” His eyes cast down with disappointment. “You know, that’s probably not much help as I have seen a few girls with the same tattoo.”

Rosie pulled a pen from her coat pocket and drew on a napkin.

“That’s it, that’s what it looks like.” Sebastian was excited now; he had helped.

“You sure? You have to be sure,” she urged. “Take your time, but be sure.”

It was exactly the same as the tattoo he had seen in Irena’s armpit when she had been touting for business in her cell. He nodded.

“That’s it. Does it help?”

“I can find her. I can definitely find her. It’s the mark of a Kazakh gang. It’s the ownership branding.” She was sombre now, resolved.

“They brand them? I didn’t know they branded them too!”

“Sebastian, I will only ask you this once. When I find her will you meet her and give her the phone? Tell her how you got it.” She entreated him to say yes.

“Why?”

She thought before she spoke as if the words needed to be chosen carefully.

“Faith, Sebastian. The forgotten ones have no faith in anything, everything is lost to them. They must believe that there is some good somewhere, especially where men are concerned. Her traffickers will have all been men, her owners likewise and all her clients. What you did was something different to what she is used to. You intervened, got involved for her. You kept the phone, you wanted to give it back. If Irena is to continue to survive she must believe, believe that there is hope."

He answered without hesitation.

"Yes."

She smiled. He had comprehended the answer.

CHAPTER 13

1

It still hurt. The tattooed man with scenes of damnation on his biceps and celestial hope on his forearms had warned him. The tattoos were taut and the pictures defined, colourful and strangely beautiful almost like the images of an adult fantasy comic. Sebastian wouldn't be around to see them sag and go inky green-blue with the lines no longer fine but blurred with age.

"It's a gun, you're going to feel a pain. It won't last long then a warm sensation, almost a glowing heat. It will then be all over." He raised the gun. It fired and he was true to his word: it hurt.

Lifting his finger to his ear lobe Sebastian felt the circular piece of metal and the butterfly clasp at the rear of his ear holding it tight in position.

"It looks good," the tattooed man said as he held up a mirror so that Sebastian could see the gold earring positioned perfectly in the centre of his lobe. The man handed him a bottle of ear care solution and talked with the seriousness of a pharmacist as he instructed him on how to keep it clean and infection-free.

Sebastian had found the earring on the side of the bed where Zoe had slept. It was the only thing that had shone since her departure. He had rolled it between his forefinger and thumb and placed it on his bedside table next to his multi-stained book. Lifting his mobile he had typed a message to her.

"Zoe, I want to be with you, near you, part of you." His finger had hovered over the send button. He recalled her last words and pressed save. The inability to speak to her and the desire to be with her had decided him on the piercing. It was the closest he was going to get to being with her until he had finished the book. Then they would be together, perhaps he would take it out then, but until then it stayed *in situ*. When he touched it he touched her.

Anneke had asked him about the earring on their now daily early morning meetings. Each morning, before Dasha had even risen for his ritual, he departed for the café. Just before he passed the cat in the window he braced his shoulders, growing two inches, and walked past without looking in the window. He couldn't resist a glance over his shoulder after passing. The cat static, watching, thinking and knowing; knowing all. Perhaps now they could be friends.

"Sebastian, I'm not sure being a resident on a static boat on a canal nowhere near the sea really entitles you to wear an earring. It's a maritime tradition. In the past it was a sign that the sailor had crossed the equator," she chuckled into the froth of her cappuccino.

Sebastian lifted his fingers to touch the earring. It was

empowering knowing he loved her. He wanted to explain to Anneke why he had done it, his reasoning, a surrogate proximity to Zoe; the motivator to finish the book so he could be with her. They belonged to each other. But the knowledge was his alone.

"It's hers, isn't it?" It was phrased as a question, but she knew it as a fact.

He looked at her, slightly startled as if she had been reading his mind. He had taken to looking at Anneke in a more questioning way since Zoe had berated her. His allegiances were confused. Anneke had welcomed him, almost nurtured him. She had not known him before he arrived in Amsterdam, she had never asked anything of his past. She had accepted him and the only things she knew about him he himself had told her. That seemed to be enough for her. Zoe had disliked her for reasons he didn't understand.

"How do you know?"

She let out a deep laugh and coughed into her coffee.

"Sebastian, if you could see the way you stroke it, no, caress it. It's obvious."

Sebastian didn't know if she was laughing at him or being kindly sympathetic. He took it as a slight. Perhaps Zoe was right, there was something odd about her. Her face always hidden behind the fall of her hair. Too much makeup masking something. What was she hiding? His loyalty lay with Zoe and he wanted to repay the slight, inflict a small reprimand wound. He felt piqued.

"Well I don't see you wearing anything of Umuntu's." He felt his cheek flush red. He knew he was being petulant.

Her hand cradling the cup paused halfway to her

mouth. She looked at Sebastian. Placed the cup back in its saucer. She smiled a smile of kind correction; it was obvious that this mistake had been made before.

"I'm flattered, really I am. Umuntu is as close to being a lover as one can be without being a lover. He knows everything there is to know about me, everything. But he is not my lover." She looked pensive, not for the lack of Umuntu as a lover but for something seemingly lost.

Sebastian felt guilty for trying to hurt her. She had been only kindness and acceptance from their first meeting at the restaurant. He saw her every day. He had wronged her.

"That was unkind of me, thoughtless. I'm sorry." His right foot applied pressure to his left under the table, hurting himself, waiting for the acceptance of his error.

"I know exactly how you feel, I know exactly why you have done it. Just beware it doesn't create an illusion, act as a substitute for the real. You must never let that happen. There is only love, Sebastian, there really is nothing else, nothing. Do you believe me?"

"Which part? You know how I feel or there is only love?"

"Both," she replied smiling forgiveness.

2

Sebastian boarded the metro at the Central Station. At each stop the crowd thinned out. Arriving at Bijlmer station it was clear to him that this was not part of the tourist route. Bijlmer was an area where the conventional routine of life was not dictated by time. By now in central

Amsterdam the streets would be quiet as the working day was underway; here it was listlessly busy with people walking, in no hurry to be nowhere in particular. Not in the pleasant head-held-high and observant way of tourists but in the tracksuit, hood up, eyes cast down way of the unemployed. Killing the day off.

The concrete slabs of high-rise blocks were built like mental asylums: drab rectangles with small windows to prevent escape and let limited light in, no requirement to offer stimulus to the inhabitants as they had been forgotten. The walls would be thin, offering no sound insulation, dismissing the purpose of individual flats as the sounds of toilets flushing, angry frustrated arguments mixed with the demands of children not attending schools flowed throughout the buildings. Although unseen the neighbours lived in each other's flats. The substitution of gardens and coloured flowers by the graffiti tag marks of the gangs reaching as high as the strength of an aerosol can. It was a desolate place.

He had taken Rosie's advice and memorised the route to the café.

"Don't carry a street map or look at your phone for directions. Dress anonymously too," she had warned.

He was dressed in dark jeans and a hoodie of brown over a white T-shirt. It was the armour suggested by Salt.

"You be careful down there, it's not safe. It's the dumping ground for all the illegals and unemployed. Why can't she meet you in town?"

He had explained to her that Irena would only meet him in Bijlmer, she felt safe there away from knowing eyes. Rosie would bring her to the café.

"Safe!" Salt had cried. "She must live a hell of a dangerous life if that's the only place she feels safe."

He turned the corner into the street of the café. Across from him a group of young men in grey ill-fitting tracksuits crowded around a teenager on a pushbike. The teenager exchanged their cash for little packets of silver foil. Sebastian walked past unnoticed. The dealer was safe here.

Entering the café the smell of last night's curry filled his nostrils, sharp and acerbic. He ordered a coffee and sat at the table to wait. Lighting his cigarette he noticed that everyone else smoked roll-ups; he put his packet of Marlboro Lights back in his pocket. So as not to make eye contact he looked at the ashtray and noticed the gnawed hope of someone's future buried in the butt ends; a small collection of thin crescent-shaped fingernails poked up from the ash, one side of the nail perfect with growth, the other jagged edged as it had been torn from the finger.

The door opened to anger from the street. A dishdasha-wearing Arab was being berated by a group of Surinamer youths. There was no exchange just a tirade of mouth-twisted hate from the youths. This was a place you could hide from the law-abiding world but not from the lawless chaos of modern metropolitan deprived living; here the differences were not celebrated but highlighted as cause for vilification. Irena was right, no one would notice her here; no one in their right mind would elect to be here.

"Sebastian!" She spoke loudly as she sat down opposite him. Rosie smiled and grabbed his hand, squeezing it, offering assurance.

Irena sat down next to her. She was wearing a sexless

loose grey tracksuit. Her blond hair pulled loosely across her scalp. If she had been in London it would have been described as Sunday morning chic, here it was dishevelled. She wore no makeup, her skin pallid with a hint of yellow over her right eye. She was not as he remembered her in the park; she was older, in her mid-twenties, reticent but assured, confident in the way that only those that survive on the street can be, almost hostile.

"Let's have another coffee," Rosie offered.

"Coke," Irena replied mechanically; no one can spike a bottle, he remembered from his student days.

"Irena, this is the man I told you about, Sebastian." Her waving arm introduced him.

"Hello," was all he could think of saying.

Irena looked at him quickly, intensely. She knew what to look for in men, whom to trust, whom not to trust. She could assess quickly and correctly… now. It was the survival instinct of the feral, lessons learnt from harsh experience.

Her smile was guarded but genuine.

"Hello Sebastian." It was an invitation to keep talking.

Rosie sat back; she had done her bit, it was his turn to take it on. Sebastian cleared his throat, drew the phone from his pocket and pushed it across the table to her.

"I've charged it up for you," he said uselessly.

Her hand, palm down, moved slowly towards the phone as if to move too fast would scare it away. Her fingers touched his. Sebastian's hand stiffened and started to move away from the phone. She lifted her hand and covered his and the phone. Her fingers were slender, youthful, and her nails short and trimmed by her teeth. He knew her hands had done more than their fair share of manual labour. The pressure of her hand almost imperceptible, but he felt it, a small squeeze. He opened his fingers and her hand slid the phone towards her. He thought he saw small red pinpricks between her fingers.

"I knew you would want it back." With the phone gone he looked up from the table top to her face. She was looking at the glow on the screen, head bent down. He noticed that she didn't dye her hair blond. A small splash of a tear landed on the screen blurring the picture.

"Is that a photograph of your parents?" Involuntarily he stroked his earring.

She inhaled deeply through her nose to gain control.

"It was a couple of summers ago, just before I came to work in Amsterdam." She made no attempt to wipe the tears from her face.

"You should go and see them. It would make them happy." He wasn't too sure if he was talking to himself or her.

She sniffed some snot back up her nose and swallowed. Her eyes closed and her head moved from side to side.

"That's exactly what I was thinking in the park." Her voice was only just audible above the noise of cups on saucers. "When I'm not working I go there, I go to watch. To watch what it could have been like. To look at the young mothers and watch their children. I pray they don't end up like me."

Her eyes opened and she stared at him with wet and angry eyes, her voice harsh escaping from between clenched teeth.

"And a lot of fucking good it does! That's the day I got

a beating." Her finger pointed to the fading yellow of her bruise. "Then the punishment. I wished they had killed me."

Rosie's arm reached out and pulled Irena towards her. Irena folded into her warm comforting chest. She whimpered into Rosie's jumper.

"I can't take it anymore, Rosie, I can't take the way they use me, the beatings. I want to die. I want to go somewhere where no one can touch me ever again." Her shoulders shook up and down. "I love them. I want to go home." She tearlessly wept into the soft wool of the red jumper.

Sebastian looked at Rosie, his eyes imploring her for guidance. She spoke to Irena; this wasn't about Sebastian.

"Darling Irena, what time do you have to be at work?" Rosie spoke it into the hair of her bowed head. "You must be on time, you can't risk another mistake."

"Christ, Rosie, she can't go to work today, look at the state of her."

Firmly but gently Rosie lifted Irena's head and kissed her on the forehead.

"She knows she has to." She said it softly.

"She can stay with me, on the *Tulp*, I can protect her. Then we can go to the police." His mind racing, grabbing at any thought that would help Irena avoid going back, back to the cell on the canal.

"No police!" It was said sharply. Irena was animated and back in control. "No police. Promise me." She was not asking, it was an instruction. Her face fierce as that of a protective mother.

Sebastian looked bewildered and felt as if he was under assault.

Rosie looked at Irena who nodded.

"Sebastian, if you go to the police Irena's debt passes onto her parents. They will have to pay it back. Then there's the pictures and videos of Irena. It would crush them. So no police."

Sebastian knew he should have thought of the consequence but he needed to help.

"OK, no police. But she can stay with me until we can come up with a plan. She doesn't need to go back to work." He pleaded for reason, he would find a plan, it would work, he knew he could make it work.

Irena looked at him kindly.

"It can't work. They always know where I am. All of the girls are given a phone. It must be with us all the time when at work so they know where we are, they install a tracker app. That's how they found me in the park. It was stupid but I just couldn't go to work, not that day. It was my mother's birthday, you see."

Sebastian surprised himself by not feeling any fear that the pimps might know where she was now and could enter the café to reclaim their possession.

"Have you got the phone now?"

"No, we all have two phones. The ones we are given and our own. Sacha has the other one in our room. I must go and get it before I go to work." She cradled the phone in her hand. "This one is mine. It has all my photographs and contacts. It contains my entire life."

The door of the café opened and two youths walked in suited in jeans and sweatshirts. Sebastian watched them walk to the counter in silence. The owner reached behind the cash till and handed over an envelope. He didn't know what made him angrier: the thought of Irena, the helplessness of the situation or the protection money being handed over.

"Right, Irena, I live at the corner from where you work. You have any trouble, I don't care what it is, you contact me." He took her phone and punched in his telephone number. "I mean it, Irena, ring me anytime."

She looked at him and smiled.

"Thank you, Sebastian, Rosie is right, you're a good man. Thank you for returning the phone and thank you also for trying to intervene in the park." She stood up and collected her bag. "I have to go to work now." She kissed Rosie Swiss-style, three times as if the parting could be delayed.

"Come see me at one of the De Rode Draad meetings, honey, they're every Thursday, all day at Oude Kerk."

Irena smiled at Rosie and nodded. She turned and put her hand out to shake Sebastian's. It was fragile and Sebastian noticed again the red pockmarks between her fingers. He hadn't imagined them.

"Remember, ring me if you need anything." He gently squeezed her hand offering protection.

"I will," she said as she walked to the door.

She didn't look back once outside; she did pause and fiddle with her phone.

"She's deleting your details," Rosie said flatly. "She would never want anyone and certainly not you involved in her life. They really are alone, the forgotten ones, all alone. It's a loveless life, they have gnawed at the carcass of parental love, there's nothing left now. Just the bones of the past."

As Irena walked away from the café the group of Surinamer youths made blowjob signs with their hands and thrust their hips as if fucking her. She ignored them as she walked past; there was nothing to see that would shock her, that's how she made a living.

Sebastian sat in silence and looked through the window into the greyness of the surroundings: grey clothes, grey buildings and grey faces. The sun was bright outside but only seemed to make the hopelessness of the surrounding concrete more pronounced. The few patches of green were weeds that even here struggled for heat and life from between the cracks in the paving stones of the pavements.

"There must be a way to get her out of this, there must be." His voice betrayed the scale and hopelessness of her situation.

"There isn't, Sebastian. She has caused trouble for the pimps, set a bad example to the other girls. They will have punished her too, more than the beating. Probably behind a closed door in the flat they all live in. The other girls will have heard the screams as they helped themselves to her. The unseen is always the more frightening." Rosie was weary, the repetition of what she heard every Thursday exhausting her. "They will move her soon or sell her. Hamburg, Prague maybe, anywhere their network reaches. She knows that too."

"Rosie, there must be something I can do, anything. Not just for Irena, for your charity. Tell me what I can do."

She smiled in a tired way and replied.

"Write, write well, be successful, make a lot of money and give some to De Rode Draad," she laughed. "Seriously,

Sebastian, be careful. Don't let your emotions get involved, you're not equipped to handle these people. No one is, that's why it goes on. The girls always have me and the charity to fall back on, we do the best we can."

They walked back to the metro in silence. At the graffiti-scrawled entrance of the station lay a beggar slumped on a bed of cardboard, his arm slashed by heroin tramlines; a mongrel dog with a head too big for its body cocked its leg and peed on the beggar's leg.

"I'm glad I got the phone to her, but the meeting didn't make a difference, did it? Nothing's changed, it's still all the same, the same shitty life for her."

Rosie looked at him gently.

"It did make a difference. Small, but it did. You showed her there is hope, there is some good in the world. You did make a difference, believe me."

Sebastian nodded but didn't agree.

CHAPTER 14

1

He knew it was impossible to solve Irena's predicament, knew that he couldn't really make her life any different, but he felt he could make it better, he just didn't know how. Rosie's charity, always too little money, offering morsels of help when what they needed was a daily square meal. He wanted to do something. Anything. The helplessness of the situation was beyond his control, the problem too big. He recalled Rosie's last comments: "Don't let your emotions get involved, you're not equipped to handle these people, no one is, that's why it goes on." There were others who were dealing with the problem: politicians, police, border controls, even the United Nations. Sebastian knew each side of the argument well; he had hashed and rehashed them. The conclusion was always the same: a slight remembered lesson in his early teens delivered by the mousey, frill-collared, twinset-and-pearls-wearing Miss Swift. It was the only time he ever remembered her raising her eyes to meet the eyes of her pupils in the classroom. She spoke it softly but determinedly.

"What man is a man who does not make the world better? It is the courage of decisions made that make the world a better place."

He had retreated into his writing with discipline to help expunge those thoughts. He could change his life for the better, through the completion of the book. He worked until the evening. It was then he knew that Irena would be at work. He felt like a man with a charge. He walked past her window. He had the same surveying role as her pimp, except he was watching over her. Sebastian's breathing was even and controlled if her curtains were open. When she saw him her enticing dance didn't stop, but her eyes shut for five seconds and she smiled softly. The unspoken but mutually understood language told him she was fine, she was coping. When the sun-bleached curtain was drawn he would walk by with a quickened heartbeat, trying to suppress his imagination. He would walk back past the window ten minutes later, the curtain now open. It never lasted more than ten minutes he had learnt. Ten minutes of soulless pleasure for the paying punter, interminable suffering for her.

It had been Anneke's idea, the walk past.

"When there is no hope and only loneliness, the slightest act of kindness and consideration can be all-comforting. The physical link may be tenuous but the thought provides the reason to go on, the means by which it can be endured."

"You don't know that, Anneke, how can you?" He was sharp with her; it sounded platitudinous to him.

"Oh Sebastian, I know. I really do know. I know what it's like to be alone. I know the feeling of desolation. The knowledge that nothing will ever be worth having again, nothing will alleviate the misery, the only thing keeping you alive is the past. But you can't live there. You can try to recreate it, but it's never quite the same."

Apart from her telling him about the meeting with Umuntu he had never heard her speak of anything so personal.

Salt and Pepper had praised him for his act in the park, the returning of the phone, but with the advantage of twenty-something age had told him he had done all he could do. The future awaited, he had been noble but it was now time to move on. It wasn't meant in any callous way, just the way it was. There was wickedness in the world but there was more good than bad.

He met Umuntu for a drink after the show.

"What do you think you can do to change her life? You can't eradicate time, you can't take her back and let her start again, this time missing out the errors."

"I know that, but there must be something that I can do." Sebastian was looking for guidance. He knew Umuntu had had a hard life but made better now. He knew Umuntu couldn't eradicate the past, he carried it with him, it formed him, made him what he was now. He hoped Umuntu could guide him to whatever the catalyst was that would do the same for Irena.

"Sometimes circumstances make people what they are. The events that happen to them are beyond their control, utterly beyond their control. It's these events that form us. Look, when I worked in the Congo, the civil war was at its height and there was lawlessness, killings, rape everywhere. In the middle of all this was a well-organised smooth-operating hell. We were mining for diamonds, no machines just manpower, digging, sifting, digging, sifting, sleep and then the same again. The death rate was high. Those that got too weak were shot and dumped in the jungle." The words were difficult for Umuntu to say; he had lived this life once.

"You know at the height of the war people left the cities and towns and tried to start again in the jungle. They felt safer there, a kind of reverse evolution. They felt safer in the jungle than the cities. I escaped and joined them. It was no different, just more chaotic and lawless, absolutely primeval. I met someone in the jungle. He knew he would never get out, knew he wouldn't survive. The machete wounds had become infected, he was dying slowly, uselessly. He only asked one thing from me: that I should live his life for him when he was gone. Live the life of two. I said yes of course."

"Did you live the life for two?"

Umuntu hesitated before replying.

"No, Sebastian, I didn't, I lived my own life."

Sebastian walked back to the *Tulp* via the street that Irena worked in. The pimps in their positions, hers a youth, younger than her and already dehumanised. The thought of "going to work" for Irena was not the tube ride to the City and warmth of an office block cocooned in health and safety regulations. Her co-workers were not the co-operative grumble of people civilised by compromise for eight hours a day. Her co-worker was the pimp, lounging against the wall smoking cigarettes and keeping his new white trainers clean. His designer jeans with a logo proclaiming their cost. All of these bought by Irena. He felt a swell of anger and walked towards the pimp. His gait was firm and his hands sweating. He was going to do it, he was going to drive his fist into that pimpled face. It wouldn't be just once, he would pound the bastard. He would pound him for her, for the man in the Congo, for him, for the thugs in the park. This bastard had it coming. His pace quickened. He didn't feel the balm of the evening, didn't see the guide leading the crocodile of spectators on their tour of the sex district, just the bloodied face of the pimp. His fist clenched as he got nearer, he was ready, it would start with one swing to the bridge of the nose, breaking it, then an upper cut to the nostrils driving the nasal bone into his brain. His army training had not been in vain.

He heard the screech of a coin on glass, not the tapping to attract business. This was a piercing screech of the coin being dragged down the glass of the door. She was looking at him. Her body danced, her hair bounced but her eyes were wide registering fear. The door of her cabin opened wide enough for her hand to reach out and grab his.

"Want to party, big boy?" Irena's hand was sweaty on his forearm. Her eyes pleading, her voice hissing and urgent. "Lean into the doorway and pretend you're negotiating." His fingers unwound from the clench. "What the fuck are you doing?"

He felt the sweat on his back cool. The adrenaline dissipated and he felt his hand shake; he closed it back into a fist to stop it. The pimp looked over, business as usual.

"Do you know what they will do to you? To me?" she

said through a smile for all to see. "Have you any fucking idea?" Her eyebrows rose, suggesting delights for him if he came inside. "Now go away! I don't need your help. Please, Sebastian, go!" She shrugged her shoulders as if another negotiation had failed. Sebastian let his arm fall to his side. He turned to walk away. The pimp indifferent to the failed negotiations, he knew that there would be another paying customer soon enough. He could have been thinking of the watch he had seen, the one with the gold wristband and the face shining with cut stones. He would have that soon; not long until she had earned it for him.

2

Sebastian hadn't obeyed her pleading. Daily, but now at night and late in the cover of darkness, he walked past her. He couldn't see the details as he was on the other side of the canal. But he could see her still there, still working. If he could at least see his ward she would be alright; not quite living but alive at least. He had convinced himself that it would be so. If he gave up the vigil something would happen; they would move her and she would be lost forever; it would be his fault. As a child on his way to school he knew that if he stood on the cracks of the paving stones his parents would die in a car crash. He did once and they didn't. But this time it was different.

The smell of cigar smoke filled his nostrils. He had been walking back to the *Tulp* having completed his sentry duty. The smell rich and suggestive of post-prandial conviviality, the smell of club land and fireside chats accompanied by shared happy memories. Perhaps a glass of brandy to ease into the early hours of the morning.

"You know you can shag your way round the world in this hundred square metres of porn. First fuck a European and last an Asian, all in less than one hour." The voice was unmistakable, the man in charge, the one they were following.

Sebastian stopped and watched. Three men in suits, all tieless and one with his shirt tail hanging out below his jacket. The penguin man swayed with each step and the toecap of his shoe caught in the cracks of the cobbles making him lurch forward two paces before resuming the motion of a tree in a heavy breeze. The leader at the front had his jacket slung over his shoulder, his face invisible in a cloud of smoke and the pinstripes of his trousers not parallel but parabolic. His ample girth counterbalancing his enormous buttocks as they moved like pistons designed by Brunel. Sebastian recognised that arse.

"Yeah right, Darren," the penguin slurred. The third man, sweating from dinner excess, leered into one of the windows.

"Wanna good time, darling? How much you gonna pay us to fuck you?" The other two laughed coarsely.

She dealt with them with dignity; her curtain closed. It surprised the trio.

"Stupid bitch," he shouted at the curtain. "I wouldn't touch her with yours." The penguin pointed at Darren's groin.

The sweating man was younger; Sebastian didn't recognise him. He must have joined since his departure and knowing Darren he was used to bolster his ego and carry his bags on business trips. Someone to marvel at his duplicity in meetings, emulate and continue that trait.

"You ever been tempted?" the youth said as he wiped the film of sweat from his forehead, just to make sure it didn't fall into his eyes and blur his vision. As they walked his head moved side to side like a man watching a passing train; too much to see and unable to focus on any particular girl, each one might just be better than the last.

"You kidding? They're all fucking slags here. Look at them, they've had more pricks than a dartboard. Touch them and you'll get itchy balls tomorrow."

The other two laughed, but without conviction. Maybe if they chose carefully they wouldn't wake up with itchy balls.

"Let's go back to the hotel for a nightcap," Darren suggested; he was more sober than the other two. The copiousness of client entertainment not enough to affect his balance.

"One more for the road before we meet with those tossers again from NMH Bank tomorrow."

Sebastian hated him when he had had to work with him, and he hated him more now. He knew where they were staying; the firm always put up the senior employees at the Prinsengracht Hotel on the canal of the same name. It was a distance of only a kilometre but worlds apart. There were no negotiations to enter the hotel; there the door was opened by a liveried man in tails accompanied by obsequious smiles. Darren would be known by name as he used the company's money to overly tip. The doorman knew the type and knew how to keep the free money flowing; he would know his name and use it often.

Sebastian felt like a ghost watching his past. The process of business: take the client out, create a transient friendship bonded over company-expensed wine. Always order the food and wine from the bottom right of the menu. Do it without knowledge but with confidence. That would show them how successful you were, eyes never looking at anything but the most expensive, nothing but the best for you, my new friend. You were successful and that's why the company let you spend what you liked. That's why the client needed to do business with you; you were a big swinger, a man that made things happen. You were important, vital. He knew what would happen next but shadowed them to the hotel hoping something would befall them; a mugging would be pleasing.

"Good evening, Mr Denton, I hope you had a pleasant one."

The doorman opened the door of the hotel as he spoke. Darren dropped his cigar butt on the pavement at the base of the outside ashtray.

"Yeah, it was fucking great. Great city Amsterdam, if you know what I mean, Dave."

He gave him a manly wink and pressed a twenty-euro note into the doorman's hand. The doorman slipped the note quickly into his pocket and looked at the nametag on his chest; in black lettering on a gold background it said Stephen in capital letters. He smiled as Darren pushed past a departing Japanese couple. The smile vanished with the arrival of Darren's back.

Sebastian knew what would happen next. The trio would retreat to the rear bar that overlooked the Keizersgracht canal, two drunk and begrudging, one commanding.

Sebastian retraced his steps to the corner and walked along Keizersgracht for a hundred metres. He could now see into the bar. He wasn't sure why he was looking; perhaps it was disbelief at the life he used to lead. No, he knew what it was: he was still hoping there would be an incident, something to damage the ego of Darren. A fatal choke on an ice cube would be pleasant to watch.

Darren melted over the bar stool and waved at the black-skinned barman, pushed the three poured whiskies away and pointed aggressively at a gold-label bottle on the top shelf. That's where they kept the expensive stuff; Darren knew that but didn't know or care what was in the bottle; it was expensive, that was enough. The barman poured another three glasses: two doubles and a single. Darren pushed the doubles towards his sidekicks, tapped his glass on the table top. He was preparing them to shoot the drinks. They held the glasses and tapped the table three times and two downed the drinks in one. The penguin looked as if he had eaten a fish too big for him. The liquid stayed in his mouth, he couldn't swallow it, he had had too much already. Darren jeered at him as he swallowed and left quickly for the toilet. The sweaty man raised his hand in defeat and after a pleading conversation tottered out of the bar. Darren now alone looked around him, waited five minutes and asked for the bill, his glass still full.

Darren looked around him alert and decided. He put his jacket on and headed towards the exit nearest to Sebastian. Sebastian walked away quickly hoping the direction to Dam Square was not the same route as

Darren's. He didn't hear following footsteps; turning he saw the piston buttocks of Darren working at full capacity. He was in a hurry and knew exactly where he was going. Sebastian followed at a safe distance and in the knowledge that Darren knew no fear as he knew no one in Amsterdam. All his actions would be anonymous. He thought.

They were back in the red light district. Darren surprisingly nimble on his feet, he was in a hurry and avoided collision with deft sidesteps. He didn't need a compass or map, he knew his destination. Sebastian followed, hiding in the crowd. He nearly lost him as Darren turned into a side street. The side street darker and less populated. Sebastian vaguely remembered being here but couldn't remember when. He slowed to a stroll. He recognised the street. The cabins were there, the windows with flirting figures, some curtains closed, others open waiting for business, the blue light above each entrance on.

3

"You're very happy this morning," Anneke hoarsely spoke through exhaled smoke.

"And you sound as if you were drinking to the early hours of the morning." She looked tired to Sebastian, with black semi-circles under her eyes. The makeup thicker than usual.

"Well yes, I was watching the match last night, Bayern Munchen won. And you?"

"I have a lunch date today," he said mysteriously.

Anneke didn't respond to the mystery. "With Rosie." He had waited impatiently for this lunch, three long but deliciously anticipated days.

Anneke's eyebrows rose; she didn't ask the question. She knew he would tell her when he wanted her to know.

"I hope to have a surprise for her. I hope it's happened," he said.

He had arrived to meet Anneke early, he had left her early and he went to the restaurant too early. There was no one sitting down. It was only 11.45. He was impatient, he wanted to know. He had asked to meet Rosie here at 12.00. He had that awful pre-exam anticipation. Would he know the answer after all that hard work or would it all be a disappointment when he opened the question paper? He looked into shop windows without seeing. He couldn't decide if the shop was selling wooden clogs or half-circles of Dutch cheese, he didn't really care. At 12.00 he walked back to the restaurant. There she was, her eyes scanning the passing people. She saw him and waved and ushered him with urgency to the table. She planted two slobbering kisses on his cheeks.

"Another one," he said laughing. "Another happy one. What's your good news?" He waited impatiently. She opened the menu, pretended to read the offering, trying to suppress her excitement. She failed.

"Ten thousand euros! Ten thousand euros! Can you imagine what we can do with that? Ten thousand euros!"

His work had paid off, it was as he had hoped, but slightly doubted. The answer was 10,000 euros.

"We can help train the girls, teach them some skills, get them out…" He nodded and smiled but didn't hear her.

He did hear the voice of the doorman at the Prinsengracht Hotel from three nights ago.

"It's too late to wake up Mr Denton now, but yes I will put it under his door this evening."

"Thank you, Stephen." Sebastian fumbled in his pocket for a note to give him.

"No need, sir."

He had walked away with anticipation and exhilaration at what was to come.

It was seven thirty in the morning when he rang. The voice at the other end gravelly from the booze of the previous night.

"Yeah, Darren here."

Sebastian knew he would be reaching for a glass of water to rehydrate from the previous night whilst scratching his balls.

"You don't know me. Just listen and do as I say." Sebastian knew the accent didn't sound the slightest like a Dutchman but with the cellophane wrapper from his cigarette packet wrapped around the mouthpiece he knew Darren wouldn't recognise his voice.

"Oh fuck off, Paul, I'm not in the mood for this, I've got a hell of a hangover. What's the market going to do today?"

"It's not Paul."

"OK who the fuck is it?" Darren's voice was now suspicious.

"Did you get the note under your door?"

Sebastian could hear the bedsheets being pulled back. The creak of the floorboards as Darren walked to the door. Sebastian was enjoying himself.

"Open it."

The envelope was ripped with haste. The breathing a little laboured as Darren moved back to the bed to take out the contents. Sebastian hoped he was sweating now, unsure of what was in it. He heard the pulling out of the photograph.

"That's you. Bottom right, it's time stamped at 23.46."

"Who the fuck are you?" Alarm now registered in his voice.

"Someone that knows what you do, when you do it and knows your little secret."

There was a pause. Sebastian knew from his business negotiations the next person to speak loses. He waited.

"That could be anyone, so you can fuck off and die." It was said too quickly, uncertain and fearful. Sebastian knew Darren wouldn't hang up. He knew he would be sweating now. He had him.

"You're right, that could be anyone. But we both know it's you. It's a frame from a video I took a couple of nights ago when you went to visit your secret, your hermaphrodite secret."

There was a silence at the other end. Sebastian knew Darren would be standing in his soiled boxer shorts from last night, brow sweaty, armpits moist and he would be breathing his stale breath. Sebastian waited.

"I'm going to hang up, whoever the fuck you are." Darren's voice was now fully fearful. Sebastian knew he wouldn't, not now.

"I wouldn't if I were you. I wonder what your two sidekicks would have to say about the photos, or perhaps your friends at NMH Bank. It wouldn't be good if these photographs popped up in the inbox of your colleagues in Canary Wharf either."

Silence from Darren. Sebastian could hear him breathing, the quick breaths of the cornered.

"What do you want?"

Sebastian knew it was over, he had enjoyed himself; he felt no guilt at what he was doing, it wasn't for him.

"If you go to reception there is an envelope addressed to you. It contains some bank details of an account in the name of De Rode Draad. You will pay 10,000 euros into the account."

"De what? What the fuck is that?" Darren's voice moved up a pitch.

"Look it up."

"I haven't got that sort of money."

"Yes you do. It's what you get paid every month."

"Do I know you?"

"No."

"What will you do with the photographs and video?"

"If you pay within the next three days I will destroy them, no one needs to know but us two."

Sebastian could hear the panic in Darren's voice. Darren was on the wrong side of this trade and knew it.

"How do I know you'll do that?"

"You don't," Sebastian replied flatly.

"Fuck you, you're bluffing."

"Am I? I wonder how long it would take your secretary Tracy to distribute the copy of the video at the water fountain. You know where everyone meets to gossip. The one next to the lift on the 52nd floor?"

"I'm not going to pay. Fuck you." Darren's voice was almost hysterical with fear and anger.

"If you don't then you will pay the consequences.

Three days." He knew he shouldn't but couldn't resist the retort; it had been last aimed at him by Darren. "Looks like you've been fucked twice in the past twenty-four hours, doesn't it? Goodbye."

"Sebastian, Sebastian, are you listening to me? Ten thousand euros!" Rosie had interrupted his reverie by shouting excitedly and grabbing his arm.

"You know something, Rosie, you are one of the most beautiful things I have ever seen." Sebastian crossed the table and cradled her head with his hands covering her ears and kissed her on the lips.

"I love seeing you happy."

He took his hands away from the sides of her face.

"You feeling alright? Your face is very hot."

She giggled girlishly with pleasant embarrassment.

"Bet you've never seen a black woman blush. You can't see it but boy we do and can you feel it! I'm smoking hot."

She took his hand and placed it on her cheek. It was hot as an Aga.

"No one has said anything like that to me for years. Don't you hesitate to say it again, even if you don't really mean it," she laughed. "You're right, I am mighty happy."

"You know you can make me happy too. If you could just..."

She interrupted him with a smile.

"I know what you're going to ask. I will. I will try to get Irena to come to the meetings. If she does I will persuade her to take part in some training, no, I will make her. I always get what I want."

Her face dropped the smile and a look of sadness replaced it.

"You be careful, Sebastian, you just be careful where you put your hope and faith. These girls have been on their own a long time. Although young they have the tiredness of old age. Sometimes like old people they can only see the end."

"I know," he said but he didn't. He couldn't believe that a twenty-something woman could even consider the option of the end.

"She's in a bad spot at the moment. She is worried they will sell her on or move her to another city. I've asked her friend Sacha to keep an eye on her. The girls tell me that you do too."

Sebastian blushed. He thought his nocturnal sentry duty went unnoticed.

"See, that's the only difference between white people and black people, you show when you're blushing but we feel it!"

Throughout the course of lunch Sebastian looked around him, the clatter of cutlery, frigid earnest exchanges between businessmen and convivial laughter between mothers lunching. That familiar surreal feeling; within less than 1000 metres men were humping prostitutes, prostitutes feigning pleasure at being humped whilst at the same time despising themselves and their clients. Some of the girls whilst groaning in thespian pleasure were fearful for their lives. Ones like Irena didn't see the end of the fuck, nor the end of the day but the desired end of their lives. Meanwhile, in the restaurant, the cutlery clattered, the waiters smiled and the conversation rose and fell. He lost his appetite and his happiness.

"It's not nearly enough to make a change is it? The 10,000 will make no difference to anything, will it?"

Rosie pushed her empty plate away from her.

"Sebastian, it will, I know it will. It can't change the lives of all of them, but if it does for one it will be the best return on the money – just one."

He tried to believe her; he hoped she was right.

"Make it Irena, make her that one."

"I'll try, but for her it's complicated. Her situation is very difficult."

She didn't know that he was behind the windfall but she felt he had a say, an ownership on how it was spent.

"If it's a good return to change the life of one, why not spend it all on one? Ten thousand is enough to pay them off, buy her from the traffickers. Surely you know how to do that."

It was the first time he had seen her angry; her face didn't go red but he thought he felt the heat from her body.

"I'm a hooker, Sebastian, not a people smuggler! What I do know is 10,000 won't even touch the sides of the debt Irena has with them, not even close."

"But for that amount of money she could get a new identity, a new passport. She can go somewhere far away from them."

The heat from her had subsided. Her reply was simple and delivered without malice just as a fact.

"And her parents would have to pay? Either way they would pay."

The plates jumped and the cutlery fell with a clatter as his fist hit the table top. Eyes turned to their table, conversation temporarily halted.

"It's hopeless." His face contorted in anger. He looked around him and shouted, "What are you looking at, you fuckers? You know nothing, you smug bastards!"

Their departure had been in silence. Outside it was sunny and warm.

Softly she touched his arm and as softly she spoke.

"Trust me, Sebastian, I'll do all I can for her. You will just have to hope I can help her. That's what the other girls are doing, hoping it will change. Most of the time it's not enough but without it there really is nothing else."

CHAPTER 15

In front of him the two headed pieces of A4 paper stared blankly at him. Apart from their headings the pages were bereft of text. One read "Love/Happiness", the other "Hope/Expectation". The pages had wrinkled and aged since they were first written at university. Looking at them he tried to recall the number of times he had crumpled the pages into a ball and sent them binwards in anger, relief, hatred, desperation. After resting there for periods ranging from seconds to days they had been retrieved, opened and flattened by his open hand and placed back in his book. Today he had repeated the exercise. The two pages formed the spine of his book from which the bones had grown to form a strong skeleton; a body he believed would be muscular and ripped with additions of characters and plot. He hadn't really known at twenty what these four words meant. Then they were out-of-focus words blurred by naivety. The intervening years had taught him otherwise; these were the essence of existence. He looked at his computer screen and was pleased with the day's editing when his mobile rang.

"It's your mother here."

Sebastian was always at a loss why his mother always announced herself, as if an attendee at a ball. He had explained to her that her name was spelt out on the phone when he received a call from her and after thirty-five years he was capable of distinguishing her voice from a call centre scammer based in Malta. But the tone of her voice was a reprimand; he hadn't phoned for a while; the implication that he might not recognise her voice was implicit.

"I hope you're paying more attention to completing you book than to phoning your mother," she said rather tartly.

He knew he had to distract her before the call developed into a one-sided berating.

"It's coming along very well actually." The "actually" he stressed to justify the absence of calling, hoping it conjured up single-minded industry.

"Well I do hope so."

He recognised the tone and knew she wanted to ask something else.

"What's that supposed to mean?"

"Nothing, darling." The pause, he waited. "I mean, Amsterdam is a… how should I put this? Unusual place. I mean drugs and you know the other thing, girls for sale. It attracts odd people."

"Thanks, Mum, so now I'm odd."

"No, darling, of course not."

Something was worrying her. He could picture her twiddling with the paperweight he had made her when he was seven. She always did when she wanted to talk to him about something important. It had a love heart in the middle, red and slightly misshaped. He knew she had been talking to Zoe.

"What's Zoe been saying?"

"Nothing."

He knew it was coming, he just had to wait. She inhaled deeply, held her breath for a few seconds. Out it came tumbling down the phone.

"She says that you have made some odd friends. She says there are girls you might have been sleeping with, then there is some butch woman that you seem attached to, they all wear makeup and drink too much. She says they're gypsies and trouble, probably all taking drugs too. Also you live in the red light district and are probably sleeping with prostitutes when not taking drugs yourself. She says that you will probably run away with this circus and end up as an usher or ticket seller living in a communal caravan with everyone. She says you'll probably have many children by different girls, maybe even set up a *ménage à trois* with a man." Her imagination was more terrifying to herself now that she had given voice to it.

"No she didn't. She did not say any of that."

The phone went silent. She would be straightening her back now, her fingers around the paperweight.

"Well not exactly. She did say they were odd."

"Mum, you have to stop worrying about me, I'm in my thirties, I can look after myself."

He had been through this all his life. The teachers at school were predatory, the sergeants at Sandhurst sadists, the bosses in the City avaricious monsters teaching greed.

"Oh darling, as a parent you start worrying the moment you have children and the last thing on your mind when you die is worry about your children. Parents love their children more than themselves, more than anything in the world, it's a boundless love."

"I'm fine, really."

He knew he had to assure her, comfort her that all was well or her imagination would drag her to endless dark corners; dark corners where muggers, killers and creatures were waiting to end his life.

"I know you are, darling."

She was clearly unconvinced, aware as she was that a child never really understands the perils that can befall them, even a child in their thirties.

"Zoe's not fine though. She seemed upset when she came back, sad even."

Her hand would be tightening over the paperweight. She had moved into intimate territory. Sebastian found comfort in the knowledge that Zoe and his mother worried about him, but Zoe talking to his mother about intimacy was no comfort. Sebastian and his mother were close, Zoe and his mother were close. Zoe and his mother were never closer than when talking about Sebastian. They had often planned subtle assaults on his previous girlfriends. The well-bred Anastasia whose family history they had studied and found a distant relation who had murdered his wife. Bad blood is what they used to say. Jane, the artist's daughter who had, according to them, an unnatural relationship with students as she posed naked on a Wednesday evening at the Clapham Arts Club. Probably a nymphomaniac.

"Well she shouldn't have been." The paperweight would be nestled in her open upturned palm.

"She was."

"Well she shouldn't have been." He knew he would lose.

"She was, she was sad."

"I told her I loved her."

The paperweight would be in the air now, a smile on his mother's face. It must have landed in her palm.

"Then why is she sad?"

She was suspicious, hands around the glass heart.

"I didn't tell her that exactly. But I told her all the same."

He knew that if his mother had been younger and exceptionally strong the paperweight would be crushed into shards. He listened for the shattering sound.

"Why are you so afraid of love, Sebastian? Don't listen to your wicked Uncle George, he's divorced and quite why it took so long I have no idea, poor Mary. Even before the marriage it was doomed. His view of a marriage is that it's a dreary dinner with the pudding served first. He's wrong."

"I didn't know he thought that. Perhaps he's right." Maybe that's why the divorce rate is so high.

"Well he's wrong, he's a lazy, selfish oaf." That was the zenith of his mother's insult. "He just wouldn't try. Look at your father and me." He did but he didn't see much love there. "He drives me mad, he is bombastic, sometimes boring, always repetitive, emotionally stillborn." Just as he thought in fact. "But I loved him when I met him and I love him now. Love is a wonderful thing, Sebastian. It starts as passion and over time takes many guises: closeness, sharing, companionability and experiencing things together. When you're our age it's about togetherness and jointly reliving all of these things all over again. Some say it makes you blind but I believe it opens your eyes. Don't be scared of it. She won't hang around for you, she won't wait forever."

He had never heard his mother talk with such enthusiasm about his father; it was at odds with what she said daily. Her passion for the subject of love was also new to him; she spoke of it with unusual frankness. He believed her; she did love his father.

"I know, I know, but I have to finish something. I know I need to complete it to feel I've changed. Does that make sense?"

"Yes, but I hope, for both your sakes, you finish it soon."

It was only after the call that he realised that Zoe had discussed the whole weekend with his mother. It put him ill at ease that his and Zoe's thoughts were now theirs – Zoe's, Sebastian's and his mother's. He wanted to phone Zoe and tell her it was between them, they didn't need a referee.

He stared at the two pieces of A4. Love was supposed to be unconditional, but it wasn't, not at any stage; it was all about hope. Young love was all hope, parenting was all about hoping for children, middle age was about hoping for companionship, old age hoping to recall all the previous hopes and death hoping the dead were at peace. Perhaps Anneke was wrong; it wasn't about love. Maybe Rosie was right; without hope no one had anything.

Too early for his sentry duty he wandered over to the Vlinder in the hope of finding someone from the cast of the Spiegel tent. He would have to wait a while as the show would be just ending. As a regular he nodded to the barman; the beer appeared with no exchange of words. Looking around him the bar seemed desolate and underpopulated except for the possums, the permanent fixtures that never left the twilight of the bar, always wide-eyed from fear of daylight. Reflected faces staring back from the mirror of those sitting at the bar alone. Tables of two and some of three with only their drinks for company. It was the ones at the bar that concentrated his attention. The old man with a face telling of labour who spoke to no one, his eyes always mirror ward, lost in the past or in hope of a different future. The young man on his own, almost furtive, chasing a whisky down after finishing his glass of lager in two gulps. He would smile at himself in the mirror later as he conjured up images of happiness, becoming happier with each passing glass. In the corner mumbling to herself the middle-aged woman puffy faced from booze and her hands scrawny and veined from lack of food. Sebastian decided it had been a bad idea to sit in the bar alone.

If there was no one in the Vlinder to offer him comfort he could offer some to Irena. He approached from the opposite side of the canal. He knew her cell, knew that she was always next to Sacha. He saw Sacha in matching white pants and bra made fluorescent by the light from within. The cell next to her had a coffee-coloured girl dressed in a soft leather basque; she was lazily flipping a whip on the interior of the glass door as she unenthusiastically tried to attract business. That was Irena's cabine. He looked at the row of cells, women dressed to cater for male fantasies but no Irena. He quickened his walk to the little bridge that crossed the canal. Crossing the water he started at the furthest part of the row of cells and studied each girl as if shopping for sex. Arriving at Sacha's cell he saw that the curtain was drawn. She was busy. He continued to the end and waited. The curtain of Sasha's cell parted and a man slipped out sideways like a coin, trying to look invisible as he fiddled with his flies. The white-gym-shoed pimp watched Sebastian approach Sacha. Business was good; the watch would be his sooner than he thought.

He had learnt from his last meeting with Irena to conduct his questioning with a leer so as not to attract attention.

"Where is she?" his eyes peering over her shoulder to check she wasn't hiding inside.

"Tap your right buttock as if you're checking for your wallet." Sacha held his hand and smiled coquettishly.

"I don't have a wallet."

"Do it now and take a look over your shoulder quickly as if you are checking that there is no one you know watching."

She pulled him into the room and closed the curtain.

He had seen into the rooms but never been in one. It was dimly bathed in red light from a strip bulb fixed to the ceiling, the room small and functional. A bed, larger than a single but smaller than a double, was fixed to a wall. There was no bedcover just a sheet and a towel with a starlight scene covering half the bed. The walls were mirrored. At the rear of the room was a locker similar to the ones in sports changing rooms but without the air vents; there was only a slit like a post box at the top. A sink with nothing decorating it. The only other piece of furniture was a flip-top bin with crumpled tissues and used condoms trying to escape. The floor was white with tiles, and the smell of disinfectant fought with perfume. It was as welcoming as a doctor's consulting room. For those that used the girls for sex the sex had already taken place in their minds before they entered. It was a soulless place.

"Sit on the towel, it's clean." She opened the lower part of the locker and put on a lilac cardigan which she held closed around her chest.

It was hot and Sebastian itched with pinpricks of sweat; he didn't want to take off his jumper.

"It's OK, take it off, I know it's hot in here but don't forget we're almost naked most of the time."

He decided to keep it on.

"Irena, she's not working? Is she ill?"

She sat next to Sebastian on the towel; it was the only place that she didn't work on. She crossed her legs. Sebastian looked at her feet, one static on the floor the other bouncing from her ankle. He wanted to see between her toes. She lit a cigarette and followed the jet of exhaled smoke with her eyes.

"No, she's not ill. They have changed her work rota."

Not for the first time the banal way in which the girls spoke of their work in industrial productivity terminology sickened him – fucked to shifts, fucked to rotas. He nodded as if this was a normal work practice. It was for them.

"Some new girls have arrived and she has to show them the ropes. They start the new girls slowly, so she will be doing the morning shift, from 11.00 onwards. It gets busy over lunchtime."

The considered induction process of the employer towards his employee: break them in slowly. *How considerate*, he thought. The new girls wouldn't be broken in slowly, they were already broken beyond repair.

"How is she?"

For the first time since he had entered the room she looked at him. The pupils of her eyes constricted to an opiated pinprick.

"You do care, don't you? You care what happens to her. But don't, Sebastian. I have someone that cares for me, you know. He wants to take me away, take me with him when he goes. He is leaving soon and he promises to take me too. But he can't, you see, it's impossible."

He knew better than to rehash his naïve narrative of escape, the possibility of re-entering the world of smiling parents on a green hilltop in the summer. He didn't know what to say to her so he just nodded and stood up to leave.

Her hand reached out to his arm and she pulled him back down onto the bed.

"You can't leave now." Her hand gripped his arm tightly. "You haven't been here long enough." She looked at her watch. "Another five minutes."

He looked confused and felt the suffocating heat of the small room; he wanted to go.

"If you leave too quickly they will see you. They will think I haven't done my job properly and you've left without paying. Stay, just for five more minutes."

He nodded. She lit another cigarette. Her work life was timed by a five-minute cigarette and a ten-minute service of a stranger.

"Do you have fifty euros?"

Sebastian patted his pockets, pulled out a crumpled twenty-euro note and handed it to her.

"That's all I've got."

She walked over to the locker, the high heels of her shoes tapping on the floor. She opened one side of the locker and pulled out a Cath Kidston rose-patterned wallet from her hanging denim jacket extracting a ten- and a twenty-euro note. Together with Sebastian's crumpled twenty she posted them into the slit letter box.

"They count the money at the end of the night. It should tally with the number of clients, fifty a go."

Taking off her lilac cardigan she opened the other half of the locker to hang it up. Sebastian cast his eyes downward. Whilst she hung it up he noticed in the corner of the locker an Albert Heijn shopping bag. The bag was forced square by neatly stacked and ironed clothes. Judging by the colours they were Sacha's.

He didn't want to see her in just her underwear so kept his eyes down. She was quiet and waited. He looked up; she was smiling gently.

"You're quite a hit with the girls. We all talk, you know, we all notice you looking out for Irena. If there is anything we can ever do for you, well just let us know."

"Oh my God, you don't think…" His face registering misunderstanding alarm.

She walked towards him; he felt powerless to move. She placed both of his hands in hers and pulled him off the bed towards her. She let go of his hands and reached for his neck; her hands encircling his neck, she pulled him towards her.

"No, we know you don't want that, we like you too much to offer you that." Her hands slipped from around his neck to cradle his face; her hands were warm and smelt of perfumed youth.

"You're a good man, Sebastian. I don't know if you can do this but the best thing for you to do is to forget us, but later when you're away from here remember us. We would like that very much," she whispered into his ear.

She tick tacked on her heels to the doorway and raised her arms to open the curtain. Under her left armpit he saw the horse's head tattoo.

"Smile as you leave as he will be watching."

More of the employer's concern. A customer satisfaction survey.

She opened the door to let him out.

"Goodbye Sebastian."

He left like the previous man, slipping sideways through the partially opened door, but he was not fiddling with his flies. The white-shoed pimp caught his eye, leered at him and smiled a crooked conspiratorial, matey smile through a fog of smoke.

Sebastian was grateful for the crowd of voyeurs and those on their way to conduct business; they swallowed him into anonymity. He moved with the crowd until the small bridge over the canal. He stopped halfway over the canal and looked back towards Sacha. As he saw her dancing silhouette in the window he remembered she was ten years younger than him, in her mid-twenties, but had spoken to him as if their age difference was reversed. He wanted to see her face again, just for a moment. He half-shut his eyes to block out the flashing neon and thought she was looking at him. For a moment, a brief moment, Sebastian saw her without her work makeup, her face rouged with health, her white teeth shining as she laughed, her hair ruffled after a walk in the wind and her eyes glistening with hope. He did, he could see her.

"Wanna watch a live porn show, mister?" a voice cracked by drugs tried to entice. Sebastian looked at the stooped man, flecks of white spittle collecting at the corner of his mouth.

"Go away," was all he could think of saying.

He couldn't see her now; a look over his shoulder told him she was busy, the curtain closed.

CHAPTER 16

The croissants tucked to his side by his elbow smelled fresh and the warmth eased the pain of his elbow. Along with the physical pain he felt a mental anguish, a desire to eradicate the previous night; he wanted that night not to have taken place.

He had avoided his normal café as he didn't want to see Anneke after the previous night's incident; she would also have known, again he never knew how, the ending of the night. Arriving at the *Tulp* he looked around him at the early morning. There was a slight mist over the canal water, almost a haar, clearing as the sun rose. It was going to be a warm day, but these mornings also gave a hint of autumn to come; leaves on the trees had an edging of brown as if outlined by a crayon. The sap was retreating.

The saloon of the *Tulp* was in disarray. He lifted the still half-full cans of beer and shook them until the butt ends of the cigarettes fell down the teardrop aperture. The ashtrays were full of crumpled Rizla papers and the packaging had a small rip from which a roach had been engineered. The sofa had two pairs of jeans draped over it;

two pairs of Converse gym shoes, both blue with rainbow laces, lay in a tangle outside his bathroom. He turned towards his bedroom and looked at his half-packed bag; the night had been as bad as he remembered.

"Come back to bed," she said through the half-opened bedroom door.

Pushing open the door he saw them both.

"Hope they are chocolate croissants, I always get the munchies after taking some dope." Salt reached for the bag.

"Come." Pepper patted the bed. "Let's have a look at your arm."

Sebastian couldn't decide which was worse: the bruising on his arm or the squad of invisible gnomes with pneumatic drills excavating his brain. It was the last gulp from a beer can half-filled with cigarette ends that had given him his hangover.

"Ouch, it still hurts." Salt rubbed the bruise tenderly; the heat helped the pain.

The bruise was a result of an encounter with Dasha. Having lost sight of Sacha the previous night he had started to walk home when he felt his elbow joint being squeezed hard, very hard. He couldn't see who was applying the pressure. The voice identified the assailant as Dasha, thick and Slavic.

"Keep walking and don't look around," he had instructed. "If you do it might just be the last thing you do." The grip got tighter as he propelled him forward. He marched him through the crowd to a dim-lit doorway in one of the side streets. Dasha spun him round without releasing his elbow, his face inches from Sebastian's;

Sebastian felt something small and circular digging into his back.

"If I hear, see or even suspect you are seeing Sacha again I will kill you." It was said simply, not hurried but controlled. The words and not the tone contained the threat. That and his breath escaping from nicotine-stained teeth with an added tang of spirits. "Don't get involved with things you don't understand, the price is high, too high for you to pay, understand?" Sebastian nodded. "Stay away." Dasha released his elbow and walked away without looking back. Sebastian stood exactly where he was, watching Dasha meld into the cross-current of people at the mouth of the side street.

"What happens now?" His voice was afraid as he spoke to the invisible man holding the gun to his back. He couldn't feel any breathing on his neck. The response was silence. He was scared and with the silence his fear grew. He expected a pistol whip to the back of his head to reinforce Dasha's message, but none was forthcoming.

"I'll do as he says, just let me go." His voice shaky.

There was no response from behind him, but he did hear a cough from the entrance to the side street. An old woman pulling a wheeled shopping bag behind her walked towards him. It was going to get complicated, even dangerous for the old woman. Sebastian reacted with the instinct of his military training. He shot his elbow backward at the same time as dragging his instep along the shins of the man with the gun standing behind him. The old woman stopped and watched. She approached him and said something in Dutch. Sebastian spun round to confront the man behind. He faced a blue door; the door knocker was a fat abbot with a swollen belly, staring back at him. The shins of the assailant were a decorative miniature bay tree in a terracotta pot.

The old woman drew a key from her pocket and approached the door tut-tutting angrily.

"It's alright." Sebastian's voice was falsetto from relief.

"Dance somewhere else, you young fool," the old lady told him as she closed the door.

He watched the lights go on in the house making sure she was safe. He wasn't too sure why he needed to make sure, but he did know that he had been watched. Watched when he went to see Sacha, watched as he walked home. He didn't want the old lady being part of it, the watching. The only other thing he did know was he needed a drink, perhaps a few.

The first few steadied his hands, the rest resulted in an imagined victorious fight with Dasha and the pimps, a rescue operation of Irena and Sacha and a triumphant reconciliation with Zoe, happy ever after. Leaving the bar the fresh air hit him; he held onto the side of the entrance; he was drunk. Like all drunks he wanted the last word, the decisive comment that told all he was right.

He tripped into the Vlinder and stared around trying to find someone he knew, particularly Dasha. The possums looked startled at the drunk and lost themselves in mutterings and reflections. Sebastian stumbled forward using a table for support; once steady he regained his posture and launched himself to the next table, arms outstretched muttering to the occupants.

"Sebastian, over here."

His head rotated like a radar trying to find the source

of the voice. It was too busy, he couldn't focus and the noise was confusing. Two hands rested on his shoulders and guided him towards a table. He needed no assistance in sitting down. He collapsed into the chair. People were talking but he was too drunk to understand. He tried to follow the conversation but by the time he sourced the speaker the conversation had moved on and he was confronted by a closed mouth. Someone held his head steady.

"I think you need to go home." He recognised the voice, the deep guttural of Anneke.

"I do not!" he shouted banging the table top. "I need a fucking drink."

Umuntu stood up and addressed the approaching barman.

"I'll deal with him."

Softly Anneke whispered into his ear, "It's time to go home."

"What do you know about anything?! I bet you didn't know that your..." He couldn't think of the word. "That bendy bastard is a fucking pimp. He nearly tried to kill me, I thought his friend had a gun at my back. I hate it here, you're all bastards. He's the biggest bastard. I just went to see if she was alright, OK, I mean, I gave her back her phone, she needed it. Then that fucker threatened to kill me."

Umuntu was standing behind Sebastian ready to lift him up. Anneke shook her head telling him to hold off.

"Who, Sebastian? Who are you talking about?" She said it quietly and in a soothing voice.

"Irena. Well she got the phone. I just went to see Sacha

to see if she was alright, Irena I mean. He followed me. Dasha followed me and threatened to kill me if I went near Sacha again. Bastard!"

Anneke waited until he had finished. She knew how to disarm a drunk male: keep it simple, logical and deliver it with calmness.

"You're wrong, Sebastian. Dasha is not a pimp. Sacha is a Kazakh like Dasha, they know each other. He tries to look out for her, help her where he can. Perhaps he thought you were… well, using her for business."

Sebastian groaned.

"Look, let Umuntu take you back to the *Tulp*. We'll talk about this tomorrow." She nodded to Umuntu who helped Sebastian up from his seat.

Walking towards the door Sebastian slurred, "Sorry, sorry", to anyone who made eye contact with him. Most avoided his fish eyes; the possums looked relieved that imminent danger was being removed.

Alone and drunk in the *Tulp* he muttered to himself justifying his actions. Just to clarify to himself that everything he had done was as it should have been done he sought a confirming drink. The rationale of the drunk. With each smoked cigarette the butt was dropped into the can, the ashtray just a stretch too far for him to reach. The cycle continued until he had opened all six cans, finished none but turned all of them into ashtrays. With nothing left to drink he had convinced himself he had done all he could to help Irena and to hell with Dasha, Anneke and the whole of Amsterdam; Zoe too. If she didn't want him book unfinished, well to hell with her. He stumbled into his bedroom and started throwing things into his bag.

"Sod them all," he muttered into the chaos of the open drawers and strewn clothes. "I'm going back to London." Although a plan, scant on detail, but a plan anyway he felt calmer. He could go to bed now that the future was mapped out. Just one more cigarette and a drink. He reached for the nearest can and poured the contents into his mouth and swallowed. His throat contracted, he couldn't breathe. That's when Salt and Pepper arrived.

It hadn't taken them long to clean him up: a shower, the basin cleaned of vomit peppered with recycled cigarette butts, a glass of water and put to bed. Throughout Sebastian had intermittently been retelling the events of the evening, his book, Zoe and his desire to go back to what he knew. They in turn followed the diatribe as best they could trying to put together the disjointed pieces of information he threw about, at the same time putting him to bed in a matronly fashion.

"I'm sorry about last night." He meant it. He was sorry for what they had had to do to get him to bed, sorry that Sacha had asked him to forget her, sorry that Irena was now getting ready for work this morning. The one thing that was common to all four was their youth. Was he destined to be guided by women younger than himself? Yes, he was sorry for them. For himself he felt contempt at his inability to help Irena and Sacha and a hungover guilt at his inability to look after himself the previous night.

"Don't be, honey," they replied in unison. Salt's finger touched his lips before he could continue with his apology.

"We know you are, so that's all there is to be said."

He felt comforted sitting between them on the bed.

Still a bit hazy about the minutiae of last night, he with some trepidation asked, "The roaches?"

"Not yours, honey, ours."

"The basin?"

"We did that."

"Was I?" His arms waved down his body.

"No we left you in your boxers."

"How did you two…?"

"Well we weren't going to leave you alone in that state and we certainly weren't going to sleep on the floor."

"Did I?"

"No, you didn't, you slept like a baby."

"Thank God for that!" He felt better for resolving the questions that had arisen on his walk back from the café.

He looked around at the mess of his room, his clothes spewing out of the drawers; he didn't have the energy to tidy up. His eyes scanned his bedside table. He felt his stomach muscles contract; they hurt from last night's vomiting; a hot wave ran through his body. Staring at him was the photograph of Zoe, watching and smiling. She had witnessed the whole episode last night and was watching the three of them in bed.

"How did that get there?" he asked guiltily.

"You were going to leave her behind. When you packed your bag you didn't pack her." Salt spoke it as a reprimand.

It wasn't clear to him what else he had or hadn't packed. He went to his bag and searched for something. It wasn't on the bedside table and it wasn't in the suitcase. He tried to think, think through the fug of last night. He vaguely remembered wanting to go back, to where he was unsure, somewhere simpler without complications. He heard a police siren close by and getting closer. It had that almost comical high pitch of European police sirens that seem to suggest the crime is a lesser event than suggested by the guttural sirens of British police cars. He looked around him in increasing panic. The computer was still there, his notes still there, but he couldn't see his book. The police siren now very loud and close distracting his memory recall.

"I can't find it, I can't find my book." His voice was high and his speech quick. The physical weakness of a hangover only intensifying his panic. "Where is it?" he pleaded to himself with a hand tugging his hair as if to extract the answer from his brain. The siren was almost directly outside and he missed what Pepper said through the bedroom door. "I need it, I can't find it," he shouted over the siren. Thankfully the siren stopped.

"It's here, Sebastian. It's fine, I have it."

Sheepishly Sebastian went back into the bedroom. The book lay on the floor like a wounded butterfly next to Pepper, opened but face down with the spine upward. She picked it up and flicked through the handwritten pages.

"Salt read it to me last night. It's good, Sebastian." Pepper nodded in agreement; Sebastian wasn't sure if the agreement was she had read it to Pepper or it was good.

"I loved it," Pepper confirmed.

"I thought I had lost it."

"Oh, I don't think you ever would. It was on top of your bag last night. When we got you to bed Salt saw it and started to read it to me. You don't mind, do you?"

He took the book and stroked it with his fingers. "It's the first draft, it was done years ago."

"Come back to bed and tell us how the final draft ends. Does the story end differently now?"

There was an innocence about her request, a companionability about it. It was warm, almost hot lying between them, a protective and comforting heat. He thought of the last time he was this hot and a slight shiver ran down his spine as he thought of Irena and the new girls at the start of their working day.

"Jane changes her mind about the marriage. One of his comments changes her mind. At the dinner when they are arguing about presents on Valentine's Day, if you remember he had given her two tickets to his favourite band. Well he ends the argument by saying, 'You do very well by me.'"

The three of them were staring at the ceiling.

"I knew that would happen! He was always an asshole to her." Salt sounded triumphant. "I can't believe she ever hoped he was going to change. He spent his whole time putting her down, subjecting her to degrading mental torture, asshole."

Almost childlike, hoping for the story to end like a fairy tale, Pepper turned to look at him. Her nose almost touching his cheek and her breath warm in his ear she whispered, "Make Jane happy, Sebastian. You can make her meet someone, someone that makes her happy. You're the writer so you can do that, can't you?"

Sebastian knew the power of a writer, the ability to give or take life, make happiness or sadness, the total power of dictating someone's life; the controller of destiny. Nothing happened that he could not control.

"She will be happy. I'm not going to tell you how but she will be, that I can guarantee."

Pepper kissed him on the cheek and rolled onto her back smiling.

"I knew you would."

He hadn't heard a knock or a door opening. All he heard was an urgent voice almost imploring, "Sebastian? Sebastian?" The slight patois-infused voice of Rosie.

He heard the door of the toilet being opened and closed, the footsteps quick towards the bedroom door. He pulled the sheet up to his chin. Salt and Pepper looked at him, not with concern but looking for an explanation.

Rosie opened the bedroom door. She didn't look at Salt or Pepper; her tear-stained red eyes pleaded to Sebastian alone.

"It's Irena. You have to come."

"What is it? What's happened?" he asked as he leapt from under the bedcover. "Has she been moved? Have they moved her? For Christ's sake, Rosie, answer me."

Rosie stood still watching him push his feet into his shoes. Her head moved from side to side, the tears silently falling down her cheeks. She raised her arms to reach out for him.

"I'm so sorry, Sebastian, there was nothing we could do."

He felt the warmth of her arms and the chilled dampness of her cheek as she hugged him close; it was a motherly hug offering protection. He tried to pull away from her but her hug was too strong.

"Come," she said as she released him.

Holding his hand they walked towards a police car, the blue light fighting the sun as it flashed silently. An ambulance with its doors open had reversed towards the four cells. Around the police car a small audience of onlookers crowded around held back by uniformed officers. Between the audience and the building a plain clothes police officer, raincoat over his arm, was talking to some uniformed officers. The officers were underemployed and wandered from ambulance to police car. The imminent danger had passed, the excitement for them, over.

"Stay here, Sebastian." She kissed him on the forehead. "I'll be back in a minute."

Sebastian stood on the periphery of the onlookers, listening to the murmurings and whispered questions being asked. Some for information: "Is it a murder?"

Some stating facts. A voice with conviction informed everyone in the small crowd, "One of them got mugged and is in a bad state."

Sebastian stopped listening and looked towards Rosie. He knew Irena was dead. All he could hear was a radio from an unseen open kitchen window; it was all he wanted to concentrate on, anything to displace where he was now. The radio was playing Mungo Jerry's song, 'In the Summertime'. The music hopeful and happy.

Rosie walked towards the police perimeter and called out to the plain clothes officer.

"Inspector Bloogard."

He looked towards his name and nodded to the officers to let her through.

"Hello Rosie." He looked tired as if he had run a distance too far. "I'm sorry, I really am." His hand squeezed her shoulder. "Is she one of yours?"

"I know her but no she's not one of mine. I tried to get her to come to the meetings."

He nodded.

"Know anyone we should contact?"

Rosie looked around her, at the buildings, the canal and the crowd. She looked at Sebastian.

"She has a friend. She will still be asleep, she works late. Let me tell her, please?"

He nodded again.

"Rosie, I need you to talk to those two girls."

Sebastian followed Inspector Bloogard's finger. He pointed to two female uniformed officers, notebook in hand talking to two crying girls. The girls, despite the warmth of the sun, were shivering and holding each other around their necks. The two were in their early twenties, heavily made-up with dark eyeliner and green mascara bleeding onto their cheeks. One dressed in jeans and a strap top with no bra wailed in a language Sebastian didn't understand. As she raised her arms pleading heavenward Sebastian saw the tattoo. Fresh vibrant colours, the horse's head the fawn colour of a palomino with a blond mane, the whole tattoo framed in red bruising. It was newly done, recent and still raw.

"I can't do anything for them unless they talk to me. Rosie, you're the only one who can persuade them to talk to us. Try."

She walked over to the two girls.

"Don't ever give up, Rosie, we need your help if we are ever to get on top of this." Inspector Bloogard spoke to her back. He knew they wouldn't talk and he knew he would never get on top of the situation.

He turned to the policeman on the perimeter and gruffly instructed, "Get rid of them. It's not a bloody peepshow!"

The crowd departed in twos and threes speculating on what had happened.

"And that one," Inspector Bloogard barked as he pointed at Sebastian.

"He's with me," Rosie spoke over her shoulder, her arms encasing the two weeping girls.

Sebastian didn't move. He watched as a policeman slipped out from behind the curtain of Irena's cell. He carried a small plastic bag containing a syringe, the plunger pushed down, the needle bent and a small residue of coffee-coloured liquid in the barrel.

A cyclist stopped and asked a policeman what had happened.

"Oh, just some hooker OD'ed."

Sebastian opened his mouth to say something but the words were spoken by the inspector.

"Get over here, Du Toit." The uniformed man walked slowly over to his boss. In tones whispered but whipping Bloogard spoke Sebastian's words. "She's not *jus*t a hooker. She's someone's child. She's a father's daughter, a mother's daughter, Christ, she's the same age as my daughter. She loves. She was loved. She is loved. She will always be loved." He paused, he transferred his coat from one arm to the other, looked at the young officer. "Get out of my sight."

Rosie came over to Sebastian and put her arms around him.

"I'm sorry."

Sebastian remained static; he couldn't return the hug.

"You ready now?" A muffled voice spoke through a white mask. The curtain of Irena's cell was pulled back.

The stretcher was lifted by two officers; the contours of her body under the white sheet outlined her young body. Her silhouette looked almost pristine as if a sculpture being moved to a final position. As they lifted the stretcher into the ambulance her arm slipped from its white covering, her hand white, fingers splayed open, and between the second and third finger a pinprick of blood glistened against the dull surrounding of blue bruising.

That's when the hot silent tears fell down his cheeks. Sebastian didn't shake or try to wipe the tears away. He just stood and watched the doors of the ambulance close.

Who would find her parents? Who would tell them? The proud father who pushed her away to a better future, a sacrifice for him but worth it for her. The mother would only remember the crucifix she had given her, the last look as the car drove away, the smiling face through the rear screen window. Who would tell them their daughter died of an overdose as a whore in Amsterdam?

The ambulance drove away in silence. The policemen got into their car and drove away. Despite the warmth of the day Inspector Bloogard put his raincoat on and walked slowly towards the police station off Dam Square. There was no evidence that Irena had ever existed, that she had once lived. Rosie and Sebastian turned to walk away too. He could see Salt and Pepper standing next to the *Tulp*, their arms folded across their chest and heads downcast. He turned to look at the cell where Irena had worked; a black woman holding a steaming bucket and mop was slopping the floor. The two mascara-smeared girls holding onto one another were being guided away by a man talking on his phone. The man on the phone stopped to crush his finished cigarette with his foot; his white gym shoe ground the butt end into a gap between two cobblestones.

"For fuck's sake, shut up!" He pushed the duo in the back. "Move it," he said to the two girls.

CHAPTER 17

1

It hadn't taken long for the world to move on from her suicide. About twenty minutes by Sebastian's calculation. After the police departed, the streets started to repopulate. The tourists arrived to see the red light district in the safety of daylight. The smell of dope and beer filled the entrance to cafés and bars. The office workers from Rokin and Spuistraat cut across the canals on the bridges of Oudekennissteeg and Karte Niezel to the north and south of Oude Kerk to collect Chinese takeaways for lunch. Their office gossip and laughter was audible to Sebastian as he sat at his desk staring at his computer and coffee-ring-stained book. He could still hear the radio playing from the open kitchen window across the canal, the songs occasionally interrupted by the noise of nails being struck by a hammer, the radio noisy and building site loud.

He looked at the three mugs: two coffee and one tea. The solace of all Brits: the offer of tea and sympathy. Salt and Pepper had asked for coffee. The cups still full and the liquid cold now with a slick of stale milk discolouring the contents. They had murmured their mutual expressions of sadness and left to apply their makeup for the evening's performance. He had been at his table unmoved for the whole of the afternoon. The arrival of dusk had made him active; the shadows being cast by the setting sun moved around the sitting room making him uncomfortable, as if they were the shadows of someone unseen.

Sebastian was undecided as to where to go. He had only met Irena in three places and none of these offered any comforting memories. Her cell workplace, the Vondel Park and the desolate district of Bijlmer. As he wandered around his room in frustration he thought about Irena; the more he thought about her the less he knew. He knew her name, her job, that was it. He didn't know anything else about her: her surname, where she came from, her favourite colour, what made her laugh, her age. He did know that her life had been hopeless and happiness had eluded her – a wasted one.

He left the *Tulp* and headed away from the harsh commercial lights of bars and porn cabine cinemas. Darkness seemed to offer some comfort; no one could see the wounds of the day on his face. He glanced around at his fellow beings with a feeling of isolation and a desire to be part of them, not alone anymore that day. The doors of Oude Kerk were open and a soft glow shone through the entrance.

He entered and wandered down the nave towards the altar, welcoming with its flickering candlelight. Underneath his feet he felt the slimy smoothness of gravestones worn by time and footfall. The names were invisible, the dates also worn away. The deceased over time forgotten by most and only alive to the small group of interested historians and charcoal stone rubbers. He sat in one of the many empty pews at the transept and stared on the altar candle lights. The air around him was thick with scent as if incense had been burnt at a High Mass. He knew from the leaflet at the entrance that Oude Kerk, a pre-Reformation construction, had been Catholic but was now Calvinist welcoming worshippers of all faiths. What little he knew of Calvinism he didn't think incense burning was part of the worship.

He looked around the dim interior, the invasion of neon from outside casting feeble stained glass reflections off the walls. There were two side chapels, one on either side of the transept. One had no one in it and only two candles burning weakly as the wax expired. The north side chapel had a votive candle rack burning brightly; each point on the rack had a new six-inch votive candle burning, fierce in its desire to be noticed. This side chapel was fully occupied, all available room on the pews full, a population of about twenty. The placing of the votive candle rack at the front of this side chapel made that congregation dim and blurred. A family remembrance perhaps.

He heard the leopard-padding footsteps of the minister patrolling the pews. His soft footfall interrupted by the hard clacking of heels moving slowly to his left. The congregation of the side chapel leaving now. He turned to look at them. The flames of the candles hesitated as they passed the candle rack before re-establishing their collective glow. The scent grew stronger as the congregation passed, the smell a diffusion of different perfumes, not the smell of incense. Some dressed in jeans, sweatshirts and trainers, almost too casual for a church. Others, unusually for the summer, with coats on and collars high and tight around their necks as if dressed for an autumn Sunday service, their stockinged feet raised on heels. All of them women, all of them young. Some held hands for mutual comfort, others cast their heads down. None looked back as they left the side chapel.

The last to leave he recognised. The candlelight made her skin glow as if a purple-green. She did look back at the chapel, crossed herself and followed the others.

"Rosie! Rosie!" Sebastian hissed at her.

She didn't seem surprised to see him.

"I'll be back in a second." She smiled at him.

He watched her walk away towards the entrance. Sebastian stood up and walked to the side chapel. Illuminated by the candlelight there was a notice in a simple unvarnished wooden frame attached to the open grill gates:

> **The Chapel of St Bridget**
> St Bridget is regarded as the patroness of fallen women, not because she was at any time of her life unchaste, but from the fact that the English King Henry VIII's palace of Bridewell in London, located beside the well of St Bride or Bridget, was converted into a House of Correction for refractory females. She is represented in Christian iconography with a lamp in one hand, typical of heavenly light and wisdom and a cross in the other, as the foundress of the first community of religious women in Ireland, or, indeed, in the

Western World. Her long white veil is such a one as was always worn by early converts. The oak which appears in the background is in allusion to her cell among the grove of oaks at Kildare, literally 'the cell or place of the oak'.

Picking up an unlit candle he reached into his pocket and dropped a euro coin into the slot of the collection box. He lit the candle off one of the already flaming ones but couldn't find a place to put it on the candle holder; all the spikes were occupied. He sat in the front pew candle in hand and looked towards the small altar to St Bridget. There was nothing much to see; a white cloth covered the altar, a picture dimly lit of what he assumed was St Bridget but could have been any one of the innumerable pictures of saints appointed by the Church to offer focal points of prayer. The confused smell of the departed women still hung in the confines of the chapel. He felt a surge of belonging for the arbitrariness of the circumstances. Nothing to do with the Church or St Bridget but the assembled togetherness in this particular space, at one with the departed women in the need for a retreat from recent events.

He didn't see her but felt the comfort of her thigh pressing against his as Rosie slipped in beside him.

"I thought it would be nice to get them together for a moment or two to think about her. Well remember her really." Her voice betrayed the futility of it all. "Some of them aren't working tonight. It's nice to see those that are coming over for a few minutes."

Sebastian remained silent. He was trying to reconcile the thought that those who were working that evening had left their workplace temporarily, their scant work clothes hidden beneath coats, to remember one of their own, now dead. They had remembered her, fleetingly, lengthily or perhaps not at all as some of them may have pondered their own predicament rather than Irena's. Those thoughts, like Irena herself, in the past now as they lay on their backs staring at the ceiling to the grunts of a stranger.

"I didn't see Sacha. How is she?"

"Quiet. Her life has been burning up one day at a time, but she has never cried about it before. Now she's just silent. Can you be more silent than silent? If you can that's her, more silent than silent now that she has lost one of the last things that mattered."

"Tell me she's not working tonight. Please?" he implored.

"Not tonight." She squeezed his hand to offer comfort for what she was about to say. "She's replacing Irena looking after the new ones on the morning shift."

Ah yes, compassionate leave for a night and training the new ones to alleviate the pain. Sebastian felt exhausted. Looking around the chapel of St Bridget, the church and the empty pews he spoke to the altar not Rosie.

"What's the point of these buildings, this chapels and these icons?" He pointed to the portrait of St Bridget. He wasn't angry, he just wanted to know.

She didn't reply.

Without moistening his fingertips Sebastian crushed out the flame of his candle, rose and placed it back in the box, the only one with a blackened wick. He started to walk back to the entrance.

"Hope, Sebastian," he heard her say. "Hope."

He pulled up his collar as he left the church. He didn't

know why, it wasn't cold, there was no wind just the night breeze of a summer's evening. Avoiding any lit part of the streets he made his way back to the *Tulp*. He drew the curtains, closed and locked the door. He knew that Salt and Pepper would look in after the show, perhaps even offer to share his bed for emotional comfort. He knew that this too was coming to an end; perhaps tonight was the end of their relationship, as he wanted, tonight, to be alone. They would be leaving Amsterdam in the next few days along with the rest of the troupe. For them this was something to look forward to, for him less so.

He looked around his room; he hadn't turned on the light. The computer screen advertised Microsoft as the logo bounced around the screen. He flicked through the pages of his original manuscript, the well-fingered pages full of crossed-out text and margins with complicated additions. Towards the end he found the two pieces of paper that formed the genesis of the novel. The two pieces of A4. With no anger or malice he scrunched both and threw them into the waste basket.

He slipped off his shoes and without taking anything else off got into the bed and covered himself with the sheet. In the darkness he reached for his phone, pressed Z. Next to her name was a bubble. He typed, "I love you", before hitting the save button.

2

He woke feeling the tightness of the sheet around his legs. The opiate of sleep wearing off, he was in that moment of half-wakefulness where the start of the day offers all possibilities. It lasted but a moment. He felt his clothes distorted and uncomfortable on his body as he had tossed and turned under the heat of the sheet during the night.

He had been awoken by a tapping at his door; it was soft and undemanding but constant. Opening the door he was surprised to see the sun rising above the Skeith weightlifter's moustached rooftops.

"I brought you some coffee." Anneke's arm reached into the companionway.

He took it and walked down the companionway into the curtain-drawn gloom. Anneke followed. Sebastian slumped into one of the uncomfortable armchairs and for the first time since his military service lit a cigarette before a sip of coffee. The soldier's three-course breakfast: cigarette, cough, coffee.

"Will you stay on to finish it?" Anneke reached into her pocket for her Marlboro Reds.

Sebastian looked at his computer, blew on the coffee to cool it. He felt no need to answer immediately.

"I don't know," he coughed through the smoke.

She waited. She always waited, knowing he had more to say.

"With you gone I'll know no one. In fact after yesterday I will know one less than no one." He drank his coffee and winced as the boiling liquid burnt his throat. "I don't suppose it matters where I finish it."

"But it does matter that you finish it."

Sebastian looked at her. He always felt uneasy that Anneke seemed to have the ability to understand him. He trusted her but her innate ability to anticipate his thoughts, to comprehend fully why he was writing, disconcerted him. At no stage had she even mentioned Irena or what had happened. Sebastian knew that was right as there was nothing to say except platitudes of consolation; nothing would change, it would be as it was no matter what was said. He knew that she knew that too.

"I'll decide tonight if I am going to stay on here to finish it. I'm unsure yet." With this lie he held something that she didn't and couldn't know. "There are a couple of things I need to do before I decide."

She dropped her cigarette into the plastic cup to a hiss from the coffee. She was preparing to leave. She pulled a black hair tie from her wrist and with both hands pulled back her hair to form a small ponytail. He had never seen her with her hair back, her face fully uncovered. She had a face at which men walking by would turn to confirm or deny their first impressions, not quite sure on just a first look.

"You will say goodbye, won't you?" She didn't look at him but rather inspected him. "I mean if you decided to leave before the show closes."

Sebastian nodded.

"Of course."

She stopped at the desk and wrote a number on a piece of paper. He knew he would ring her but not when.

"Be careful," were her last words as she disappeared up the staircase.

3

It didn't take him long to pack. One rucksack, neat and

circular like a tube, contained all his clothes. That would be for the hold. A small holdall open and lined with Zoe's scarf, otherwise empty now but later tonight would contain his student manuscript, computer and photograph of Zoe. That would be hand luggage.

He wiped down the kitchen surfaces, brushed the floor. The bathroom could wait until tomorrow morning after his shower. He washed the vases that had held the flowers when Zoe visited. All the glasses were put away in the cupboards and the two plastic coffee cups from earlier were put in the bin. The bin bag tied and ready to be disposed of at the communal bin when he went out, for the penultimate time. He rearranged the furniture as best he could to the positions they were on his arrival. He was done with the *Tulp*, as if he had never been there.

He walked towards Oude Kerk. He knew that breakfast for the homeless would be over. Rosie would be elbow deep in soapy water. He wanted to say goodbye to her. He wanted to see her like that, not at work. In the kitchen her hands usefully employed. He pushed open the metal-studded oak door. He could hear her, confident and commanding in the kitchen. Her orders kindly given, unquestioningly obeyed as the table was wiped and the chairs stacked by willing hands.

"Hello Rosie."

She turned and wiped some sweat from her brow. A handful of white soapsuds stuck to her fizzy hair.

"Give me a moment."

She turned back to finish the dishes; she hadn't noticed the new addition to her hair. Sebastian could see her in years to come, her hair like the soapsuds: white.

Grandchildren in her lap resting against her bosom as she told them afternoon stories of princes and princesses. They would never know her story; she would always protect them from that story.

"Come, you can buy me a mint tea." She busied herself taking off her apron and putting on a cream cardigan. Her fellow volunteers discretely studied Sebastian and speculated. She slipped her arm through his and giggled quietly. "Let them guess," she whispered into his ear.

They walked in silence. She didn't look at him but squeezed his arm.

"You OK?"

"So, so."

Those two words were enough. There were no other words to describe how he felt about the suicide of a young woman whose life he had impinged on, and at the periphery. "Selfish", "waste", "sinful", "sad" were the words for those who heard of her suicide and spoke briefly of the anonymous woman's death. They hadn't ever been part of her life, not even on the periphery; that's what gave them the authority to use those words.

Before the waiter left Sebastian changed his order.

"Forget the coffee, two mint teas please."

"Oh, and a large piece of chocolate cake for me please." She looked guiltily at Sebastian. "I know I shouldn't. If I get any bigger I'll never get any customers," she chuckled.

He looked at her shiny full face, her cardigan buttons trying to escape the buttonholes as flesh pushed against them. He hoped she would eat a thousand chocolate cakes every day.

They sat in silence waiting for their drinks. His

eyes wandering around the street, watching nothing in particular. As if the thought had just come to him he turned to Rosie.

"Do they ever talk to them?"

She look quizzically at him.

"The inspector," he said. "Don't ever give up, Rosie, you're the only one who can persuade them to talk to us. Well do they?"

"Aart – Inspector Bloogard – is one of the finest policeman on the force. He's worked the red light district as long as I've been working. We started at almost the same time, in fact we could be called work colleagues," she laughed. "We're friends really, he's a good man, he speaks at the meetings offering guidance and help if the girls need it. For years he has tried to get the trafficked girls to talk to him. He really wants to crush those bastards. They never do though, the girls never do. They're just too scared."

He had heard it all before, the fear that was instilled in the girls. The undiluted fear.

"Well I agree with him. If they are ever going to talk to him it's up to you, Rosie, you're the only person they are likely to trust. So don't give up."

She smiled at him.

"I never will."

He stirred his tea; the scent of mint filled his nostrils as he lifted the glass to his mouth. She was right, it was cleansing. He didn't know how to approach the subject. Didn't know the response he would get, but he did know that he would be sad.

"I'm leaving tomorrow. I've come to say goodbye."

She looked at him with kindness.

"It's good that you're going, Sebastian. Not from Amsterdam I mean. You're just not really made to cope with my world. To cope with it you have to be born into it or placed into it young. Young enough to learn there is nothing else. Then it's up to me to un-teach what they have learnt."

She shrugged with resignation.

"Maybe I'm not a very good un-teacher. But I'll learn to be one."

He reached over and held her hands.

"Rosie, you are the only thing they have, the only hope. I think you are the most wonderful person I have ever met. I will always remember you, always."

She laughed quietly. She lifted one of his hands from his embrace and placed it on her cheek.

"There you go again saying things no one has ever said to me before." She pushed his hand against her cheek. "Feel it?" He felt the intense heat of her cheek.

"I'm right though, you are wonderful."

She waved her hands dismissively, embarrassed but happy.

"You're a good man, Sebastian. Can I ask you something?"

"Ask me anything and for you the answer will always be yes."

Her gaze intense on his face, waiting to see if there would be a change.

"Did you have anything to do with the 10,000 euros?"

He answered too quickly, he knew.

"No! How could I?"

She shrugged her shoulders waiting for an explanation.

"Rosie, I'm an unemployed wannabe writer. Where would I get 10,000 euros from?"

She nodded in understanding; a peaceful smile covered her face.

"I'll miss you, Sebastian." She paused. "I just wish I had found someone like you long ago."

He flushed as the blood ran to his face.

Rosie laughed victoriously loud, drawing the attention of their fellow morning coffee drinkers.

"It's my turn to make you blush!"

The waiter took away their empty glasses and wiped the table, leaving the bill attached to an ashtray with a clip.

They fell into silence as both watched the retreating waiter.

"I'm not very good at these goodbyes, Sebastian, I've said too many before. I think we should say it now. Give me a kiss and off you go."

He stood up and hugged her hard feeling her body flesh almost wanting to wrap him. He kissed her on both cheeks and started to walk away.

"Sebastian, can I ask one more thing?"

He turned to look at her.

"Anything, Rosie. Anything."

"When you walk away promise me you won't look back."

He nodded.

"And don't lie this time."

Of course he didn't. He walked away until he arrived at a tram stop. Hiding within the anonymity of the waiting passengers he looked back. She was still sitting at the table. A broad smile crossed his face. She had ordered another large piece of chocolate cake.

CHAPTER 18

Sebastian knew there were two more goodbyes he had to make that day, both of them time sensitive. He had already decided how he was going to deal with one, but on the other he was undecided.

He took the first tram that arrived. It rattled and tinkled its way towards the south, each stop announced by a female mechanical voice. He heard the voice announce, "Jodenbreestraat. Museum Het Rembrandthuis." He decided to get out at the next stop. There was still time to say goodbye. He stood by the doorway as the voice told him he was at "Waterlooplein". The doors hissed and like a collapsed concertina, they opened. He stepped out onto a busy junction, feeling disorientated. He was lost. He heard the bells chime on the church opposite the tram stop. He looked up to the church clock; it was 12.00. His time window was closing. Next to the entrance of the church he could see a large board of a street map of Amsterdam.

There were no pedestrians, just cars, motorcycles and vans waiting impatiently at red lights leaping forward like greyhounds at green. He waited at the pedestrian crossing looking at the amber-hatted pedestrian light and the countdown in neon from thirty seconds until he could safely cross.

He studied the map to find out where he was, and the quickest way to get to where he wanted to go. It was a map aimed at religious or ecclesiological tourists, all the churches, of which there were many, marked with a grey cross. The only two synagogues identified by the Star of David. There was a red spot and an arrow stating, "You are Here" next to a cross and the name Sant'Egidio Church; a Star of David highlighted the Portuguese Synagogue close by. The board, like so many in cities, was supposedly there to help but not orientated to the map-reader's position left the onlooker none the wiser as to where they were. His eyes moved from one cross to the next until he found Oude Kerk. Oude Kerk sat in the middle of a cradle of churches. Oude Kerk the compass rose, to the north the Church of St Nicolas, to the south De Waalse Kerk, to the west De Nieuwe Kerk. The east had none, just the exit to the sea. The irony of so many places of sanctuary so close to an area of such suffering confirmed why this goodbye was essential.

Sebastian entered the foyer of the church looking for help. Behind the counter selling crucifixes and religious icons a small woman with grey hair sat reading the *Catholic Herald* through half-moon glasses. She gave a smile welcoming the pilgrim.

"Hello, I need to get to Oude Kerk. Can you tell me the quickest way to get there?"

The smile beamed back at him. "Welcome, you're safe now," it said. He knew she hadn't understood him.

"O-U-D-E-K-E-R-K," Sebastian spelt out slowly.

She pointed to a small board at the entrance telling the times of services at Sant'Egidio Church.

"Yes, I know this is Sant'Egidio Church. But I want Oude Kerk."

He was getting agitated. With each second passing the chance of saying goodbye was diminished; he needed to get to Oude Kerk.

"Ja, Ja," her hand pointing into the church. "Hier Sant'Egidio."

He felt his feet dance the quickstep of frustration, his weight moving from one foot to the other like a boxer warming up. He tried again.

"O-U-D-E-K-E-R-K."

His phonetic accent betrayed the passing of the information. He looked around the counter for visual aids to his request. The table top was covered in brochures telling of African droughts, application forms for Christian Aid, a rack of postcards showing the interior of the church. None helped. Amongst the pleading literature was a small display case with a glass flip-top lid. He scanned the contents of the display case; the neat rows of medals shone and underneath each medal a small plaque stated the saint whose face was stamped on the metal. He saw her in the second row, St Bridget. The oval medallion had her in profile dressed in a habit with a halo behind her head, her hands clutching a cross to her chest and a staff running from the base across her body with a lantern at the top.

"How much?" he said reaching into his pocket.

This she understood.

"Ten euros." She smiled.

Sebastian dropped the money on the counter and picked up the medallion and pointed at St Bridget.

"The red light district?" he asked hopefully.

Her eyes registered relief at understanding him at last; her mouth turned downward at the understanding of his question. For a septuagenarian she was swiftly on her feet. The newspaper had hardly hit the counter by the time her hand was firmly on his back pushing him towards the exit. On the step she waved disapprovingly in the general direction of central Amsterdam. Sebastian headed in the direction suggested. He turned to thank her; she formed a cross from her forehead to chest to shoulders. His mouth closed before the first words could be spoken. She had taken a position on the steps; her legs apart and with her arms across her chest she was prepared for the pagan masses who might try to besiege her church.

Her eyes reflected the fallen as he impatiently looked for a taxi. She smiled at the invisible hand of God who had removed vacant taxis from the roads. Sebastian wanted to tell her, explain to her why he needed to go the red light district, needed to get there before the time window closed. It was important.

The taxi smelt clean and with the bribe of an extra fifty euros if the taxi driver got him to Oude Kerk without obeying the lights, the pine tree swung violently from side to side on the rear view mirror wafting the fresh scent of alpine spring air, purging the smell of previous passengers. He knew that for Sacha it could never be. The smell would remain. The smell of the previous customer would linger not just for the rest of the day and night, it would cling to her and slowly suffuse to become part of her; over time his smell would become hers.

He didn't feel the brakes being applied as his body shot forward. His shoulders rested on either side of the gap between the front seats and his head bent forward on the arm rest as if awaiting the executioner's axe. Raising it, he looked through the windscreen at the zebra crossing. Inches from the bonnet of the car a man in a long black cloak was reproachfully staring at the driver from under his black Fedora; the only other expression of animation was the bobbing up and down of ringlets. It was Dasha's rabbi.

The rabbi turned his back to the car and formed a crucifix with his arms to halt any motorised movement. They were like a Roman battle formation; a testudo of twenty black-coated and Fedora-wearing men crossed the road. Their flanks were protected by their black ankle-length coats; from above, the rims of their Fedoras protected them and their only weapon was a Torah clutched in their right hand held at chest height like a Pila. At the rear, not in rank but separate and alone in a new sharp-edged coat with the shine still on the fur of the Fedora, was a face without ringlets. It lacked the resolution of the others; a newbie in his new clothes, the nose askance to the face and his step out of sync with the others Sebastian thought he looked like Dasha.

"Sorry, my friend. I had to stop," the taxi driver spoke over his shoulder. "Does the fifty still stand?"

"Yes." The taxi leapt forward. Sebastian stared through the rear window to confirm it was Dasha. Neat and tidy in his new sharp-edged black armour Dasha looked as if he belonged.

The taxi drew up at the Krasnapolsky Hotel; Sebastian threw the money on the passenger's seat and ran towards the revolving door. Rushing through the foyer, knocking into late-check-out businessmen he looked for the clock; the multiple time zones confused him – New York, London, Tokyo and Amsterdam. The clock read one thirty for Amsterdam. He ran to the rear of the hotel and the cut through to Oudezijds Voorburgwal. As he got closer he knew he needed to slow down. The red light district, unlike the prostitutes' cells, was not an area with fast-moving people. The ponderous sex shoppers would notice a runner as would the pimps; they would be on alert to the unfamiliar.

He stopped to light a cigarette. The smoke made him cough after his run and the nicotine made his already fast heartbeat increase. He stubbed it out and inhaled the air in deep breaths. *Calm it down, calm it down*, he thought. He walked towards the little bridge over the canal; his eyes ahead, the curve of the bridge gave him a slight height advantage to see into the distance. He knew who he was looking for but couldn't see him. The four cell windows covered with the bleached curtains, the white-shoed pimp absent. His fingers glided over the medallion in his pocket; he could feel the benevolent face of St Bridget on his fingertips. He knew he would only have to wait ten minutes before the curtains would open again. He leant on the wrought iron railings of the bridge, trying to convey nonchalance and the natural state of someone enjoying the summer sun post lunch.

He heard the clock of Oude Kerk ring for two o'clock. He had been on the bridge for over twenty minutes; not one of the three curtains had opened. He thought of Irena, thought of Sacha and the new girls under her charge. His mind ran across the possibilities; Sacha had overdosed, but why would the other curtains be closed? It was impossible to have four overdosing, wasn't it? Had Sacha been moved or sold? No, as Rosie had told him she had been put in charge of the new girls. His eyes concentrated on the curtains willing them open. The thought that she had finished her shift and departed depressed him as he would never say goodbye, never be able to offer her… offer her what? He didn't really know what he would say to her or what he could offer to her.

He saw one curtain drawn back; he waited for the departing man. No one came out. He started to walk slowly towards the other doors. There was still no one exiting. He stopped to check if the pimp was in his usual place. He wasn't there. His disappointment increased as he imagined a bucket and mop being put outside the door before a cleaner emerged having cleaned the room for the next girl renting the room. It wasn't a bucket and mop placed on the cobbled pavement, it was an Albert Heijn plastic shopping bag, full and square shaped.

She was wearing a pair of jeans and blue Jack Wills hoodie. The hood was down and her hair was pulled back untidily in a ponytail; her face with no makeup was red raw as if she had been scrubbing it hard. She picked up the bag and knocked on the curtained doors to her left and right. The door to her right opened immediately as if the occupant had been awaiting the knock. A girl of about nineteen emerged with her eyes cast down to the pavement and the mascara on her eyes smudged. She didn't talk to

Sacha, just walked past her and called a name to the drawn curtain.

"Natalia."

Nothing happened. The young girl called the name again. The curtain remained closed. Sacha walked towards the closed door and opened it slightly. She spoke whispered soft words into the small opening. Her hand went into the room and as she turned she gently pulled out a track suited girl. The girl had a baseball hat pulled low over her face, the tracksuit was a size too big for her. Sacha lifted the peak of the baseball cap slightly and kissed her forehead. Sebastian saw the girl's face, blotchy and swollen around the eyes, and with her makeup partially removed her face looked like a bruised peach. He thought she must be around sixteen or seventeen and seemed to have been crying for all those years.

Sacha started to walk away from Sebastian, Natalia and the young girl following behind her in silence. Sebastian followed them in the hope they would separate and he could talk to Sacha alone. He followed them to the Central Station willing them to part. He knew once they arrived at the concourse he would lose them in the crowd. Before the entrance to the station next to the large lettered sculpture of "Amsterdam the Happiest City in Europe" Sacha stopped at a kiosk to buy cigarettes. As she put her change into her Cath Kidston purse he knew he had to talk to her or lose the opportunity forever.

"Sacha." He spoke it gently so as not to surprise her.

Natalia and the young girl who had been standing waiting for Sacha looked up in alarm, their faces were fearful and their eyes looked at Sacha, pleading for help.

Sacha looked at him blankly; she was emotionless, nothing would frighten her again and nothing would make her safe and happy again. She was functioning only.

"Sacha, it's me, Sebastian."

She stared at him as if he was something she had lost and now couldn't remember why she had worried about the loss in the first place. She said nothing.

"We met when you were at work."

The two girls looked startled and stepped away from Sacha, trying to hide in the migratory population of travellers.

"I was a friend of Irena's. I mean I am a friend of Irena's."

Her eyes lit up in recognition, not of Sebastian but of the name Irena.

"She's dead," she said flatly; the only part of her body that moved was her mouth. Her arms rested by her side; the open Cath Kidston purse spilled her change onto the grey concrete concourse.

"I know."

She didn't move, she just stared at him. She looked like a confused child; her feet were turned inward and her knees pressed together. He wanted to hold her close and by a process of osmosis absorb her misery; he would take it from her, he would bear it for her.

The tannoy rattled off a list of stations to be visited by the soon-to-be departing train from Platform 10.

"Haarlem. I have to go," she said mechanically as if the name of Haarlem had triggered something in her brain.

Sebastian didn't know what to say. He had anticipated she would remember him; the goodbye would have been easier. He took a step towards her; she remained static. He picked up the change from the floor and put it into her purse snapping it closed.

"Sacha, the phone, Irena's phone? The park? Remember me now?"

"Irena is dead," she replied placing the purse into her hoodie pouch. "Dead."

He took a risk, he knew time was running out. He placed his hands on her shoulders and looked directly into her eyes.

"Look, Sacha, we've met before. You once told me something when we met. You said, 'I don't know if you can do this but the best thing for you to do is to forget us, but later when you're away from here remember us.' Do you remember?"

Her head moved sideways and her eyebrows moved closer together as if trying to recall the conversation. He knew if she thought harder she would remember, if not now but later definitely.

"Sacha, I am leaving now, going home. But I want to give you something."

He put his hand into his pocket and placed the medallion of St Bridget into her hand. She looked at it blankly. He took it from her open palm and hung it round her neck. He felt as if he was dressing a mannequin.

"When you touch this you will know that I am thinking of you and Irena. I may not be here but I will never forget you both. I will always remember you both."

Her hand touched the medallion nestling in the soft indentation of her collarbone.

She looked up at him; her eyes were moist. She was fighting to stop them leaving her tear ducts.

"I remember you. You're a friend of Irena's." Two tears fell, one from each eye, and rolled to the corner of her mouth. To gain control she inhaled the teardrops into her mouth. "She trusted you." Her voice so quiet he could hardly hear her.

The tannoy repeated the list of stations. As soon as she heard Haarlem she turned to go. She didn't look back. Sebastian watched them go towards Platform 10. The only motion he saw from Sacha was her right arm see-sawing across her neck with her hand holding the medallion between her thumb and index finger.

He watched them disappear down the stairs to the platform. It was as if he was watching her presence fading, slightly at first and then totally, as he exited a labyrinth, leaving her, forever trying to find the exit. The goodbye felt like a betrayal. It lacked a future for Sacha.

He consoled himself that the last goodbye of that day would be easier; he knew how to handle that one. It would be quick, decisive and leave him satisfied. He just needed the night.

CHAPTER 19

1

He turned out of the station towards the north end of Prinsengracht; he couldn't face the red light district. The bohemian and alluring decadent atmosphere that first struck him when he arrived in Amsterdam now seemed comprised of misery and hopelessness. The working girls, he now saw, were having their souls slowly dug out of them with each joyless jab of a commercial cock.

He needed somewhere quiet, somewhere normal. Prinsengracht in late afternoon offered both.

The electronic confirmation of his two o'clock flight to London stored in his phone burned through his breast pocket. He knew that he would only have the next morning to say goodbye to Anneke, Umuntu, Salt and Pepper. They would already be making plans to move on after the show closed, next stop Hamburg. He wanted the time available to be constricted; the goodbye would be easier in the hurry of limited time.

He knew he wanted to do more than say goodbye

to Anneke. He wanted to thank her for her tutelage. To thank her for her discrete hand of guidance, making him see what he somehow knew but couldn't see. The book now so nearly finished, the prize on completion as he presented it to Zoe – that was the gift she had given him. It was irreplaceable. She had changed him, and slowly and imperceptibly she had given him back his ability to take decisions, decisions that channelled his future. He wouldn't know how to say that to her. He bought a packet of cigarettes, a notepad and a small red Swiss Army knife from a corner shop. He would tell her though, he would write it and give it to her just before he left for the airport.

The start of the letter was hesitant. Each sentence ended in a drag on a cigarette. He paused, thought and paused again. Ordering another coffee he allowed the waiter to take away the crumpled pages of his previous efforts and his dirty cup. The delight of secret laughter as a young couple walked by distracted him; his eyes followed after them as they walked down the length of Prinsengracht. The soft net curtains of street-level kitchens waved from the open windows in the light summer breeze. Outside many of the houses placed directly on the doorsteps or cobbled pavement were deckchairs. One house had a two-seater sofa promoted from the interior darkness to a place in the sun. A woman passed the café terrace pushing a pram; she spoke softly to her sleeping baby. The elderly woman on the sofa was joined by her husband; he handed her a cup of tea in a small, fine delicate china cup. She smiled at him as she took it from him. There was no need for a sugar bowl or milk jug, he would know how she liked it. Her free hand patted the cushion next to her.

The waiter returned and placed the coffee on the wiped-clean table top.

"Thank you." Sebastian smiled at the waiter.

He lit another cigarette and felt a bite at the back of his throat as he inhaled. Flipping the cigarette packet lid open he was surprised to count only ten left. He stared at the notepad; the most recent letter hadn't progressed further than, "Anneke".

Looking at the retreating waiter he thought of those simple two words, "thank you."

His previous attempts at writing the letter had all failed. The contents of the previous letters weren't about Anneke. The thanks may have been, but the sentences all led to what he hoped from his return to London. It all revolved around Zoe. Anneke's nurturing, encouragement and café tutorials had all been about finishing the book. He remembered some of her comments: "You now know who you are writing it for", "There is only love, there is nothing else".

He pulled out his phone, found Zoe's telephone number and typed, "I'm coming back. Can we meet next week?" This time he didn't save it, he pressed the send button.

Crushing out his cigarette he started to write:

"Dear Anneke,

Thank you.

Love Sebastian."

He knew he didn't have to add anything else. She already knew he was grateful, and by how much.

He folded the letter into an envelope, wrote Anneke on the envelope and put it in his pocket.

2

The deckchairs and sofas were gone, the windows shut and the streets quiet now except for the occasional rattle of the contents of a bicycle basket as late night returnees cycled over the cobbled streets. The daylight had long since been stolen by the advancing shadows. Sebastian had traced and retraced the horseshoe canals: Prinsengracht circular route back to the Central Station, the same with Keizersgracht, Herengracht and Singel. He watched the lights in the houses go out downstairs, the bathroom and then the bedroom. The houses were dark and the people safe inside unaware that this goodbye was imminent. Sebastian knew he would be there, *in situ*, waiting for the close of business.

He walked past Madame Tussauds and laughed as the headlights of the only car on the road highlighted Arnold Schwarzenegger sneering at the world in his Terminator costume. The restaurants were closed in Damstraat, and the only suggestion they had been busy were the fat black polythene bags stacked at the roadside ready for dawn collection. Oudezijds Voorburgwal was almost empty of people; the neon red and purple lights still flashed but only onto the canal water.

Sebastian kept his eyes lowered. He counted off the cobblestones as he walked. Each stride covered eleven cobbles. He needed to concentrate. The mostly nocturnal Bulldog was closing to the scrape of zinc chairs being stacked. He was getting closer. Eleven, another eleven, he would see him soon enough.

Most of the working girls had left, their curtains drawn. Those that remained made no effort to stand at the window; there was little business to be had. They sat on their bar stools in the recess of their rooms making calls to each other. They didn't even look as he passed. There was a Friday afternoon ten-to-five feel; business nearly over and just going through the motions until they could leave. He passed two drunks with football scarves wearily chanting.

He kept his eyes down, counting.

Arriving at the bridge that crossed the canal he looked towards the familiar cells. Two had their red lights on, the others dark and the offer-of-business light were off.

He saw him. The white trainers supporting his squatting body as he played a game on his telephone at the alley entrance.

Sebastian reached into his side pocket and opened the knife. The blade felt cold against his hand; it frightened him. He estimated it would take him less than five minutes to get there. He walked slowly at first, quickened his pace and then ran. The pimp looked up as Sebastian's foot caught him under the jawbone. He felt the outline of his chin on his instep. The pimp slumped backwards, his mouth open to cry out. Sebastian put his hand over the pimp's mouth and pulled him into the darkness of the alleyway.

He felt with pleasure the warm blood on the inside of his hand.

"Lie still, you bastard," he hissed.

The pimp stared up at him from the prone position. His eyes bloodshot and scared. Sebastian reached into his pocket and pulled out the knife with the open blade. The pimp's eyes widened with an end-of-life stare. Sebastian half-smiled, almost a sneer of satisfaction.

"Move and I'll cut you. You understand."

The pimp's head nodded.

Sebastian leant forward. The pimp's eyes tried to follow the blade, his forehead sweaty, and the smell of urine filled Sebastian's nostrils. Sebastian moved the blade down the shiny black shirt, over the damp patch of his groin and rested on the white trainers. With two swift upward strokes of the blade he cut the laces and pulled off both trainers holding them like a trophy.

He stood over the pimp, his legs straddled across the prone pimp's torso.

"I'll be watching you. You so much as lay a finger on one of those girls, I'll know. You understand me?"

The pimp nodded.

"And buy your own fucking trainers, you little shit," Sebastian snarled at the pimp.

His adrenaline now dissipated, he had achieved what he had set out to do. He placed the knife inside one of the shoes and with a swing of his arm threw the trainers into the canal. With the splash from the water he knew this had been an error. He first felt the sharp pain of a fist hitting his testicles. The pain made him double over, presenting a perfect target for his opponent. The pimp crashed his forehead into Sebastian's face at nose bridge level. The pain like an electric shock sending waves of pain into his brain. He couldn't think. He knew he was out of his depth, his upbringing had not taught him street survival; that's all the pimp's upbringing had been, from some hellish decayed town to the hellish pimping world of trafficked women. He represented street-style natural selection at its evolutionary apex.

Sebastian curled into the foetal position exposing only his back, his face barricaded in his arms and his hands covering the top of his skull. The pimp still found a way in, raining punches onto his jawbone, kidneys and liver. Sebastian was thankful that he had thrown away the shoes or the kicking would have been more severe. His body screaming in pain from all quarters. The pounding continued but the pain didn't increase, it couldn't.

He heard the heavy breathing after the last punch connected with his temple.

"If you ever come here again. If I ever see you again, I'll kill you." The voice thick with a foreign accent made almost unintelligible by the fat swollen lower lip.

The pimp reached into his inside jacket pocket. The lighter flicked alive and the cigarette glowed. After the first inhalation of smoke the pimp coughed and spat an oyster of bloody phlegm smelling of tobacco into Sebastian's face.

"Understand?"

Sebastian whimpered.

Sebastian didn't hear him leave the alley on his stockinged feet. He did see his shadow approach as he walked away towards the lights of Oudezijds Voorburgwal. He remained stationary, curled into a ball, aching.

He heard the bang on the windows.

"Get your coat. We're done for tonight."

A female voice raised a protest.

"No, you can't get changed. Get your fucking coat. Let's go."

Sebastian heard the clicking of heels recede down the street.

The last thought as he passed out was one of uselessness. He had failed as a street fighter and with the two essential human functions inoperative – his balls aching and his eyes swollen – he really wasn't much use in the red light district either.

3

He didn't know how long he had been unconscious. He did know it had rained. His clothes were wet, his hair damp and a cold chill made him shiver. He struggled onto his hands and knees and crawled onto Oudezijds Voorburgwal. The pain was ubiquitous. He slumped into a doorway.

Sitting in the doorway he looked down into the pool of rainwater pixelated by the cobbles. Slowly his eyes focused on the hydra-headed reflection. The faces were fractured and gaunt and the iris of their eyes held in bruised orbits of off white by fissures of red. There was a sheen of sweat on the faces making the many images seem almost in relief as the dimming red lights of the whore's cabin melded with the slit yellow hint of sunrise.

Christ, he hurt; liver, kidneys, eye, nose and head ached. The lower part of his legs filthy with grime from the street, his right foot rested on a used condom. He wasn't conscious of the act just felt the heat of tears running down his cheeks.

He sensed he was slipping into unconsciousness when he felt the welcome warmth of a fur-cuffed hand wrap around his shoulder, the end of which glowed with five perfectly painted scarlet nails.

"Sebastian, what are you doing here?" she said.

"Saying a goodbye…" were the last words he mumbled before passing out.

CHAPTER 20

1

"OK, so what are we going to do with him? We can't leave him here. Anneke, I been planning this for ages, he can't ruin it, it's too important." The voice was foreign, angry and vaguely recognisable.

"We can handle it," a deep voice replied, a voice of authority.

"Well you had better!" It was said accusingly.

A door opened and shut with a bang.

Sebastian felt the bed open up and swallow him. It wasn't an uncomfortable feeling; the sheets seemed to wrap around him like a shroud. He sank further down; it was warm and safe where he was going.

"We can, can't we, Umuntu?" Her voice searching for an answer.

2

It was dusk when he woke to a sharp pain. His kidneys felt

as if a stiletto blade had entered them – short, sharp and twisted. He turned in the bed. The sheet had been tucked tight around his body and an eiderdown kept him warm. He wriggled his arms out from under the sheets and with each movement a new pain announced its presence.

Sebastian tentatively sat up in bed. Even in the purple light of dusk he could see the walls were white with a photograph perfectly centred on each. His arm reached out for a bedside table; there was no side light, just a glass of water and a bowl of lukewarm water with a flannel neatly rolled up. A pool of yellow light invaded the room from under the closed door.

"Hello?"

He groaned as he shuffled towards the door. The pain was everywhere.

Opening the door onto a small hallway he tried again.

"Hello?"

There was no response.

The light reflected off thc bathroom mirror making the room seem much bigger. He looked down to undo his flies for a pee and was surprised to feel the flannel of striped pyjama bottoms. It hurt to pee; inspecting the arc of liquid he noticed it was not the usual yellow but a rusty brown. The water in the bowl turned a weak red.

Turning to the washbasin a partially recognisable face looked back from the large medicine cabinet mirror. Staring back at him was a face that had taken a beating. Both eyes swollen and red like the inside of a pomegranate, a darkening skin topped his nose.

"Christ." He placed a hand on either side of the washbasin as he half swallowed a bitter reflux of bile escaping his stomach. He gagged and spat. He remembered too.

He heard keys being placed on a table and the rustle of plastic shopping bags. Before he could speak he gagged again, a dry back-of-throat gag.

"Sebastian, you OK?"

When he looked up at the mirror Anneke was behind him. He nodded at her reflection.

"It's too early for that, I'd avoid mirrors for a while. Those are going to become spectacular bruises." Her hands reached and glided over the swelling without touching the skin.

"Come next door, I've got something from the pharmacy to dress those."

She led him into the sitting room. The room was lit by uplighters and a collection of lamps on pale blue side tables giving a gentle glow rather than illumination to the room. Like the bedroom the walls and the wooden floorboards were painted white. The centre of the room was occupied by a blue lacquered table at knee height covered with perfectly spaced fashion magazines, the table surrounded by cream sofas with colourful silk cushions. Every surface had a vase of flowers, the vases empty of water and the silk flowers shining with the light. The room had a sense of order that told of the recent visit of a cleaner.

He sat on one of the sofas as Anneke opened cotton wool packages and a bottle of Dettol.

"Do you remember anything of last night?"

He winced as she applied the liquid to the bruising over his eyebrow.

"Unfortunately, yes. Almost all of it, well up to when

I passed out on Oudezijds Voorburgwal." He raised his hand to touch the bridge of his nose. "How did I get here?"

"It was our last night. After the show we started the packing up. You know we are off in the next two days?"

Sebastian nodded and realised he hadn't managed to leave before them after all.

"By the time we had finished the initial pack up it was late. On the way back the troupe went to some club for an end-of-show party. Umuntu and I walked back and he was just about to enter his apartment when I saw a crumpled heap. I didn't know it was you. Umuntu told me to cross the canal in case it was a comatosed junkie. Lucky for you I didn't. As I got closer I recognised your jacket."

He kept perfectly still as she dabbed gently with the cotton wool. To alleviate the pain of the medicine he concentrated on a photograph on the sideboard. The photograph was of a smiling couple at the end of a fashion runway. The model was attractive and her makeup exaggerated. Standing next to her was a neat and precise, almost feminine, man of the same height with dark hair perfectly cut around his ears and parted at the side. He was wearing a black suit and a white shirt with the top button undone. His arm raised in salutation acknowledging praise.

"Umuntu carried you back here and put you to bed."

He leant forward to look at the dimly lit photograph. He thought he recognised the woman. The man vaguely familiar but undefined when he tried to recall the face from his memory.

"Keep still, Sebastian, I can't do this if you keep moving."

A drop of Dettol got into his eye.

"Sorry about that, you OK?"

Sebastian rubbed his eyes creating tears and blurred vision.

"Well it's the best I can do for the moment. Look, why don't you have a shower and I'll make us some food. You must be starving. There is a spare towel in the bathroom."

Turning the light on in his bedroom the four photographs came alive from a cluster of spotlights held in an orb set in the ceiling. Each photograph was of the same model as the one in the sitting room, the same setting, a catwalk setting. The clothes she modelled were extravagant and of the unwearable type beloved of the fashion world. He approached each in turn. He did know the model. She was the one in the photo pinned up behind the bar at the Vlinder. The one above his bed showed her arriving at the start of the catwalk; the soft curtains at the entrance to the walkway seemed to cling to her as she made her entrance. A board above the curtained entrance announced, "The Jurgen Collection". He leant closer to the picture. In the right of the photograph looking from backstage and almost obscured by the curtain was the same man, dressed in black with a white open-necked shirt. With his eyes still smarting from the Dettol the face was vaguely familiar but Sebastian couldn't attach a name.

He heard Anneke clattering around in the kitchen preparing supper as shower water hissed down. He felt a hint of a coming headache and opened the bathroom cabinet looking for painkillers. The inside was neat, disciplined and contained an impressive array of makeup. It had been arranged on the shelves in order of use. On the top row was a selection of cleansers and moisturisers from Clinique. He was surprised to see on the next row a collection of Mehron paint sticks next to containers of foundation, concealer and highlighters all made by Kryolan. Both brand names he was familiar with from his student days as the head of makeup at the university theatrical society. The Kryolan brand had been founded by a 1920s chemist, Arnold Langer, who had been mesmerised by the glitz and glamour of 1920s Berlin. He had combined both interests to specialise in the production of makeup for the stage, cinema and television. It was not everyday makeup. A small tube of eyebrow wax had a set of tweezers next to it. The final two shelves had a selection of coloured skin toners, mascara, eyeshadows and lipsticks.

He stood under the shower and felt better as the water washed away the dried sweat from the previous night. The slight pain of his head remained. He looked for a laundry basket to put his pyjamas into. In the corner was a wicker basket with the arm of a silk shirt hanging out. He lifted the lid and was embarrassed to see a bra. As he pushed the washing down in the basket his finger caught the bra, not on the strap but in a slit of a pocket at the back of the cup.

Back in his bedroom his clothes were washed and ironed in a neat pile on a white chair. He searched through his jacket pocket for his lighter. The note to Anneke from the inside pocket had gone. Standing close to the photograph he flicked the flint of the lighter to get more light onto the photograph. The man in the corner shone back at him. He knew he recognised the face, not as it was in the photograph but what the face could become.

"Are you ready for something to eat?" Anneke asked from the kitchen.

He dressed quickly.

"Give me a minute."

Sebastian returned to the bathroom, closed and locked the door. He looked around him, looking for some drawers or another cupboard. Below the sink was a small unit with one drawer. He knew what he was looking for. He opened the drawer and neatly placed on a towel was a cellophane package containing two perfectly formed small, nippleless breasts made of silicone gel.

He raised his face to the mirror; he didn't see his battered face. He saw Anneke crush a cigarette with her Doc Martens; saw her tired and overly made-up after a night of watching football; saw her always let her hair drop to cover her face. He heard Pepper say, "Anneke, shy, reserved and not what she is", Umuntu's speech after his tour of the red light district, "Things are never quite as they seem. Are they?"

He inhaled deeply, shut the drawer and closed the cabinet door on the makeup. Straightening his back he pushed his shirt further into his trouser waistband and then did something he hadn't done since an earlier age: he buttoned his top shirt button.

"It's ready, Sebastian, you can tell me what happened over supper."

He walked into her small kitchen where she had placed two bowls of soup on a neatly arranged table. She turned with a smile half-formed on her lips. She looked at him standing in the doorway, studying him closely and in silence. Her face seemed to relax totally, the muscles around her mouth and cheeks at ease. Sebastian thought she looked peaceful, almost serene.

"Sit down," she said softly as she reached for her cigarettes. Sebastian slowly and quietly sat at the table with his hands in his lap. She lit two cigarettes, handing one to Sebastian.

He drew on his cigarette; his hand shook slightly as he pulled the cigarette from his lip.

"You never suspected, did you?" She spoke gently.

Sebastian's eyes roamed her face. Her makeup was perfectly applied to alter the main differences between a man and woman; he knew how difficult that process was to achieve. He had never quite managed that; there had always been one feature that had betrayed his efforts and the character under the stage light was never as convincing as he had wanted. Her hair cut with the wispy bangs had narrowed her forehead and the bony bridge that runs across the forehead above the eyes had been softened and smoothed. The eyebrow wax and plucking had moved her eyebrows from their natural position on the orbital rim bone to above the bone making them finer and curved. Her eyes showed her skill to the fullest; she had overcome the deep set of men's eyes by using eyelash curlers and mascara. Her application of eye makeup removed the shadow from the brow ridge making her eyes seem less deeply set in their sockets. The use of shadowing and contouring had lifted her cheekbones and narrowed her nose which rested on fuller lipstick-covered lips narrowing the distance between the base of the nose and the top lip.

"No. I wasn't looking. I suppose I never look beyond my assumptions."

She poured two glasses of red wine and placed one in front of Sebastian before she sat down opposite him. They sat in silence.

"Who are the people in the photographs?" He felt foolish asking, but wanted to know why Anneke had become who she was.

She took a sip of wine and carefully placed the glass in the exact place she had raised it from.

"The one in the suit is me."

Anneke had always struck him as rather sexless, but perhaps not to other women.

"Tell me about her."

Anneke looked away from him to stare through the kitchen window into the orange yellow of the streetlit night.

"I love her. I loved her with my entire soul." She spoke slightly above a whisper.

She started to talk, not to him, but to some invisible listener beyond the room.

"I had left the ESMOD fashion school in Berlin. Like so many others I wanted to design my own range of clothes. I didn't want to work for one of the big established fashion houses. I was broke, of course, so did the design, cutting and sewing in my flat. I thought my creations could sell themselves. It took me time to understand that the creation of such beautiful designs can only be fully appreciated if worn by someone of matching beauty."

She walked through to the bedroom and placed the photograph of the girl with the curtain clinging to her in front of Sebastian.

"Don't you agree?" There was a hint of a smile.

She didn't wait for an answer and sat down.

"I met her at a fashion party. I knew the moment I saw her I wanted her to be part of me. I had never been more assured of anything in my life. I think you know that feeling, Sebastian, don't you?"

This time she did wait; she looked at him almost willing him to give the answer she wanted. If it was the answer she wanted he would hear the rest of the story. If it wasn't, the story wouldn't be told. He knew what she meant; he now knew that she had always known. She had recognised it in him when they first met at dinner in the Envy.

"Yes, I know that feeling exactly. Did you know when we first met?"

She nodded her head and continued the narrative.

"She started modelling my clothes. Over time the Jurgen Collection became quite famous amongst a cult following. We had a shop here in Amsterdam, one in Berlin and were thinking about opening one in London. The range grew, the cut altered and the style morphed though not with current trends. We were always trying to be different to the mainstream. I really had two ranges. One was designed and cut for distribution for retail. The other was for her."

She pecked at her wine as if to finish it would end her recollection.

"The relationship between the designer and model was turned upside down. Normally the model complements the design but for me, because of her, I tried to create the most beautiful clothes that I could. I tried to capture and enhance her beauty. I don't know why I tried it as I knew it couldn't be done."

She wasn't speaking to him, she was explaining to herself.

"With each attempt and failure the designs went to our shops for resale. I didn't care who wore them. It didn't stop me trying. She was really the inspiration for all the clothes I ever made, even the ones I made before I met her. You do understand, Sebastian, don't you?"

He nodded.

"What happened to her?"

She reached for her glass and took a mouthful, swallowing quickly. Her face reflected the distaste of too much wine at once. She sat in silence and squared her shoulders.

"She died, Sebastian, she died."

She didn't look at him but raised her palm off the table top to stop him speaking. She needed to tell it all without interruption.

"We had moved to offices in the Mitte district in Berlin, the design studios on the first floor, my office on the third overlooking the street. It had a wonderful view. It was late autumn, the grey sky was sunless. It's the time of year you feel as if you are living inside a cloud unable to see out. The weather was cold, frosty, the streets had small glaciated puddles of icy rainwater. It was just after the rush hour, she was always late. I saw her walking whilst searching in her bag for something. The man in front her had just stopped to light his cigarette, I remember the brand, it was a West. He held his yellow plastic lighter in his right hand, his left held the red packet with the red lightning strike through the black lettering. He wore a heavy navy overcoat and I could see his blue shirt and his paisley-patterned tie pulled slightly to the right of his collar. He stopped by the curb waiting for the traffic to clear. A yellow single-decker bus blocked my view of them both. It was a bendy bus, you know the one divided by the rubber seal. It wasn't full, well it wouldn't be at that time of day."

Her hand reached for the glass but she didn't raise it, she held the stem.

"I heard the screeching of brakes. I couldn't see anything, but I knew. By the time I got there she was surrounded by people, no one doing anything, just looking. I pushed my way to the front of the crowd."

She picked up her glass and swallowed.

"At the inquest the man with the cigarette said she had slipped on the ice while trying to cross the road. She was hit by a Mercedes, a grey one. It was no one's fault. That's what makes it harder, no one to blame."

She turned her head from looking out of the window to face Sebastian. He expected to see tears in her eyes but there were none; her eyes were dry.

"I've relived that day every day since it happened. It's odd, you know, when you first think about it it's like being stabbed in the stomach, the pain is sharp and spreads. Later on it's like being punched, a dull pain. Over time the pain is the same intensity but for some reason it doesn't take over the whole body, it's as if it's localised but it's not really, it's not contained. The pain lives elsewhere." The red-painted nail of her forefinger tapped her temple. "It lives here."

She finished her wine and reached for the bottle to top up her glass. The neck of the bottle hovered over Sebastian's full glass before she refilled hers. Sebastian struggled for something to say; he thought and dismissed every fleeting reply.

"You want to know how I became who I am now, don't you?" It was said kindly with no hint of the pervasiveness of his thoughts.

"You don't have to tell me, only if you want to, I mean if I'm intruding there's no need."

She didn't look away to the window, she just looked at him knowing he would understand.

"It started with one of her cardigans, a soft cashmere emerald green one. She had gone and I was bleeding, my soul was bleeding and drop by drop it was disintegrating. The only things I had of hers were her clothes, I mean *her* clothes not the ones I had made for her. Her clothes were all that was left of her. They had her scent and when I touched them I could see her, I could feel her. To be close to her I slept with some of her clothes. Over time her scent got weaker, I had to bury my head into her clothes, deeper and deeper to reach her. It was harder to feel her, harder to visualise her. I could only conjure her up feature by feature and never the whole, never the essence of her. I couldn't let her go, to let her go was to let go of myself. If I could just be part of her we would survive."

She let out a resigned laugh.

"Of course I couldn't be her, I knew that, but I could be part of her. If I was part of her, she would be part of me and together we would still be alive. The process was slow at first. I knew what I was doing and I knew where it would end. In my apartment at night I started to wear her cardigans and jumpers. I bought and started to use her perfume. It wasn't long before the makeup, then the wardrobe of new clothes in the same style as hers. The first day I went out there were looks from passers-by but over time I learnt more and now most don't notice anything untoward. You see, Sebastian, we had to survive, we were made to be together."

Sebastian looked at Anneke and saw the woman from the photograph, not exactly as she was in the photograph but almost her. He couldn't decide if the familiarity was due to Anneke's physical appearance or if it was the result of her telling.

"Do you feel and see her now?" He hoped.

Anneke closed her eyes.

"I feel her. I can sometimes see a hint of the essence of her when I look in the mirror or catch a reflection of myself. Most days I can form her from others. When I sit early in the morning watching the passing women I can see a feature, an expression and sometimes a gesture. They all remind me of her but only individual parts of her. I can never see her whole, as she was, I never will again. I am as close as I can get to her. It is as simple and as complex as that."

Sebastian touched his earring and remembered Anneke's comment: "There is only love, Sebastian, there really is nothing else, nothing."

His hand reached out and covered hers.

"Anneke, I'm so sorry she died, I cannot imagine ever losing a lover, someone I loved as much as you loved her."

Anneke looked down at his hand and then upward to his face. Sebastian saw the untouched tears fall from her eyes as they rolled over her cheeks to dampen the collar of her blouse collar. The Kryolan remained intact, her eyes as beautifully made-up as if she had just completed her toilet in the morning making the tears seem unrelated to the pain etched on her face. He reached out and with his finger wiped the drops from her cheeks. She turned her head to the window to speak to the unseen listener.

"I never told her, I waited too long, I missed it. Oh, I could have, but I wanted so much to create the perfect design for her, to complete her beauty, then it would be time to tell her."

She turned to look at him with moist eyes. She squeezed her eyes shut as if to close out a memory too painful to recall and as she did two perfectly formed tears ran from the side of each eye down her cheeks.

"I loved her so much but we were never lovers," she whispered.

CHAPTER 21

He was awake when he heard the soft clunk of the Yale lock close; it had been pulled softly so as not to wake him. She had asked him to stay over, she didn't say why, but he knew it was important to her. The early morning sun was bringing the photographs to life. He lay in his bed and watched the sunlight creep along the wall opposite, the photograph slowly illuminated. It had been taken from an aisle seat; firstly the seated crowd was revealed and sitting in the middle was Jurgen in his customary uniform: black suit and open-necked white shirt. On the catwalk the clothes seemed to flow from her almost like a silk web extension to her limbs; her eyes stared straight ahead almost devoid of emotion. His efforts had not fulfilled his aim and the clothes hadn't complemented her beauty, Sebastian could see that in the perplexed looked on Jurgen's face. A face not of frustration but a face that expressed the daunting scale of his task.

Looking at Jurgen's face he found it difficult not to see Anneke now. It was as if their roles had been reversed; in the photograph Jurgen looked like Anneke concealed as a man, their roles symbiotic. He was undecided if this symbiotic relationship was mutually beneficial or a parasite-to-host relationship where only one of the two benefits.

He felt an overwhelming desire to speak to Zoe. Looking at his phone there were no messages, no reply to his asking about meeting next week. He knew that to wait was to take a risk. There was no time for procrastination, no new message to be sent and the reply awaited. He pressed her name and waited for the ringing to cease and her voice to answer. The ring continued; he knew where she would be, she would be putting on her makeup, hopefully placing the bracelet he had given her, the one she always wore, on her wrist. He could see the dressing table and knew she would still be in her towel, her hair wet. She would apply her makeup, blow dry her hair before slipping on her shirt. The phone would be plugged into her bedside table and his name would be flashing green.

"Hi, it's Zoe here, please leave a message."

Sebastian pressed the cancel button and retried, after ten rings he was no closer to talking to her. He didn't want to leave a message, he wanted to talk to her, he needed to talk to her, he wanted to tell her that he loved her and that he was coming back to be with her, that he wanted to live with her and finish his book just as she had suggested. He didn't want to make the same mistake as Anneke, he would tell her.

"Christ, give me break!" he shouted to the sunlit room. The glass on the photographs reflected the sun's glare making the individual figures hard to identify. He pressed the call button again.

He felt his earring press hard against the phone; he pushed the phone closer to his ear believing it shortened the distance between them. He didn't hear the door unlock or hear the footfall in the corridor. The knock at the door surprised him.

"Sebastian? You awake?"

He would wait to see if the phone was answered before he replied.

"What?!" His voice angry and beaten as he cut short her answer message.

The doorway was filled by the frame of Umuntu; his muscular presence. Sebastian put the phone down and got out of bed pulling on a jumper. Sebastian followed him to the kitchen through the hallway. Stacked neatly by the front door he saw his rucksack and holdall.

"I got those from the *Tulp*. I think I got everything, I found an old book along with a photograph and computer and put them in that one." He pointed to the holdall. Sebastian rummaged around to check they were in the bag.

"I spoke to Rosie yesterday and the girls told her what happened the other night. I thought it for the best to get your stuff as you seemed to have made some dangerous enemies. It's probably best you don't go back there again. It might make things a bit difficult to manage, well I mean to arrange." He looked as if he was withholding some information, his eyes not meeting Sebastian's. "It's really very important you don't go back unless someone tells you to, do you understand?" He was looking at him now, directly and although it was posed as a question it was more like an order.

Sebastian wasn't really listening, his hands busy in the holdall. He also had no intention of going back to the *Tulp* or to the misery of the red light district, ever. He just wanted to go back to Zoe.

Sebastian nodded as he rewrapped the photograph of Zoe in her scarf and replaced it carefully and safely in the bag.

"Did she love him? The model I mean, did she love Jurgen?"

"I don't know, Sebastian, I've never asked Anneke." He busied himself making a cup of coffee as Sebastian waited for more information; he had learnt from Anneke, to wait was to receive. "I don't suppose it matters, does it? I mean he loved her, he still does. Just because someone dies it doesn't mean that the love dies too. Perhaps he has to forgive himself for not telling her."

Sebastian interrupted, speaking quickly.

"He should have told her."

Umuntu placed a cup of coffee in front of Sebastian; as his hand left the handle he let out a wry snort.

"Oh Sebastian, all those missed opportunities! How different all our lives would be if we had spoken what we had thought rather than what we felt the listener wanted to hear. The course of our lives would be forever changed and we would all be different people now. Is it the unspoken words that make us who we are or is it the words spoken that make us who we are?"

"He should have told her," he insisted, almost angry. "She would be alive today. If he had told her she might have moved in with him. She wouldn't have been late that day and the accident wouldn't have happened. Even if the accident did happen they would have both died together, would that not have been better?"

"Then there would be no love left, would there? No one to talk of his love for her. As it is the love affair goes on even in her absence. Jurgen holds onto her as Anneke and perhaps over time, maybe never, he releases her and forgives himself for those words unsaid."

"I would have told her." Sebastian stared at Umuntu facing down the lie.

Umuntu returned the stare but kindly and asked, "Even if you thought that there was even the slightest chance that the unspoken words of love would not be reciprocated? Would you risk it, would you?"

Sebastian sat in silence. He turned his head towards the holdall.

"Yes, I would," he lied.

Zoe had made that choice, she had climbed up to the last rung of the ladder and from there, her feet firmly on that rung with her knees bent, she had jumped into the air with full belief that there would be something unseen to catch a hold of her; that something was him, Sebastian. He had not been there to catch her outstretched hands; he had placed his arms by his side holding his book in his hand and watched as she fell. She had shown complete faith in him, in his reply. He had failed her. She had wanted him unconditionally, as he was, but he had wanted to change, the book being the catalyst. Would the completion of the book change him, make him not what she wanted? He didn't want to end up like Anneke, a surrogate life and lived vicariously because of a missed opportunity.

"I've got to make a call." Sebastian grabbed his phone, pressing the keypad as he retreated into his bedroom.

He listened to the ringing. It was eleven o'clock in Amsterdam, ten in London, she would be at her desk looking at emails. Her phone would be at her side on the desk or in her jacket pocket; even if it was in her pocket she would hear it. What if she had put it to silent mode after his calls earlier?

"Come on, come on," he hissed into the mouthpiece.

"Hi, it's Zoe here, please leave a message."

His hands fumbled with the keypads, he punched in her work landline.

"Hello, this is Pinkerton and Smith Auctioneers, Jane speaking, can I help you?"

"Oh God!" Sebastian groaned.

"Hello?"

"Hi Jane, it's Sebastian here. How are you?"

There was a pause and rather alarmingly she replied brightly, "Oh! Sebastian, how nice to hear your voice."

He knew with that reply she knew something to her advantage.

"Hi, I'm looking for Zoe, is she around?"

Her reply succinct.

"Yes."

"And?"

"She is quite close by actually. Why?"

Sebastian felt like a bull being jabbed by a picador.

"I need to speak to her."

"I'm not sure she wants to talk to you." She was triumphant as her lance struck him.

"Well can you ask her please?"

"No. She has left instructions that if you were to ring she didn't want the call put through." She had perfected her picador aim; he was enraged.

"Put her on the line!" he shouted.

"No." Another tear in his flesh.

Sebastian saw the red cape hanging on the Muleta and charged.

"You'll die a virgin, you know that! You bitch."

The earpiece echoed to a buzz from London.

"Christ!" he roared into the now sun-warmed room as the doorbell rang.

He smelt her rather than saw her. The scent of Stroopwafel crept under his bedroom door; the smell of syrup sandwiched between two waffles reminded Sebastian of somewhere safe and simple, the opposite of where he was now.

He overhead a mumbled conversation and the squeaking of her soft-soled shoes on the wooden floorboards; it was like being a patient in a hospital bed awaiting the arrival of a nurse with a painkiller. She would always be able to soften the pain of a blow. The door opened with a knock.

"Hello Sebastian," she said softly, offering him the chance to share her nibbled Stroopwafel. "You haven't got very far, have you?" She smiled as her tongue wiped the side of her mouth clear of syrup.

"I don't know, Rosie, perhaps I am destined to never get away from here. Maybe there is no point in leaving." He spoke glumly as he pocketed his phone.

She sat on one of the wooden chairs watching him pace around the room.

"Well you will because you can, remember that. But before you do go I need to ask something from you. It's just a small thing, it will help Sacha." He knew he couldn't refuse her; whatever she needed from him he would oblige.

"Sebastian, stop pacing around, sit down." She looked around for another chair. "There on the bed." As he sank into the soft mattress he had to look up to her. Her tone was more business-like than her normal maternal speech; she had something to say, wanted it listened to and she wanted to hear the correct answer. He nodded his acceptance of whatever she would ask of him.

"Thank you." She paused and placed the half-eaten Stroopwafel in the bin. "I know what you did to the pimp and why, but, Sebastian, you have to understand the whole situation is complicated, we've been through this before. The Kazakhs who control the girls, the trafficking and the pimping are organised on a global scale. It was an act of foolish bravery. In fact it could have altered the course of Sacha's future." It was a criticism and it hurt him.

"Has something happened to her because of me?" He wanted to be cleared from the error, innocent to anything else that might befall Sacha.

She paused, then smiled a taut smile of forced absolution.

"Thankfully no. But it could have altered something we have been working on. Since Irena's death Sacha has been collapsing into herself. If we don't get her out of Amsterdam I think she will walk the same path as Irena."

"You've got a way of getting her out, away from all of it? How? I'll do anything to help. What can I do, tell me?"

She didn't reply but she did assess his enthusiasm.

"You said you had been working on something, you and others, what others?"

She pushed her head back and looked at the ceiling, her assessment over.

"I can't tell you that. I can tell you that what you did has opened up an opportunity for you to help us."

He had a feeling of indignation that she wanted his help but would reveal nothing; he had a right to know. He felt an ownership of Sacha's future. Before he could protest he heard the creaking of the floorboards as Umuntu entered the room.

"It's not a question of trust, Sebastian, it's a question of protection, protecting some of those involved in what we are going to do," Umuntu said as he leant against the doorframe blocking the view of the corridor. He had been listening to their conversation.

Sebastian felt at a disadvantage sunk into the mattress having to look up at Rosie and now at the room-shrinking presence of Umuntu.

"So you're involved too? Who else? And what are you going to do?" He felt piqued that a plan involving Sacha had been made without his involvement. He was tempted to tell Rosie the source of the 10,000 euros.

Rosie looked at Umuntu and Sebastian thought he saw a slight nod of her head.

"When we leave tomorrow and we are taking Sacha with us." Umuntu's voice was as certain as he was in achieving the plan.

2

The table had been cleared of the glasses, cutlery and strips of ribbon that had represented the important features of the red light district; the plan had been discussed; each person involved represented by coloured beads had been put away. Everyone knew where they were supposed to be and at what time. Sebastian was impressed with the minutiae of the planning by Umuntu and Rosie. Unknown to him prior to the briefing was that the outline of the plan had been Anneke's. She had formulated it, approached those required to pull it off. There had only been the four of them in the room: Anneke, Umuntu, Rosie and himself.

"I know there is bad blood between you and Dasha. He is not happy with you participating and he doubts you can pull off your part."

Sebastian interrupted Anneke.

"Look, it was a mistake. I went to see Sacha to ask about Irena. I don't know what he thought, maybe he thought I had been, well you know, using her." He looked at the other three. "Christ, you don't think…"

"Sebastian, don't be so stupid!" It was a rebuke from Anneke, not in anger but frustration as her thoughts were elsewhere. His crass assumption they would think such a thing had interrupted her thinking. She lit a cigarette and drew on it. "It's important to him that this goes as planned. She is important to him."

He felt like an outsider; first Rosie and now Anneke, both had concealed the planning from him.

"Oh, I see."

"No, Sebastian, I doubt it."

This new tone of Anneke's annoyed him. He wasn't sure who he was talking to, Anneke or Jurgen. He thought of the photographs in the bedroom, Jurgen looking perplexed as he saw his creation on Anneke. Perhaps it wasn't a perplexed look, maybe it was a look of weakness, watching all that he wished to hold walk down the runway away from him. The weakness of not telling her he loved her. Sebastian decided that he didn't like Jurgen; he had had it all to hold but had never had the courage to close his fingers around her. Sebastian felt the uncontrollable rush of indignant blood in his brain; his temper was now lost.

"Well for fuck's sake try me then! Just tell me." He stared an Anneke in a threatening way.

The heavy voice of Umuntu started to speak but before many words were spoken Sebastian interrupted.

"Not from you. Him." He pointed at Anneke.

It lay on the table in front of them, that one pronoun; it couldn't be seen or retracted. There was silence as they stared at the centre of the table. To Rosie these were not shocking words. Over the years she had seen the changing personae of so many in the dark world of prostitution. Umuntu had changed as a result of circumstances. Sebastian had never had to adapt to survive.

Anneke looked at Sebastian registering no surprise at his outburst. Her face was calm, her speech even and patient as if he had not said anything. She continued.

"Dasha has refound his Jewishness. Since he has been in Amsterdam he has been tutored by a rabbi to welcome him back to the faith. Part of that is the Golden Rule, 'That which is hateful to you, do not do unto your fellow.' Perhaps that was the cause of the altercation between you two. As to Sacha, well he has been helping her try to get out of prostitution, trying to show her acts of kindness to show her that not all men are made equally evil. He believes in redemption for his lapse from his faith, but in his mind that redemption is inexorably linked to the salvation of Sacha. He believes that if he can save her from the circumstances that are destroying the value of her human existence he will have earnt his redemption. That, Sebastian, is why she is so important to him. That, Sebastian, is why we cannot fail tomorrow." Her hand reached across the table and covered Sebastian's.

She looked at him questioningly.

"Do you understand now?" she almost whispered.

He stared at the table, it was clear to him now why he had been excluded from the planning; he really was an outsider. Rosie wanted to get Sacha away from Amsterdam, away from the world of prostitution. Dasha needed that to succeed for his reconciliation. Anneke was needed to make it happen. Umuntu was needed to execute the plan.

His eyes alighted on her red nails. He was the one who had tried to draw blood with his comment, he was the one who had tried to inflict the wound on Anneke. It should be his hands covered in red. He couldn't look at her; he was willing but his neck wouldn't move. His eyes fixed on her red fingernails.

"Anneke, I can't tell you how sorry I am for what I said."

Her hand squeezed his; her nails disappeared into the palm of his hand.

"I know. It wasn't about me or Sacha, was it?" He didn't look up, he knew what she was going to say.

"It was about what you haven't done."

She was right of course. They both knew that.

CHAPTER 22

1

He knew where he was supposed to be, and when, the timing essential for the successful execution of the plan. He walked slowly, looked at the clock on the Royal Palace in Dam Square and quickened his pace. He would be late. After a short spurt of speed he fell back into the amble of the tourist. He needed to get the arrival right. Small as his part was, it was integral to its success. He would execute his part without fear of the consequences to himself.

His mouth was dry and his packet of cigarettes half-empty; a tracker dog could have followed his path backwards to Anneke's flat by the half-smoked stubs. The route had been circuitous to avoid any sighting by the pimp; he had looped around Oude Kerk turning into Lange Niezel and left on Warmoesstraat to Dam Square. Standing in the square he looked towards the corner where the shop had been, the one where he had bought Zoe the bracelet. He looked at his phone. No missed calls. The speaking bubble of the text message had no red circle indicating a message. He knew then that he would never return to Amsterdam. If all went according to plan he would be on the last plane this evening to London, to what he wasn't quite sure.

The square was active with people. He felt an envy as they moved to their destination in full knowledge that they would be greeted by a familial kiss, perhaps a passionate lovers' intertwine. His future was opaque and grey as October; he could only see as far as his arrival in the Babel-like chaos of Heathrow Terminal 4 under harsh lights. In his case illuminating nothing.

He entered the Krasnapolsky and sat in the foyer with his eyes locked on the multinational clocks to avoid the curious eyes scanning his overly made-up Kryolan face, bruises hidden behind the makeup. He was early; he didn't have to start to get into position for another twenty minutes. His eyes wandered around the guests. He watched a businessman shake hands with a fellow suit, formally with an unspoken commitment to be in touch with each other soon. The goodbye between Sebastian and Anneke carried a commitment to be in touch again at a time unknown too. He had woken early; Anneke was already up and dressed when he entered the kitchen.

"I'll miss you, you do know that?" She said it quickly as if she had rehearsed and waited with impatience to say it. He wasn't sure if this was a comment of forgiveness for his lash-out the previous day.

He took it as forgiveness and didn't want to jeopardise the inner cleanliness he now felt. He just nodded without knowing what to say to her.

"I think we've helped each other, don't you?"

Before Sebastian could answer, the doorbell rang and she rose to open it. *There is never enough time when you need it and always too much when you don't*, he thought. He needed to talk to her to explain that he was not angry with Jurgen for the fatally missed opportunity. He had superimposed his fear of never having Zoe again onto her. But then she probably knew that already, but he wanted to tell her all the same, to tie up the loose ends, make the ledger balance.

Umuntu entered the room looking awake and urgent.

"Hello Sebastian. Here is your ticket to London. Before we set off I need to have a contact number in case something goes wrong." His voice was officerial.

Anneke looked at Umuntu.

"Well you have mine and I have yours. How about you, Sebastian, what number should we use if anything goes wrong?" Her eyes held his, her eyebrows pulled slightly together. He knew it was a test, a test that could affect his future.

"My mother." He slowly dictated the number so they could program the number into their phones. As Anneke tapped the number into her phone her eyes never left Sebastian's. He felt as if she was rummaging around his brain rewiring his thought process. He broke away from her eye contact and said, "If you can't get a hold of her, try a friend of mine called Zoe."

Anneke smiled.

The contingency planning over Umuntu took charge.

"Right, Anneke, you need to leave now. Rosie will meet you at Oude Kerk, she is there now with Dasha and the rabbi. They want to run through the plan to iron out any potential problems. Hugo and Ricard have already left with the lorry and are on their way with the Spiegeltent to Hamburg. Salt and Pepper are on the way to Oude Kerk and Philippe is checking the van."

It was happening so suddenly, events overtaking time. That was the curse of being a small part of something bigger: events controlled time.

"Everybody know what they're doing?"

Anneke and Sebastian nodded.

"Right, let's go."

Umuntu picked up the luggage and took it downstairs to the car.

Anneke with her hair pulled up in a ponytail looked at Sebastian, walked over to him and kissed him on both cheeks.

"Before we meet again say it, don't make the same mistake as I did," she whispered into his ear, then turned and left.

Before he had time to reply he heard Umuntu shout from the stairwell.

"Come on, Sebastian." It was an order.

His eyes moved back to the clocks behind the check-in desk of the Krasnapolsky. It was time to go.

2

He walked through the foyer and out of the hotel through the covered walkway of Servetsteeg; at the junction with Oudezijds Voorburgwal he stopped at the tobacconist to buy another packet of cigarettes. The combination of adrenaline, cigarettes and coffee had made him skittery; he wanted it all to start and end now. He looked around him nervously, studying the passing people and those hanging around outside bars. He knew there was no need but the fear and responsibility of getting it right made him view everyone as suspicious. There were two men standing outside a bar; one listening to a dull story stared over the teller's shoulder and caught Sebastian's eye briefly. Sebastian cast his eye down to the pavement. Hopefully he would not be remembered; just another punter on his first trip to the red light district, anonymous, bruised after a stag-night outing, like so many others. Just now he needed to be small; later he would have to expand to fill a large space.

He waited until a group of men passed him, their faces red with anticipation and a combination of sunshine and drink. He kept his shoulder to the shop faces and used the group as a cover until he arrived at the Bulldog. The walk past the prostitutes had been quiet, no tapping of coins on the window to attract business. As the group passed the girls their comments had been ignored, the prostitutes looking towards Oude Kerk. There was no touting for business, it was as if the torpor of summer had won. Sebastian sat in the shade of the awning outside the bar and lit a cigarette. He looked across the canal at the girls in their cells. Most had their curtains open but the girls weren't prancing to entice; with each solicitation from a passing punter the dialogue had been short and met with the curtain being drawn with access denied to the potential client. The curtain reopened shortly after.

"You look stressed, man." He hadn't noticed the dry-haired dreadlocked man sitting at the table next to him; he had the look of a public schoolboy who on his gap year had arrived in Amsterdam, gone straight to the Bulldog and never left. The sight of his bruises deserved no comment, a familiar sight at the Bulldog. Sebastian didn't want to get into a conversation with him.

"I mean it, man." His nicotine-stained fingers held a crushed roach end. "Look at the ashtray, man, you've got one in your mouth and two burning."

Sebastian turned to look at the man; his face shone with drug-induced inner knowledge and his smile confirmed he understood all of the workings of the world.

"You'll die with all that stress, man. You need some of this." He held out a black-ended roach.

The bells of Oude Kerk rang out.

Sebastian crushed his cigarette out and stood up.

"Sooner than you might think!" was his parting shot to the oracle.

He left the dreadlocked man tutting and worrying about his life expectancy as he positioned himself at Dollebegijnensteeg alleyway adjoining the Bulldog. From here he could look along the full length of Oudezijds Voorburgwal in both directions and remain unnoticed as he hid in the constant stream of potential clients seeking out the sexual privacy that the dark alleyway offered. He thought it strange that it was through a similar alleyway that Umuntu had revealed what to him had been unseen: the true world of the red light district. Here, now, he was part of a plan to make a small correction to one individual. It wouldn't change the world but it would change her world.

He looked across the canal. Sacha was in her window looking almost childlike, her imploring expression turned towards the church; her small body although only partially clothed looked innocent and sexless as she waited, expectantly. Her hair was not its usual flow to her shoulders but held up in a bun as if a hat was about to be placed on her head. Rosie would have briefed her with Dasha; both would have had to persuade her it was possible as the repercussion for failure would be obvious to her. Her pimp, shoed in brand new white trainers, had his back to her talking on his phone, his arms resting on the railings and his eyes behind the two pools of circular darkness of his sunglasses. He looked bored until he saw a group of thirteen-year-old girls, arms interlinked, walk past him obviously lost from their host group, clutching their city maps for safety. The black reflecting eyes of his sunglasses took each in turn and roved over their bodies from feet to groin, groin to breast and then a cursory look at their faces. He licked his top lip with anticipated thoughts. Sebastian flushed with anger.

"You bastard," he muttered to himself.

"You see, man, it'll kill you, all this worrying." The dreadlocks bounced with confirmation. Sebastian nodded to him; he couldn't get into a discussion, not now. He threw his packet of cigarettes to him in the hope that he would occupy himself rolling joints.

For the first time all of the girls' curtains were pulled back; each cell had a girl inside and none was touting for business; each client approach was thwarted with a gentle push away.

"Where are they, where are they?!" Sebastian muttered.

“Thanks, man. Try to kill the inner monster or I’m telling you it’ll kill you,” the voice drifted from the hair-covered mouth of this joint-rolling Jesus.

Sebastian’s ears were ringing as he strained to hear the noise; it should have started by now. He thought a drinker had dropped a wine glass; a tinkling noise penetrated the silent ringing in his ear. Another drinker must have done the same and another one too. He let out a held breath.

“See, my friend, breathe deeply and peace will come to you, exhale your troubled thoughts to the wind.” His fingers fumbling to crumble the hash into the open cigarette.

The tinkling increased. It had started. The source of the noise came from the cells nearest Oude Kerk and flowed slowly from cell to cell: the tapping of coins on glass. From the side of the Kerk he saw him in his full hierophantic glory. The rabbi alone in his black ankle-length coat, his Fedora alternating from black to a colourless shimmer as the sun fell on it from parting clouds. His face as resolute and certain as he remembered him at the opening night of the Spiegeltent. The noise of metal on cell windows announced his arrival. If the tapping of coins on glass had been rose petals they would have been strewn to herald his route as now the chorus of tapping had been taken up by the prostitutes on both sides of the canal. The rabbi didn’t look behind him, he knew they wouldn’t let him down. Voyeuristic and sex-shopping tourists stopped to observe the lone figure. Fingers started to point at Oude Kerk as the testudo formation of black-coated and Fedora-topped battle group appeared. It consisted of eleven ranks, each rank made up of three people, except the middle rank which contained one open space between the two manned flanks – a total of thirty-two persons.

Sebastian's heart was thumping as he watched the advance. There was no turning back now. He noticed that the arrival of a mass of religious figures had seen the guilty slip off Oudezijds Voorburgwal through alleyways to question why they were in the red light district.

The noise of the glass being tapped was in stereo as the cells on both sides of the canal tapped their windows in unison. The noise got louder with each advanced instep footfall of the testudo; it sounded like the support drumbeat of an advancing army. The chorus of noise heralding the approach of the testudo joined with the tapping that confirmed its passing. The noise seemed amplified by the canal water. Sebastian had heard no laughter from the working girls before; he had seen feigned smiles, but now like the most appreciative audience he saw the girls' faces light up. For the first time in their working lives it was the girls that anticipated the pleasure. Scantily clad, they looked more like a party of friends changing for a swimming trip rather than selling their bodies, their postures animated at the thought of the near future.

The pimp turned to see what the commotion was about, his face unconcerned. He looked around at the girls; he obviously mistook the girls' tapping as a spontaneous mocking of the *feh* of Jews invading the red light district. He spat at the advancing feet of the rabbi, turned back to the water and mockingly updated the listener on the phone; his face sneeringly described the scene before the conversation returned to business.

The rabbi walked past the pimp, his eyes firmly fixed on the horizon, confident in his plan.

Sebastian smelt the acrid fauna scent of marijuana as the inmate of the Bulldog had finished his surgical rolling of a joint.

"Hey man! This stuff is strong. What's that huge black beetle doing over there?" His eyes were glazed with the hit and his pointing arm shaky as the drug coursed through his bloodstream.

The black-clad group had halted in front of the now stationary rabbi. The rabbi had positioned himself five metres beyond Sacha's workstation. The testudo stretched for ten metres behind him. Sacha's cell now blocked off from the pimp's view who had been pinned against the railing unable to move.

Sebastian knew his time was coming, it had been a success so far and he couldn't let them down. He screwed up his eyes to block out the sun as it reflected off the canal water. By raising his hands to block it out he saw what he was looking for; the middle rank with the empty space in the middle was protected on either side by two smaller members of the group, one with a large stomach. These two didn't satisfactorily fill their black coats, which hung off them as if off a coat hanger while their Fedoras sat like oversized cooking pan lids on their heads, easily mistaken as young apprentices to the faith. The anticipated sign could only be seen by those who knew what to look for; a small wisp of red hair blew gently in the breeze from under the rim of one of the Fedoras, the one nearest to Sacha's cell.

The rabbi extracted his Torah and addressed the

stationary group; his voice thundered like Moses with the tablets clenched in his hands. Sebastian watched but didn't listen. The crowds who had been following the advance were now stuck behind and those in front were equally stuck, unable to navigate past the group at prayer, unwillingly increasing the size of the congregation. The noise of the coins on glass persisted, reaching a crescendo as the rabbi started to read from his book. The pimp looked around him and scratched his groin; these crazies would be away soon.

"Come on, come on! Do it now," Sebastian whispered.

He watched as the black-clad figure with the distended stomach and red hair fiddled with the coat buttons. The hands that slipped out from the sleeve were almost doll-like in their size; the fingers fumbling with the buttons, they were failing to undo. The figure leaned forward to concentrate on the stuck buttons; the Fedora slipped backward revealing more red hair.

"For Christ's sake, Salt, your hair. Pull your hat back on your head," Sebastian hissed as he moved forward ready to cross the small bridge to the other side of the canal.

Salt's fingers finally released the buttons and passed the package through the black-coated armoured perimeter to the unseen Sacha. Salt's coat hung even looser now that she had got rid of her stomach.

"Man, it's weird to have Satan's black beetle roaming the streets." The voice was relaxed and dreamy as it drifted through the exhaled smoke. The now thoroughly stoned hippie looked lightly through his half-closed eyes at the testudo. He raised his two black yellow-stained fingers to his lips and popped a little pink pill into his equally yellow black-teethed mouth. "It's scary. I hope it goes away. Just imagine if it laid an egg and the whole city was taken over by little black beetles. What do you think, my friend?"

Sebastian nodded without looking at him; his eyes were fixed on the pimp. He had made a series of calls, all short, and during each his eyes had looked along the canal railings. Sebastian noticed five almost evenly spaced alert, not curious, heads looking back and forth. A smaller separate congregation, a backhand of pimps.

Sacha's pimp, bored of the disturbance to business, waved his arms around trying to usher the group away from his domain. He knew that no souls would be saved by prayer; they had long been sold by someone else. He wanted business to resume, money made.

The booming voice of the rabbi ceased with the closing of his Torah. On cue as at a theatre the coins restarted the tapping on glass. The testudo shuffled without moving forward as if waiting for the waters to part. It was only as the rabbi set off along Oudezijds Voorburgwal towards Damstraat that it broke into step following its leader. The ranks were closer now making it impossible to see the individuals, just a phalanx of righteous avengers. The testudo Sebastian now knew was a full complement, thirty-three in all and the middle rank the smallest in height. That rank he knew was made up of two redheads on each flank and a nervous addition in the middle, all three struggling to look taller and fuller of body.

"They've done it!" Sebastian hopped from foot to foot. Rosie's plan of distraction had worked; the girls of De Rode Draad had fulfilled their part of the plan. Sebastian looked towards Oude Kerk and could just make out Rosie smiling, her skin a sheen in the sunlight. He waved his arm in victory. He wanted to celebrate the success; he walked over to the now very animated pink-pilled druggie, picked him up off the chair and hugged him.

"I told you, man, speak the words and the wind takes them away. See there, the beetle goes away, leaving no eggs. The wind listened to me. We're all safe now." His eyes moist with safe and beautiful chemical visions of the future.

As the testudo made its way to Damstraat laughing tourists, now released from their forced participation in the prayers, snapped photographs with their iPhones. The alleyways surrounding Oudezijds Voorburgwal started to empty as the guilty returned now the eyes of God had departed and couldn't review their souls.

The girls were slow to start their business of tempting customers. Their doors were ajar as they leant out to discuss the recent events. Sebastian watched as the rear wall of black coats rounded the corner of Damstraat and felt a glow of success; he wouldn't be needed after all. His eyes looked towards Sacha's cell, the curtain drawn and a contented pimp knowing business had returned to normal, money being earnt so quickly after the interruption. The pimp basked in the evening sun with his back to Sebastian, his arms behind him resting on the railings. The whole body position told all that this was the way to make money; life is easy if you're smart.

Sebastian knew what should be happening now; the middle rank would break away from the testudo, the black coats taken off and the Fedoras handed to the old Yiddish driver of the bus. Thanks would be offered by the two redheads as they kept a tight hold of Sacha. The car with Anneke behind the wheel would be outside the Krasnapolsky Hotel, the two rear doors open in welcome to Salt, Pepper and Sacha. It had been decided to overrule Umuntu who had wanted to drive. Anneke felt that only the presence of women would put Sacha more at ease, as the last time she departed in a car to a destination unknown it had been the start of her captivity to the sex traffickers. The bus would depart with a wave from the quartet; a different future lay ahead for Sacha than the one when she last waved at her mother from the rear of a car.

"Do you want a beer?" asked the dreadlocked stoner.

He wanted to celebrate; he had time for one last schooner of Amstel before he left Amsterdam for good. The beer frosted the side of the glass.

"You'll have to pay, I don't have any money." His arms shrugged and disappeared into his matted hair.

Sebastian dropped his last fifty euros onto the waiter's tray. The waiter deftly and single-handedly withdrew the change from a pouch held loosely around his middle whilst balancing the tray of empty glasses in the other. Sebastian tipped the waiter five euros and gave his new friend the remainder. He held the glass up to the opposite bank of the canal to toast a hoped-for befalling to the pimp. His finger stroked the frost from the glass giving him a sepia view through the liquid to the other side of the canal. He could see the prowlers ambling past the windows making their choice, office workers striding past like Giacometti figures through the glass's distorting lens. He heard the voice rise in anger. Lowering his glass he saw the pimp knocking on the door of Sacha's curtain-drawn room. The curtain had been drawn for longer than fifteen minutes; the pimp would have noticed that, he knew the timing of the visits. Sebastian knew that the door was always locked from the inside when a punter was busy. Sacha had used her key to lock it when she left. He heard the voice accompanying the banging of a fist on the window.

"Open the fucking door!"

Sebastian placed the glass on the table; he was going to be needed after all.

The pimp put his hand in his pocket and took a key from his rear pocket. As the tail of his coat rose the sunlight caught the knife blade in his waistband. He turned the key and, shoulder to the door, burst into the cell. He closed the door.

"What's all the noise about? It's peace time now." The words slurred from the top of the beer glass as the chemically contented man found his peace being disturbed.

The cell door swung open; the pimp was standing in the street with legs splayed ready to run in either direction, his head looking up and down the street. Had they had enough time? Were they driving away, away to safety? He knew he couldn't take the risk; he had to buy them some time, any time. It was his time to make himself large; he had dreaded this moment but had wanted to be a contributor to her escape.

Sebastian stood up from the table knocking the table and glass over to a clattering of zinc and broken glass.

"Hey, arsehole! Remember me! I told you if you touched her I would get you. Want to know where she is? I know!"

The pimp's black sun glassed eyes locked onto Sebastian as his hand reached behind him to his waistband. Sebastian felt the alertness of adrenaline; he looked left towards Oude Kerk, that was one route, the other was to Damstraat on the right. He looked at the pimp, he knew what he was thinking: would he run to the bridge that crossed the canal nearest Oude Kerk or the one nearest Damstraat?

"Come on then, you fucker!" Sebastian goaded him by gesturing himself as the target with his arms.

The pimp looked left, right, made a decision and ran towards the bridge nearest Oude Kerk.

"Run, Sebastian, run," Rosie's voice screamed from Oude Kerk.

Sebastian was trying to think, think what to do. The screaming from Rosie made him shiver; the last time he had heard similar words Sacha had pleaded with Irena.

"What's going on, man? There's a lot of shouting."

"Listen to me, my friend, I need to ask you a favour. I don't have long so listen to me." Sebastian had pulled the dreadlocks back and was trying to squeeze some sense into the fuddled brain inside the docile face of the drifting resident of the Bulldog. "If you look over there," he pointed at the running man with the dark glasses, "there is a man with black eyes like a beetle. See him?"

"Yeah," he replied vaguely looking at Sebastian's fingertip rather than in the direction it was pointing.

"He is what the big beetle left behind, and he is going to roam the city sewing destruction. Get it?"

"Yeah man, I get it," he drawled.

"Well when he runs past here you have to push this table in front of him. OK?"

"Yeah, beetle, destruction, table. I get it." He nodded the way a toy dog nods through the rear windscreen when the brake is applied.

The pimp was across the bridge and pushing past pedestrians. He was fit, fast and closing in on the Bulldog.

"I have to go. Remember, beetle, destruction, table."

"Yeah, yeah," he slurred into his beer. "Be happy, man."

Sebastian knew he had been wasting his time; the man was beyond sense. He turned and ran towards Damstraat. With every stride he imagined he felt the hand on the shoulder dragging him to a walk and then the pierce of the blade as it sunk into his soft lower back. He was unclear if it was fear, exertion or imagined blood that soaked the back of his shirt. He risked a look over his shoulder, hoping not to be able to see his reflection in those sunglasses. It was like looking down a railway track; the pedestrians had parted as he had run forming rails on either side of the pavement; the gauge offered a perfect view of his travelled escape route. He didn't hear it but he did see it. A flash of light as the sun shone on the falling zinc table top. The pimp tripped over the table outside the Bulldog, his knife pointing to the shouting dreadlocked Medusa.

"Over here!" Sebastian shouted more to protect his new friend than out of desire for the pursuit to continue. He took advantage of the pimp's fall and started to run. His mind was racing, where to run to? Where to find safety? He just needed to get to Damstraat and turn right into Dam Square; there would be tourists there; where there were tourists there were police – he hoped.

His left buttock started to buzz with the ringing of his phone in his back trouser pocket. He nearly dropped it as he fumbled to see who was calling. He couldn't see the name of the caller on the screen as sweat was in his eyes making it impossible to focus. He pressed the green answer button. The phone slithered in his sweaty hand, his breathing irregular as he ran.

"Sebastian, it's Rosie."

He felt a sense of calm; she always had that effect on him.

"Run to the Old Stock Exchange. Umuntu will be there with a car. Keep running, don't look back, just keep going."

He couldn't reply, there was not enough wind in his lungs to run and speak. His legs ached, his chest screamed in pain and his mind tried to work out how to get to the Old Stock Exchange. Which was quicker: Damstraat on to Damrak or was it Pijlsteeg on to Warmoesstraat on to Beursplein? *Why can't the Dutch name their streets properly?* he thought.

He needed to stop, just for a second; if he didn't he wouldn't be able to continue. At the junction of Damstraat he turned right and stopped. His hands resting on his knees, sweat pouring from his forehead and a slick of tobacco-tasting saliva fell from his lips. He walked back two metres and looked down Oudezijds Voorburgwal; he couldn't see his pursuer. The onlookers were following his gaze down the same street, their faces expressing surprise at seeing a man running at full pelt away from some invisible foe.

Sebastian weighed up the consequences of the non-sighting. Perhaps the pimp had been hurt outside the Bulldog; hopefully he wouldn't be taking it out on the hippie. No, that wouldn't happen, the Bulldog staff had dealt with every conceivable event over the years, the staff would handle this one too. For a fleeting moment he thought that perhaps the pimp couldn't pass over the invisible line between the red light district and normality. Damstraat was the border of the red light district, maybe he would be safe here in the normal world. Either way he needed to get to the Old Stock Exchange.

He jogged up Damstraat constantly looking over his shoulder; no one was following him. His legs were shaking as the adrenaline dissipated; he was in the clear. Even if the pimp was following there was safety in the crowds in Dam Square. He stopped at the corner of the Square for one last look over his shoulder, all clear. He walked quickly towards the Krasnapolsky Hotel pushing sweat from his forehead into his hair. Only 300 metres to go and he would be safe.

The doorman at the hotel guarded the revolving doors as he watched him with a disapproving look knowing that no one that dishevelled ever checked in; he would bar him access if he tried to enter. As Sebastian drew up to the hotel entrance the doorman fell onto the disability ramp as the fixed side door opened from within. Sebastian did see the reflection of himself in the sunglasses; he looked scared. The pimp must have seen him turn right into Damstraat and had cut through Servetsteeg, the covered walkway that led into the back of the hotel. Sebastian knew he never wanted to see his reflection in those glasses again.

He turned and ran past some departing guests knocking their bags over behind him to act as an obstacle to his pursuer. He knew this race couldn't go on for long; he struggled to breathe and his legs weighed heavy on his will. He danced and pirouetted between traffic-jammed cars and taxis in Warmoesstraat. Why had he taken the long route? His legs wouldn't hold out. He could hear the pimp's coins rattle in his pocket, his footfall silent on the rubber soles of his white trainers. He must be no more than two arms' length away; a spurt from the pimp and his collar would be grabbed and down he would go, the blade would go in and the pimp would vanish; it would only take twenty seconds and he would be dead.

He could see Umuntu in the piazza outside the Old Stock Exchange walking round in small circles attentive and searching. Sebastian wanted to cry out, to let him know he was close; his mouth opened, no voice came out, just a lungful of phlegm. The crowds in the Old Stock Exchange piazza admiring the historic building, eyes turned upwards. He could see but not hear, his ears were filled with the deafening bass drumbeat of exertion; he couldn't go for much longer.

He felt it. There was no warning just a drag on his shirt collar. The shirt pulled back and the V-shape of his open-necked shirt stabbed into his larynx. He couldn't breathe; the pull of the shirt had cut any entry or exit of air to his throat. He was exhausted. He could see Umuntu's back, big, broad and strong. He would have got away. Sebastian stopped and tugged at his throat, he couldn't go any further. He was so close to Umuntu, he could almost feel him. He was standing in front of two lovers with their legs intertwined, making one. Sebastian knew he had bought time. His eyes misted with lack of oxygen, the lovers blurred, he knew he had failed. His muscles relaxed and he waited for the sharp pain.

The pain at his throat eased as his collar was released. He didn't care anymore, his throat screaming heat as he tried to draw breath. He was bent double looking at the paving stones. An arm grabbed him by the elbow and pulled him towards the curb side. He heard a door open, felt himself pushed into the rear seat.

"I've got him!" he heard from the driver's seat.

Some running feet, a clunk as the passenger door shut. Sebastian choked and spat into the floor well of the rear seat. He felt a raincoat land on his lap as the engine started and the siren cried.

"There's a handkerchief in the side pocket."

"Let's go," the deep voice of Umuntu.

Sebastian wound down the window to get some air into his lungs. His eyes ran across the piazza; surrounded by onlookers he saw the pimp, sunglasses askance to his eyes wrestling in the unbreakable lock of two policemen.

Looking into the rear view mirror he saw the driver, intense and concentrating with the hint of a smile on his lips as he weaved through the parting traffic at speed, the siren of the police car opening the way.

"Thank you," Sebastian croaked, his throat like sandpaper.

Umuntu laughed.

"That was a close thing, Sebastian. Thank the Lord that Rosie has friends in high places, Inspector Bloogard here has saved our skins."

The inspector nodded in acquiescence.

"I have been after those bastard pimps for as long as I've worked the red light district. Every time I get one they're out on the tailcoats of some lawyer or the silence of the girls. Thank God I am retiring soon. That bastard will also be out by tomorrow, I don't doubt." He added to the noise of the high-pitched siren by hooting his horn. "You know what? This is the most fun I've had since I was a rookie!" He sandwich filled the car between two BMWs.

The car screamed as the gears changed. What the sirens didn't part the flashing lights did; even the smugly sacrosanct cyclists knew that this was not a time to assert their right of way. They crossed the fan of canals leaving behind the picturesque narrow streets of Amsterdam and as if by a click of a finger they raced through the utilitarian blandness of the concrete outskirts of the city. Sebastian saw the signs to Schiphol airport. He couldn't think of anything to say, it had all been done, there was really nothing to say. They followed the signs onto the main three-lane motorway and for some reason Sebastian couldn't work out why they kept in the slow lane. A sign told drivers of a fuel stop in one kilometre; the indicator ticked as the now sirenless police car turned onto the concourse of the petrol station and pulled up next to a white car with four passengers, all women.

Umuntu was first out of the car; he approached the boot of the female car, opened it and extracted Sebastian's bags.

"Quickly." Inspector Bloogard spoke through the half-open window.

Umuntu transferred the bags to the police car boot. Sebastian tried to open the rear door but the lock wouldn't open.

"It's on an automatic suspect lock," the inspector informed him. "There's no time to say our goodbyes, your flight leaves soon."

Sebastian heard the boot of the police car shut. Umuntu walked over to the white car and leant through the front passenger window checking the passengers. He returned to the police car.

"Go safe and be happy, Sebastian." He reached his hand over to Sebastian and squeezed his shoulder. "You can do and be whoever you want to be, remember that."

Sebastian wanted to get out and hug him; the nomads were packing their tents: Umuntu, Anneke, Salt and Pepper. Sebastian needed something to remember them by, something that would always enable him to remember them with clarity.

"I never asked, does Umuntu have an English equivalent?"

The reply was a deep-throated laugh.

"Not on its own, it's from a Zulu saying, 'Umuntu ngumuntu ngabantu'. It means, 'A person is a person through other persons'.

Before he could reply he felt the police car gears engage.

"We have to go." Inspector Bloogard checked his watch as he let the clutch out.

The police car moved past the stationary car; Salt and Pepper smiled at him waving their hands from their wrists like wind vanes. Sacha offered a tentative smile. Anneke smiled and blew a silent kiss through the window with her phone cradled between her chin and shoulder. Her smile offered something Sebastian didn't understand, a hint of a different future perhaps. The last thing he saw as they joined the stream of cars on the motorway was the five scarlet nails of Anneke waving goodbye.

CHAPTER 23

Sebastian sat at the end of the bed watching her applying her makeup. The mascara brush held delicately by her fingertips, her eyelashes closed onto the brush and after each flutter she reviewed the application for any clogging on her eyelashes.

"I'm rather nervous about meeting her again. The last time I saw her was at the Vlinder." She spoke to Sebastian's reflection in the mirror. "We both owe her a lot. Don't we, darling?"

He used to love to watch her apply her makeup when they were students, had dreamed of doing it again and now it seemed as if there had never been a break between the doing and the desire. He knew he owed it to Anneke.

He had arrived at Heathrow; the arrivals hall was clogged with excited waiting family members of all colours. He walked through the door with the usual absurd feeling of being an adored star, with crowds of people craning their necks, children being lifted for a better view. The air was crackling with excitement, whoops of recognition, tears of reconciliation and reunion. There was no one to meet him. The crowds thinned as he walked past; no placard welcomed him home, no arms opened to engulf him. Amongst all the happiness he felt bereft. He couldn't go back to his flat as it was still rented out; he didn't want to go to his family, not yet; that would have been to admit to repeated failure. He walked toward the brightly lit kiosk offering last-minute discount hotels in London. He fingered his credit card; nothing had changed, the book was unfinished, his fiscal deficit remained. The harsh overhead strip lights seemed to concentrate on him as he studied the marker-penned cards offering rooms in optimistically named bed and breakfasts around Victoria Station: River View, Rose Cottage, The Churchill. He remembered that area for its once grand stuccoed houses now divided into pokey flats for the desperate and dispossessed. Perhaps he deserved to be there amongst the disposed.

He felt a tap on his shoulder, rather urgent in its desire for attention. He had spent a long time looking at the cards; it was his turn to walk to the counter to choose his bed for the night. He didn't want to look around; he knew it would be a happy pair of backpackers with the wonder of youth beaming from their excited, flushed faces.

"You could stay with me." The voice soft with a slight quaver of uncertainty.

He turned to see her, her face flushed with exertion, her hair ruffled as if she had been dragging her fingers through it. She was wearing jeans and a T-shirt covered by a suede waist-length jacket. She wore no makeup. She had the look of someone who had been in a hurry; to Sebastian Zoe had never looked so beautiful.

He looked at her, his vision blurred with tears.

"How did…?"

Zoe put her arms around his neck and pulled him towards her. Her lips were wet and Sebastian tasted the salt from her tears as she kissed him.

"Your German friend Anneke phoned about three hours ago to say you would be arriving."

Sebastian knew now why Anneke had not got out of the car to say goodbye at the petrol station.

The memory of his arrival back in London had made him want to see Anneke; though he knew he didn't need to thank her, she would know his thanks.

"Come on, Zoe, we need to go or we'll be late. I really don't want to be late. The table is booked for 7.30 at Giovanni's on George Street." He walked around the hotel room impatiently. Since he had left Amsterdam he had exchanged text messages with Anneke as the Spiegeltent had been struck and unstruck from locations throughout Europe. It had now arrived in Edinburgh; the tent had been erected in St Andrew Square. He had arranged dinner and wanted to get there before Anneke and Umuntu.

He heard the click of her makeup bag. Grabbing her coat he looked at her and thought without Anneke none of this would be happening. The fulfilment of his love for Zoe was down to her intervention. He loved them both equally, Zoe for being Zoe and Anneke for being the catalyst.

It was cold when they left the hotel, the streets lit up by Christmas lights; groups of office parties tottered and staggered with their arms interlinked for support mostly. Hats and tinsel decorated their faces red with the weather.

Arriving at the restaurant it was hard to see the tables

as the bar was crowded by drinkers. The hostess greeted them and shouted above the noise.

"Yup, got your reservation. Your guests are already here. I'll take you over."

She surgically dissected the crowds and guided them into the restaurant, noisy but with the semblance of controlled jollity. Sebastian spotted the large presence of Umuntu and in his enthusiasm pushed past the hostess, pulling Zoe behind him. Umuntu saw him coming and rose from his chair, his arms open wide with his face beaming. The arms wrapped around them both squeezing them close to his body.

"Sit, sit down and tell me your news!" He was laughing, the laughter of delight heard so rarely and when heard remembered with pleasure.

"Well," Zoe and Sebastian started in unison.

"One at a time."

Sebastian looked around the table.

"Anneke is here, isn't she?"

Umuntu waved his hand around the restaurant.

"Just gone to the toilet. Tell me, Zoe, how has he been? Has he finished the book yet? Tell me all."

Sebastian let Zoe talk; his eyes wandered in search of the ladies' toilet. He was paying attention to what they were discussing but his eyes couldn't leave the toilet door. He wanted to see her without her knowing she was being watched. He needed that moment to remind himself just how much he owed her.

He didn't look up as a pair of black trousers imposed themselves between himself and Zoe. He didn't want a drink at the moment, he didn't want to miss the moment she opened the toilet door. He wished the waiter would go away. The toilet door opened and two women walked out swapping a story; one held the forearm of the other as she expressed disbelief looking over her shoulder back into the toilet.

"Hello Sebastian, hello Zoe." The voice was deep and smoky.

Sebastian looked confused. He turned to the black trousers and raised his eyes upward. Standing with an arm on his shoulder and one on Zoe's was a handsome, precise and neatly dressed man in a white open-necked shirt and a black suit. His hair was cut carefully round his ears and a foppish lock of hair drifted across his forehead. Sebastian raised his hand to cover the one on his shoulder. Five neat fingers applied a gentle pleasure to his shoulder; the smallest finger had a bright scarlet-painted nail.

"Umuntu ngumuntu ngabantu," Umuntu laughed.